SHEILA ROBERTS

HOME
on Apple
Blossom Road

MIRA

ISBN-13: 978-0-7783-1879-8

Recycling programs for this product may not exist in your area.

Home on Apple Blossom Road

For questions and comments about the quality of this book, please contact us at CustomerService@Harlequin.com.

www.MIRABooks.com

Printed in U.S.A.

Praise for the novels of Sheila Roberts

"A cast of endearing characters, a warmly humorous look at the myriad forms mother-daughter relationships can take, and a delightful small-town setting come together enchantingly in Roberts's latest sweetly engaging novel."
—*Booklist* on *A Wedding on Primrose Street*

"Sweet, affecting, and emotionally charged, this multi-threaded story highlights the complex relationships between mothers and daughters, and while more women's fiction than pure romance, this is sure to appeal to fans of both genres."
—*Library Journal* on *A Wedding on Primrose Street*

"Whenever I start a Sheila Roberts book, I know that I won't be able to stop until the very last page. *A Wedding on Primrose Street* is no exception. I love the Life in Icicle Falls series, and with every story it's like going home and visiting with old friends."
—*Fresh Fiction*

"*The Lodge on Holly Road* is the ultimate in feel-good family drama and heart-melting romance."
—*USA TODAY*

"This amusing holiday tale about love lost and found again is heartwarming. Quirky characters, snappy dialogue and sexy chemistry all combine to keep you laughing, as well as shedding a few tears, as you turn the pages."
—*RT Book Reviews* on *Merry Ex-mas*

"Homing in on issues many readers can identify with, Roberts's women search for solutions to a common challenge with humor."
—*Publishers Weekly*

For Lorraine

Dear Reader,

I love a treasure hunt—the thrill, the fun! Where will we look next? What will we find? I actually designed one for an annual fall party once with some of our crazy friends. At the time we were living on our family island property with lots of woods to crash around in and a beach, where I buried treasure in the form of tiny bottles of rum and gold coins. (Did I mention we had a pirate theme going for this particular bash? Yo-ho-ho and a bottle of silliness!) I created a map, tore it into pieces and hid them all around the property, then sent the players in search of clues that would lead them to those pieces of the map. There was only one fly in my ointment… I forgot about the tide. By the time my pirates got to the beach, it was coming in with a vengeance and there was barely any beach left. We did manage to rescue the rum and chocolate, though.

Remembering how much I enjoyed creating that search for treasure, I thought I'd give two characters a bit of a treasure hunt and send them all over Icicle Falls. I hope you'll enjoy going along for the ride as Colin and Mia search for their inheritance by way of many of the places and people you have come to know. (And if this is your first visit to Icicle Falls, please come back soon!) I hope as you join their adventure, you'll find an entertaining and inspiring read. Thanks for coming along!

And if you'd like to hang out together in between books, check out my website (sheilasplace.com) and my Facebook page (Sheila Roberts Author). We have lots of fun!

Sheila

HOME
on Apple Blossom Road

April 3, 1960

Dear Mother,
We've done it! We bought the apple orchard that was for sale outside town. Mother, it's perfect. The orchard is lovely, and Gerald's already talking about planting some cherry and pear trees in addition to the apple trees. I can see myself in the house that comes with it. It has four bedrooms. Four! And a front porch for sitting on in the evening, just like folks do back home in Pittsburgh.

The owner wouldn't come down very far on his price but, thanks to the GI Bill, we were able to swing it. I'm going to make yellow-checked curtains for the kitchen window, and I plan to bake my very first apple pie this fall. Of course, we'll also have a vegetable garden, since the house itself sits on a quarter acre. Gerald and I are going to be very happy here.

I do hope you and Daddy and Emmaline will be able to come out for Thanksgiving or Christmas or maybe even the Fourth of July, so we can all be together.

Do write back and say you'll all come out and see us in our new home.

Love,
Justine

volunteering for the town and at church, baking for the

Chapter One

At thirty-one, who wants to think about death? Colin Wright sure didn't, and the last thing he wanted to do was go to a funeral, especially when that funeral was for his grandmother.

The Icicle Falls Baptist Church was packed with people who'd known Colin since he was born, all dressed in their Sunday best on a Thursday afternoon to honor Justine Wright. Justine only had two kids, Colin's dad, Dylan, and his aunt Beth, but to hear people talk you would've thought she'd had a dozen. All the testimonials made her sound like Mother Teresa. In a way she was, with all the foster kids she and Gramps had taken in over the years. They'd never kept a penny of the money they received as foster parents, opting instead to put that money in savings for the child. Colin couldn't begin to count the number of people who'd called her Mom. Or Grandma.

It wasn't only former charges blowing noses and dabbing at eyes. Gram had inspired countless people in Icicle Falls—giving cooking lessons to young brides, volunteering for the town and at church, baking for the annual Raise the Roof fund-raiser that helped maintain historic buildings. She was one of the old-guard movers and shakers, and everyone loved her.

August had just begun, and a blazing afternoon sun was reaching in through the windows. That, combined with all the body heat, made the sanctuary hot enough to bake a pie in spite of the fact that the doors had been opened.

The heavyset, fortysomething guy two rows back who'd stood up to share his memories was sweating as if he'd been stuck under a broiler. "No one could make an apple pie like Mom," he reminisced and mopped his eyes and his forehead. Colin had no idea who he was, but the tears and the use of the word *Mom* proclaimed him to be one of Gram's many projects.

The sweaty pie eater had barely sat down when a woman called out, "I can. She taught me how."

This produced a chuckle from the crowd and momentarily lightened the misery.

Except for Colin. He tried not to look at the closed casket at the front of the sanctuary, loaded with lilies. Not looking couldn't save him from remembering what a shit he'd been the last time he'd seen her. Not a major one, he tried to comfort himself, just a minor one.

Who was now having a major guilt attack. If only he'd known Gram was going to die so suddenly a month later, he would never have told her to mind her own business. Oh, man. Had he really said that to his grandma?

"But you *are* my business," she'd said sweetly. "My favorite business."

He'd shaken his head and said, "I love you, Gram, but I gotta go." At least he'd kissed her goodbye.

Next to him Aunt Beth was sobbing quietly and blowing her nose. He took her hand and she squeezed it, cutting off his circulation and turning both their hands slick with sweat.

Gram was in heaven for sure. He, on the other hand, had to be in purgatory. He still couldn't believe she was gone, and he had no idea how he was going to fill the gaping hole in his life.

And then there was Mia Blair, the woman who'd broken his heart, sitting on the other side of Aunt Beth. She was another reason Colin didn't want to be in this overheated sanctuary smelling of battling perfumes and sweaty armpits, pulling on his shirt collar with his free hand. She'd moved away, made her choice years ago. Why hadn't she stayed away? Who'd invited her here, anyhow?

She was still slender and delicate, with the same huge brown eyes and long dark hair, same full lips. Those lips used to drive him wild. Not to mention her other body parts. The light coming in through the stained glass cast her in subtle rainbow hues, making her look like an escaped fairy from one of those Lord of the Rings movies.

"Don't wear black," Aunt Beth had instructed everyone. Mia hadn't, but if you asked Colin, she shouldn't have come ready for a picnic, either, in that dress splattered with pink flowers, showing off so much leg. She leaned forward to dig another packet of tissues out of her purse and he could see cleavage. A woman shouldn't be showing cleavage at a guy's grandma's funeral.

And a guy shouldn't be looking. He directed his eyes straight ahead. But oh, man, there was the casket again. He lowered his gaze to his hand, the one that wasn't numb and sweaty.

"Justine had a long, wonderful life," said the minister, "and we all know how happy she'd be to see so many of you here to honor her today."

It would've been better to honor her when she was alive and not been a smart mouth, even if Gram had provoked him. It seemed she was still provoking him from beyond the grave, summoning Mia back to Icicle Falls, dredging up memories of their childhood, those intense teenage years, the final hurt and frustration.

"When we celebrated her eighty-sixth birthday last month, she told me she was ready to go and meet Jesus," the minister said. "Everything was in order down here. She'd done all she could."

To get her grandson squared away, anyhow. Sadly, he hadn't squared the way she'd wanted him to.

"'And now I'm leaving things up to God,' she told me. How's that for a great attitude?"

No one could deny Gram had her shit together. Which was more than Colin could say.

Now he was looking in Mia's direction again. *Cut that out!* He forced his eyes to move away. Again. Back to staring at his sweaty hand.

Boring.

Too bad, he told his wandering eyes. *We're not looking at Mia, so deal with it.*

"Justine wanted us to all celebrate her life," the minister said. "So, at her request, we'll sing 'Amazing Grace' and then proceed to the fellowship hall for pie and ice cream."

Pie and ice cream. As if it was a party. Colin had no interest in partying. Gram and Aunt Beth had been his mothers growing up, and Gram had been the queen bee mother, keeping everyone happy and connected. He didn't want to celebrate the fact that she was no longer here by eating pie in her memory. It would taste like ashes.

If it wasn't for the reading of the will the next day and strict orders from his dad to stick around, he'd be on his way back to Seattle.

This was…awkward. Why had Aunt Beth insisted Mia sit with her?

Because she was family, of course. Not blood-related, but family just the same. Aunt Beth had been Mama's best friend, and when Mama got sick and Mia's loser dad took off, both Aunt Beth and Grandma Justine had been there for them. They'd finished raising her after Mama died. Mia had spent as much time playing in the family's orchard on Apple Blossom Road as Colin had. She'd helped sell apples at the fruit stand and worked alongside Grandma Justine, canning applesauce and apple-pie filling every fall.

Still, she was very aware of Colin sitting there, glaring at her as though she didn't belong. Well, as far as Aunt Beth was concerned she did, darn it. Colin might have dumped her, but his family hadn't. Most of them, anyway. And just because she lived in Chicago, that didn't mean she loved Grandma Justine any less than he did. He'd moved away, too.

Okay, only as far as Seattle, but he'd still moved.

Behind her an old lady was singing so shrilly it made Mia's ears hurt. Next to her, Aunt Beth was blowing her nose. And next to Aunt Beth, Colin was frowning. Mia realized she was, too. *Oh, Grandma, I wish you weren't gone. I wish you could have stayed around to hear about my latest success. I wish you could've stayed until I finally got the whole love thing right.*

Except at the rate Mia was going with the love thing, Grandma Justine would've had to live to be two hundred. How easy it was to take wrong turns, and it seemed that once you did, there was no turning back.

Never mind the painful past. Mia was here to pay tribute to a wonderful woman, not to sneak glances at the woman's grandson, the man who broke her heart.

"We've no less days to sing God's praise than when we first begu-un," warbled the woman behind Mia. It would've been more tolerable if she'd been singing in the same key as everyone else. Hopefully, this all sounded a lot better up where Grandma Justine was than it did down here.

The service ended, and people began to make their way toward the fellowship hall. Aunt Beth still had Colin's hand, so Mia figured she should slip into the crowd for a while.

She was just about to when Colin said, "Uh, Aunt Beth, my hand's gone numb."

"Oh, Colin Cootie, I'm sorry," Aunt Beth said, freeing his hand and latching on to Mia's arm at the same time. "I don't know what I'd do without you two here."

Since Uncle Mark had been seated two bodies down, next to Colin's dad, Mia was fairly sure that she would've managed. In fact, it was kind of odd that she wasn't sitting beside her husband.

Now she had both Mia and Colin by the arm and was walking them down the aisle, making it pretty darned obvious what had motivated the seating arrangement. "I'm so glad you two are staying over."

"Did we have a choice?" Colin retorted.

"Oh, nice," Mia said. "Be rude to your aunt at your grandma's funeral." Sometimes Colin could be so thoughtless.

He kept his mouth shut, but his scowl said, "Who asked for your opinion?"

Nobody. And she wasn't his mother. Or his girlfriend. Not anymore. "Sorry," she muttered.

Aunt Beth was always happy to cut them both some slack. "We aren't ourselves. Mark," she said over her shoulder, "I think we're going to need more ice cream for the pies."

She was some kind of magician. In the space of a few seconds she'd stepped back a pace to confer with her husband about ice cream and move Mia and Colin together as if they were a couple. Awkward. Oh, so awkward.

Well, they *were* adults. "I'm sorry about…" *Our grandma?* No, technically that wasn't right. And y*our grandma* sounded…removed, as though she didn't care. "Grandma Justine." That was who she was, to Mia and many others.

He nodded.

It would have been helpful if he'd said something. Anything. It was his turn.

And then he did. "Nice dress. You going to a party after this?"

So now he was a fashion expert? Who'd crowned him the next Clinton Kelly? "As a matter of fact, I am. A celebration of life."

He scowled again. Then grudgingly said, "You look good."

"Thank you," she said stiffly. "So do you." No lie. He'd been cute as a boy, even cuter as a teenager. As a man he was ridiculously handsome. Blond hair, blue eyes that crinkled at the edges when he smiled, a square chin with a strong mouth that made a girl dream of kisses. Ugh.

They were in the foyer now. Some of the mourners were already heading toward the addition known as the fellowship hall; others milled around, visiting. She scanned the crowd for someone to talk to besides Mr. Thistle Britches. It wasn't hard. She knew almost everyone.

There was her old friend Bailey Sterling-Black, only a few feet away, standing with a man who looked like an escaped model. Todd Black, the new husband, of course.

"Bailey, hi!" she called.

Bailey turned and smiled. She took the man's hand and towed him over. "Mia, when did you get to town?

And why didn't you tell me you were coming, you jerk? Your hair looks great! I love the bangs," she gushed, hugging Mia.

"You look great, too," Mia said. Was that a baby bump her buddy was sporting?

"You finally get to meet Todd," Bailey said, beaming at the gorgeous thing beside her. "He owns the Man Cave."

"I've been in there," Colin said. What was he still doing here? "Cool place," he added and the two men shook hands.

"We also have a tea shop together," Bailey told Mia. "You definitely have to come by now that you're finally back in town." Bailey's sunny expression disappeared. "Gosh, I'm acting like this is a party. I'm sorry you lost your grandma."

"Thanks," Colin said right along with Mia. She ignored him. Or tried to.

"I wish you were here for happier reasons," Bailey finished.

She was kind enough not to say, "I wish you'd made it back for my wedding."

Mia should have. She'd missed her old friends, missed Icicle Falls. But the wedding had fallen on the weekend of an important business conference, and she'd had to settle for sending a present. Plus, there was the Colin factor. She'd had no desire to risk another encounter like her last one with him.

She'd come out for Aunt Beth's surprise birthday party, newly engaged and nervous about seeing Colin for the first time since their breakup in college. It turned out she'd been right to be nervous. Their meeting had been ugly, nothing she wanted to repeat, so she'd kept her distance.

She wasn't going to do that anymore. If she wanted to see Aunt Beth at Christmas, she was going to. And if she wanted to visit for Mother's Day instead of sending flowers, she was going to do that, too. No more chickening out.

She'd almost chickened out on coming for the funeral, except Colin's dad had insisted she come. She was in the will. Maybe Grandma Justine had left her a small piece of jewelry or something. But why Dylan couldn't have sent it to her, she had no idea.

Cass Wilkes, the owner of Gingerbread Haus, passed them, bearing a pie. "Mia, great to see you back in town. How are you?"

"I'm fine," Mia said. She was, darn it all. She'd set out to prove herself and become a success, and she was well on her way to doing exactly that.

"You look good. Chicago must agree with you," Cass said. "Your aunt tells me you're moving up the ladder at GF Markets."

"I am." She was thrilled about her new responsibility and had been about to share her good news with Grandma Justine when Beth called to tell her Grandma was gone.

"Of course you should go to the funeral," Andrea Blackburn, her new boss, had said. "We can start work on the Sprouted Bliss campaign when you come back on Monday."

That was last Tuesday. Mia had flown out on Wednesday. That gave her until Sunday to mourn, commiserate and get her Icicle Falls fix before she jumped back into the world of marketing food products to the nation.

GF stood for Good Food, but you had to use the term loosely when it came to some of the GF products such as Zombie Bites, a sugary corn cereal like half the other sugar-buzz treats on the shelves. Its distinguishing features were the cartoon zombie characters on the box and the goofy zombie-shaped bits of cereal inside. Then there were Yum-balls, a cheap rip-off of another company's snowball-shaped cakes, complete with marshmallow coating and coconut. Yes, they were yummy but hardly what you'd call a nutritious snack.

Yum-balls were only the tip of the company's sugar iceberg. A variety of GF Markets goodies lined the shelves of grocery store baked-goods aisles, and some of them owed their continued existence to Mia. During a marketing brainstorming session on how to reinvigorate sales, she'd suggested simply acknowledging that, other than sensory pleasure, those goodies had no food value whatsoever.

"But people still love treats." Herself included. "So why not appeal to that with a slogan like 'Indulge Yourself.'"

"Go on," Andrea had said.

So she had, outlining an ad campaign that would show happy food consumers on picnics in the countryside, their Fiats parked nearby, or soaking in a bubble bath surrounded by candles, drinking champagne, all of them consuming decadent GF Markets goodies.

Sales increased, everyone was happy, and she got

a raise, along with a case of various GF Markets cake and cookie mixes.

The company also offered nutritious products, and Sprouted Bliss Bread was the newest addition to that family. The marketing department was under orders to give it a big push, and this one was Mia's baby. She'd been excited about both the product and the opportunity. The news of Grandma Justine's death had drowned the thrill.

"So you like it there?" Cass asked.

It wasn't Icicle Falls, but then what place was? "I do." She had a sweet little apartment, nice friends. No boyfriend. Who had time for a man, anyway, when you were working sixty-hour weeks?

"And Colin, it's always good to see you back," Cass continued. "I'm sorry about your grandmother. We hated to lose her."

The reminder of why they were all there brought fresh tears to Mia's eyes.

"Thanks," Colin said. He looked as if he wanted to cry, too. But, of course, he wouldn't. That guy thing.

"I guess I'd better get this pie over to the kitchen. See you later," Cass said and moved on.

Mia was flying out on Sunday, but she'd make an effort to get to Gingerbread Haus and order a gingerbread boy for old times' sake.

More people stopped by on their way to the pie pig-out. Harry Defoe clapped Colin on the back and gave Mia a big bear hug. Harry was several years older than they were, and he was one of Grandma Justine's many success stories. He lived on the other side of the mountains in the wealthy community of Bellevue. Mia had once eavesdropped on a conversation between Grandma Justine and Harry as they all sat on Grandma and Grandpa's front porch, Mia and Colin playing gin rummy, and Grandma and Harry on the front porch swing, having an earnest conversation about his future. It had been June. School was out and many of Harry's friends had had plans to go away to college. Not Harry. His grades hadn't been good enough.

She'd patted his shoulder and said, "Harry, college isn't for everyone."

"I just wish I was smart," he'd mumbled.

"You are. You're smart in practical ways." Mia had peered over in time to see Grandma take his hands in hers. "You're smart with your hands. You know how to put things together, how to fix things. That's an important gift. Let me talk to Everett Jenson. I think he could use a strong young man with clever hands."

Grandma had, indeed, talked to Everett Jenson, who owned Jenson Plumbing. Harry became a plumber. He eventually started his own business in Seattle and now he was a very rich plumber.

Harry was one of a dozen success stories standing in the church foyer; kids who'd been lost until Grandma Justine helped them find their way. Kids like Mia, who'd needed a mom. Now here they all were, related by grief.

Mia stood politely, hugging, fielding condolences. Colin disappeared. Good, she told herself. Now she could relax and enjoy reconnecting with people she hadn't seen in ages.

But how did you enjoy yourself when such an important person was gone from your life?

If one more person told Colin what a great woman his grandma was and how lucky he'd been to have her, he was going to sit down in the middle of the church foyer and bawl. He got into his restored Corvette and peeled out of the parking lot. When he was a kid, he would've climbed the maple tree in his grandparents' backyard and hidden in the tree house or run off into the orchard to lick his wounds. That wasn't possible now. The old farmhouse on Apple Blossom Road had passed out of the family years ago. So the next best place was the river.

He drove away from town and parked in a scenic pullout alongside one of the turbulent bends in the Wenatchee River and made his way down the bank. That roiling mass of water crashing past boulders in the riverbed perfectly reflected how he felt inside. Why did Gram have to die when she did? Even though he still had Dad and Aunt Beth and Uncle Mark, he felt… abandoned. He picked up a stone and tossed it into the angry rush of water. He was like that stone, sunk in the riverbed while his dreams raced past. While people he loved were rushed around the bend and out of sight.

His cell phone vibrated and he checked caller ID. Lorelei. He didn't want to talk but he knew she'd keep calling until he answered. "Hi, babe."

"How's it going?" she asked.

"Rotten."

"You should've let me come up with you."

"Nah. No sense both of us missing work."

"I don't mind," she insisted. "It's not like I can't re-schedule people."

As a personal fitness coach, his girlfriend had a certain amount of flexibility. He could have taken her up on her offer. Somehow, and he wasn't even sure how, it hadn't felt right.

"That's okay. We've got the reading of the will tomorrow, and then I'll head back." He almost added that he'd be home in plenty of time to do something. Except he didn't want to do anything. Going for a bike ride or out dancing felt disrespectful of his gram. It seemed wrong to have fun now that she was gone. In fact, it all seemed a rather obscene mockery that the sun was out and the birds were happily singing, cars were driving by up on the highway, filled with people ready to come to Icicle Falls to hike and shop and enjoy themselves. He wanted to yell, "Don't you all know my grandma is dead?"

Life goes on. How many times had he heard that expression? Yeah, it did go on, but that philosophy seemed callous now.

"I'll call you," he promised vaguely, and then said goodbye.

He knew people would be coming to Aunt Beth and Uncle Mark's place after the affair at the church for more talking and eating, but they'd have to talk and eat without him. The last thing he needed was to stand around and make nice when he wanted to hit something. Losing Gramps had been hard enough, but at least he'd had plenty of warning that Gramps was on his way out. Gram's death had struck like lightning. She'd been the linchpin of the family and now she was gone.

He picked up another rock and hurled it. Then he sat down on a boulder and cried. And wished he'd come to Icicle Falls to visit Gram more often.

Too late. He'd have to do better in the future with Aunt Beth. And Dad, too, of course. Checking in via phone every once in a while really didn't cut it. He needed to go fly-fishing with the old man, take him out for burgers at Herman's, come see his aunt and uncle more than once in a blue moon.

He should probably go back to Aunt Beth's. She'd expect him to.

He stayed on the boulder and watched the river roar past.

Late that evening, as night crept in to steal the last glimmer of daylight, he went back to town and slipped into the house where he'd grown up. All the lights were off and he assumed his dad was still over at Aunt Beth's until he walked down the hall past his father's office and a voice said, "You back, son?" scaring the crap out of him.

The door was slightly ajar and he pushed it open. "Dad? What are you doing sitting here in the dark?"

"Just sitting and thinking."

He heard a click as Dad turned on a lamp, revealing a lawyer's lair. This was Dad's private office, the inner sanctum his clients never saw. There was his big mahogany desk and the requisite green-shaded reading lamp. Tall barrister bookcases filled with legal tomes and literary classics lined the walls.

Dad was in his favorite leather reading chair in the corner. He looked sad and worn-out, like some John Grisham hero, ready to give up the fight.

Colin fell into the matching chair opposite him. "You didn't go to Aunt Beth's?"

"For a while." Dad sighed heavily. "I needed to be alone. Your grandma was one of those people who…" He broke off and glanced away. "Of course, we all knew she couldn't go on forever." He shook his head. "Damn, but the heart attack came out of nowhere." He swirled the remaining amber liquid in his crystal glass, then downed it.

Colin watched as Dad moved to his desk where the bottle of Scotch sat. "Care to join me?"

"I think I will."

As Colin fetched another glass from the liquor cabinet he couldn't help remembering the time he and his buddy Neal got into that cabinet and did some sampling. Dad caught them working their way through a bottle of brandy and just about broke it over their heads.

His father filled the glass, then lifted his own. "To your grandma."

"To Gram," Colin said, and they solemnly took a drink.

Dad returned to his chair, crossed one long leg over the other and downed some more booze. He was fit and lean and still pretty good-looking. And still single.

Colin knew his father'd had a few dealings with women—a short-lived fling with someone in Seattle, a date or two here and there—but he'd mostly kept his life female-free. Colin had once asked him why he'd never remarried after Mom left. "No reason to," he'd said. Not exactly a shining testimonial to marriage.

Colin got it, though. Dad had gambled on love with Mom and lost. He could hardly be blamed for not wanting to throw the dice again.

Mom certainly wasn't much of a poster girl for the wedded state. She'd been through a couple of husbands and had given up. Now she was in the process of moving to Italy to live with some business shark who owned a villa in Tuscany. A "relationship of convenience," she called it. Colin didn't expect to hear from her again anytime soon. Not that he'd heard from her very much in the first place.

"Don't get married young," she said one of the few times she'd met up with Colin for a visit, hoping to earn some good-parent points. "It never works out."

Gram and Aunt Beth took a different view. As far as they were concerned, everyone's life should be like a Vanessa Valentine romance novel. They'd considered Dad's single state a condition in need of curing, throwing various women at him. Dad had remained incurable. It left the women in his family mystified, but after his own experience Colin understood.

"I'm glad you came, son," Dad said. "It means a lot to your aunt Beth."

Colin perched on the edge of the desk and took another slug of whiskey. "I get having to be here for the funeral, but I still don't see why I have to be here tomorrow. What could Gram possibly have to leave to me? I already got Gramps's coin collection and that signed Babe Ruth baseball." Uncle Mark had inherited the tools and Dad had Gramps's classic Ford truck. What else was there that a guy would want? Colin had no interest in Hummel figurines or quilts or jewelry.

Dad shook his head, a look of disgust on his face.

"What?" Colin prompted.

"It'll all be clear tomorrow. Meanwhile, I've got a mother of a headache. I'm going to bed." Dad tossed down the last of his drink, stopped to lay a hand on Colin's shoulder as he passed then walked out of the room. "Turn off the lights when you come up."

And that was that.

All this mystery. Why couldn't Dad just tell him what Gram had left him and be done with it?

Oh, well. A few more hours, then he'd be out of here. He'd go back to Seattle and recover his equilibrium.

At least he wouldn't have to see Mia again. She'd be gone, too. And that was fine with him.

April 26, 1986

Dear Mother,
I'm sorry to have to tell you that Bethie lost an-
other baby. This is the third miscarriage, and I
don't think she and Mark will try again. Two boys
and now this one a girl. She's heartbroken. I feel
so horrible for her. I remember how swamped
you feel by sadness, how your arms ache to hold
that child. It's a cheat, a horrible, evil cheat.

Her best friend, Anna, had her little Mia ear-
lier this month and she asked Bethie to be Mia's
godmother. I do hope that will turn out to be a
blessing and not a constant reminder of what
Bethie herself almost had. Anyway, please pray
for Bethie and Mark.

On a happier note, the orchard is in bloom
and it's beautiful. If all goes well we should have
a bumper crop of Gala apples this year.

Well, that's it for now. I have to go restock the
information booth.

I hope you've finally resolved the issue with
the neighbor's tree overhanging your fence.
There's the advantage of living in the country
like we do. No fences!

Mother's Day is right around the corner and
I'm looking forward to coming out and spend-
ing it with you.

Love,
Justine

Chapter Two

"Are you sure I need to be at the reading of the will?" Mia asked Aunt Beth as they sat at the vintage red Formica table in Beth's sunny kitchen, enjoying coffee and blackberry scones with homemade boysenberry jam for breakfast.

It was probably the hundredth time she'd asked, but Beth nodded patiently and said, "Yes, you really do."

"I can't imagine what Grandma Justine would leave me that you couldn't have sent me in the mail." This was going to be awkward.

"Trust me when I say you need to be here, not just because of what's in the will but because you're family."

Mia felt the same way. The Wrights were the only family she had. Unless she counted an aunt and uncle and some cousins in Mexico whom she'd never met and a father who wasn't a father.

"I hope you know how much you all mean to me," she said. "Taking me in after Mama died, raising me like your own."

"Honey, you make it sound as if that was a hard

thing to do. You were already part of the family. You've always been like a daughter to me."

Mia studied Beth over her coffee mug. She was in her early sixties now, but she'd aged well, with laugh lines around her eyes and a few threads of gray mixed in among the blond hairs. She'd put on some weight but not much, and to Mia, she looked the same as she had when Mia was a child. She'd been a great second mom, and Grandma Justine had been a perfect grandma.

"You're not about to start crying on me, are you?" Beth demanded. "I just put my contacts in, and if I start crying again they're going to get glued to my eyeballs."

Mia wiped at the corners of her eyes and smiled. "Not me."

"We're all going to miss her, but she wouldn't want us being unhappy."

"It's hard not to be. Without you and Grandma, I don't know what I would've done."

"Oh, you'd have managed," Beth said with a knowing nod. "Grandma was very proud of your success. We all are."

Career success—the merit badge she'd worked so hard for. Once upon a time, it had been a means to an end. Now it was important, because it had become her identity. The only identity she had these days.

She took the last bite of her scone, savoring the combination of flavors and textures. "These are so good."

Aunt Beth beamed at the compliment. "My latest creation."

Aunt Beth truly was a domestic goddess.

Spending time in the kitchen with her and Grandma

Justine had always been an experience that combined culinary artistry and female bonding. The Wright women took what happened in the kitchen seriously. "We're not simply feeding the body when we make a meal," Grandma Justine liked to say, "we're feeding the soul, as well. So many important conversations take place around the dinner table. So much love is shared."

A lot of love had been shared teaching Mia how to cook. She remembered a particular Saturday afternoon when her mom was still alive. The three women had gathered in Grandma Justine's kitchen and were making apple pies to put in the freezer. She'd been five, but Grandma Justine had given her the rolling pin and leftover pie dough to roll out. She'd been wearing the apron Aunt Beth had made especially for her—red fabric with a teacup print. It was both her Wright family uniform and her magic cape that turned her into a grown-up, doing grown-up things.

"Never overwork your pie crust," Grandma Justine had told her. "That makes it tough. Roll from the middle out." She'd put her hands over Mia's and helped her get a feel for it, wrinkled hands with veins that stood up like miniature blue mountain ridges covering small, smooth hands. Practiced hands guiding a beginner into a new world of taste and texture and camaraderie.

Mia still liked to play around in the kitchen when she had time. Maybe that was because it brought back such good feelings.

Beth glanced at the rooster clock hanging on the kitchen wall. "We'd better get going. Dylan wants us all present and accounted for by ten."

They put their dishes in the dishwasher, then walked down the street and around the corner to the old Victorian that housed the offices of Dylan Wright, attorney at law, specializing in elder law and wills. He was the attorney of record, and Aunt Beth was the executrix of Justine Wright's will.

Uncle Mark wasn't mentioned in the will, and he had his sand and gravel company to run, so the only ones present were Beth, Dylan, Mia and, yep, here came the awkwardness. Colin. The look he gave Mia as Dylan's secretary showed them into the conference room said, "What are you doing here?" She was asking herself the same question, but she raised her chin and reminded herself that Grandma Justine had wanted her here and that was all that mattered.

A long wooden table occupied the center of the room, which had originally been a dining room. A couple of plants took away the severity of the space, and the view outside the window showed them a well-maintained yard with plenty of shrubs and flowers and, beyond that, the mountains that held Icicle Falls in their craggy hands.

Dylan had set out water bottles, and they all took a seat, Colin slouching in one to his father's left and Aunt Beth opposite them, with Mia settling in next to her. Right across from Colin. Mia focused on her water bottle.

"For the most part, this is a pretty straightforward will," Dylan said. "So." He adjusted his reading glasses, shuffled the official-looking papers in his hands and then began to read. "I, Justine Wright, being of sound mind…"

It *was* pretty straightforward. Tesla stock to Dylan and a hundred shares of Apple to Aunt Beth. The money in savings to be divided equally between the two siblings…

When did Gram get together enough money for stocks and savings? Colin was under the assumption that all she had was her house and her social security. She'd always lived so frugally.

Dad read on, "The house at 23 Pine Street is to be sold and the profits from said sale divided equally between my children, Elizabeth Ann Mallow and Dylan Hartman Wright."

Okay, so what else was there? Why was he here? And why on earth was Mia here?

The contents of the house were also to be equally divided with the exception of Justine's jewelry…

Ah, she'd probably left a necklace or something for Mia. Maybe she had some old ring of Gramps's for Colin.

The jewelry went to Aunt Beth.

"I still don't get why we're here," he grumbled.

"Because your grandmother has left an unusual bequest to you and Mia jointly," his father told him.

"Jointly?" Colin echoed.

"Jointly?" Mia said faintly.

Dad sighed. "Yes, and it gets more…interesting." Dad's euphemism for *weird*.

It sure did. As Dad read, it quickly became clear

that Gram expected the two of them to go searching for their inheritance.

"Searching?" Like in some goofy movie?

His father pinched the bridge of his nose, and Aunt Beth grinned like a kid about to go on a neighborhood scavenger hunt.

"I don't get it," Colin muttered.

"Oh, come on now. This is just the sort of thing you kids loved to do at Easter," said Aunt Beth. "You remember those Easter basket hunts Grandma and I made up for you."

Did she think he was still twelve? He frowned. "I'm not a kid anymore, Aunt Beth."

"Don't worry. You won't be hunting for Easter baskets," she assured him. "This is on a slightly grander scale."

"Grander scale," Colin repeated dubiously.

"A treasure hunt," Aunt Beth said.

Colin envisioned himself and Mia running around Icicle Falls dressed like pirates, searching for buried treasure. All they needed was Johnny Depp. "Okay, this is seriously whacked out. And what's left that's worth searching for?"

"I promise you, there *is* something of value at the end of your search," Aunt Beth told him.

Dad frowned at her. "If I can continue?"

She shrugged. "Don't let me stop you."

Dad looked sternly at her over his bifocals, rustled his papers and then said basically the same thing. "There's another stipulation. Both parties must still be single with no serious commitments. If either is married or engaged at the time, then the bequest goes to whichever one is single to do with as he or she sees fit." He stopped and asked Mia, "Are you engaged?"

Her cheeks turned rosy. "No."

Dad asked Colin the same question, even though he knew Colin was nowhere near popping the question. Gram had known it, too.

"No," Colin said firmly. In a way, he would've loved to say yes, just to see Mia's reaction.

Dad nodded and continued. "If one of the beneficiaries refuses to participate for reasons other than the aforementioned, then the other is free to search alone and will become the sole beneficiary."

That worked for Colin. "You probably have to get back to Chicago," he said to Mia.

"This shouldn't take long," she said. "But maybe you'd like to return to Seattle and...whoever."

As if on cue, his cell phone pinged. He checked the screen. He had a text message from Lorelei.

Mia raised her eyebrows as he put the phone in his pocket. "Are you sure you're not with someone?"

"Being with someone isn't the same as being engaged," he fired back. "And how do we know *you're* not with someone?"

"Don't worry, I'm not," she said almost bitterly.

No way was Colin letting her push him out of the picture. "Me, neither, so I'm in."

"Me, too."

Dad continued, still looking as if he'd been forced to suck on a bushel full of lemons. "There is one more condition. Neither participant may bring in outside help. That means if either of you brings in another person and goes looking with that person, then you disqualify yourself from continuing the search. It must be done by both of you—together."

What the hell was Gram up to? "Together, as in…"

"If you don't want to do this," Mia began.

"You are not making off with my inheritance," Colin snapped.

"Our inheritance," she corrected him.

"Let's try and focus here," Dad said, returning their attention to the will. "Once you two find your inheritance, it'll be up to you to decide what to do with it. As executrix, your aunt will be able to guide you when the time comes, and I'll handle the necessary legal matters."

What the heck did that mean? Who knew? All Colin knew was that he wasn't going to back out and leave whatever *his* grandma had left for Mia to make off with.

"So, do you both accept the conditions laid out in the will?" his father asked.

"Yes," said Mia.

"Yes," said Colin.

"Then I need you to sign this." Dad pushed a piece of paper loaded with legal gobbledygook Colin's way.

He scrawled his name and returned it. "You sure you don't have to get back to Chicago?" he asked Mia. "You're something big and important now, right?" At least according to Aunt Beth.

"I'm not leaving," she said as Dad passed the paper to her. "Anyway, I can't think of a better place for a minivacation than Icicle Falls," she said, smiling at Aunt Beth. "I'll check into the Icicle Creek Lodge."

"You'll do no such thing," Aunt Beth told her. "You'll stay with us."

And Colin would stay with Dad. Just like the old days, when everything he ever wanted was here in Icicle Falls, when life consisted of neighborhood baseball games, playing hide-and-seek in his grandparents' old apple orchard and snarfing down Gram's apple crisp loaded with whipped cream. He'd ridden his bike around the corner and down the street to his aunt's place to hang out with Mia and Gram's various foster kids about a million times when they were growing up. They'd both logged in a lot of holiday meals and Sunday suppers at Gram's. Hanging out had been simpler when they were kids.

"So what do we do now?" he asked his dad.

"I'm to give you this," Dad said, producing a long pink envelope. "We'll leave you two to read it. Take your time. Come on, Beth," he said, and they left the room.

Colin tapped the envelope. "Whatever this is, it can't be much. Seriously, if you want to get back, I can find whatever Gram hid and buy you out." That would be so much easier than traipsing around together, stumbling over the past.

Mia frowned. "That's not how she set this up. And besides, I don't care what it is. It's from Grandma Justine, and that makes whatever she's left is valuable to me. I loved her, too, you know," she added softly, and he could see tears in her eyes.

Colin suddenly felt about two inches tall. "Okay."

He opened the envelope and took out what looked like a letter. Mia walked around the table and took the chair next to him to read over his shoulder. She was wearing a black T-shirt and a little white sweater, and white shorts that showed off just enough leg to tempt him to run a hand up her thigh. He got an up-close whiff of her perfume—something spicy that whispered, "Sex."

No, no! No thinking of sex, not when he had a girlfriend in Seattle, and not with Mia. Especially not with Mia. He forced himself to focus on the spidery writing on the pink notepaper.

Dear Ones,
You are both very special to me, so I'm leaving you something equally special, which I hope you will appreciate. I have fond memories of those treasure hunts your Aunt Beth and I sent you on when you were children. And I won't mention a certain little boy being afraid to go in the hen-house.

"I remember that," Mia said.

Or a certain little girl running so fast that she tripped and fell in a mud puddle one rainy Easter.

"And I remember that," Colin retorted, pointing to the sentence in case Mia had conveniently missed it.

*I also remember two happy children work-
ing together to figure out clues, swapping jelly
beans after they'd found their baskets and posing
for pictures with their arms around each other.*

This made Colin squirm.

*You two were so close. I'm sorry that, for
some reason known only to the two of you, things
changed when you got to college. But I hope you
work well together on this final hunt your aunt
and I designed for you. I love you both and want
you to find that valuable treasure you deserve. I
wish the best for each of you. And now, let reminiscence lead you to your first clue.*

*Much love,
Grandma*

Colin frowned. "What the heck is that supposed
to mean?"

Mia tapped her chin. "Reminiscence. Remembering.
Memories." She cocked her head and looked at Colin.
"Where do you find memories?"

He shrugged. "A scrapbook? Photo album?"

"Grandma had a ton. I say we walk over to her
house and go through them."

Colin nodded. "Good idea. Aunt Beth has a key."

Aunt Beth had been hanging out in Dad's office,
waiting for them. "Is there something you want?" she
asked, with a teasing smile.

"As if you don't know," Colin retorted. "The key to Gram's house, please."

She dangled a beaded key chain holding a single key. "You said the magic word. Good luck, you two."

They both reached for it, but Colin was faster and snatched it. Mia frowned and followed him out of the room, muttering, "Grabby."

Okay, maybe that was kind of immature, but he wasn't ready to admit it. "Does it matter who takes the key?" he said irritably.

"Obviously, it does. Are you just going to take over this whole hunt? Really?"

"Are you?" he retorted.

"I wouldn't dream of it. I'm lucky I get to tag along," she said, baiting him.

He clamped his lips shut and hoped this would only take a couple of hours. The sooner he was away from Mia and her perfume, the happier he'd be.

Beth and Dylan watched as the two squabbled their way out the door.

He shook his head. "If I didn't know better, I'd have questioned Mom's testamentary capacity."

"Ah, but you do know better, brother dear," Beth said with a smile.

"You should never have encouraged her." He rolled his eyes. "You and those Vanessa Valentine novels. This is ridiculous."

"No, it's sweet."

"Harebrained."

"Clever."

"Doomed to fail, if you ask me."

"Fortunately, nobody did," Beth said. And with that, she kissed him on the cheek and left him to sit in his office and stew in his superior lawyerly juices.

He'd tried to talk their mother out of her idea, but Beth was glad he hadn't succeeded. The will had been updated less than a month before Mom passed. She hadn't been feeling well, and she'd had a premonition that her time was coming to a close.

"I suppose you think I'm being silly," she'd said to Beth the morning they'd first hatched the plan. They'd been sitting at Beth's kitchen table enjoying the morning sun streaming in through the window and the lattes Beth had made them using her new frothing machine.

With the morbid turn the conversation had taken, Beth had found herself pushing away her mug. "Believing that you're going to die? Yes."

"We're all going to die, dear, and I'm afraid my time is almost here."

"Mom, please don't talk like that."

Mom had only shaken her head. "It's not a bad thing to accept when it's your time to go. I'm ready. Last night I was drifting off to sleep and I saw your father. That's how I knew."

Maybe she *had* known, Beth thought now. Her mother seemed to have a sixth sense about a lot of things.

Dylan, the more practical—translation: cynical—of the two siblings didn't believe in Mom's premonition, and he certainly hadn't been on board with this latest idea of hers. For all his education and smarts, Dylan could be very obtuse. Mom had been determined to have her way, though, and there was nothing he could do but follow her wishes.

Beth smiled, remembering how much she'd enjoyed helping Mom with this last treasure hunt for the kids. And while Beth, and a couple of times even Mark, had been her legs, hiding some of the clues, Mom had planned each one and taken care of several herself. And she'd loved every minute of it.

This would be an opportunity for Colin and Mia to resolve their differences and inherit something special to boot. Dylan might have known about wills and legal documents, but Mom knew about hearts and what people really needed. And Beth was sure the kids would find what they needed right here in Icicle Falls.

December 29, 1987

Dear Mother,
Happy New Year! I'm sorry you weren't able to make it out for Christmas, but I understand your not wanting to travel alone. This first Christmas without Daddy had to be very hard for you. Sometimes I still can't believe he's gone! Anyway, I'm glad you could spend the day with Emmaline and Joey. I'll fly out for your birthday next month and we'll have a belated Christmas then. I'm so looking forward to that. As for moving in with them, I think it's an excellent idea. You know we would happily have had you live with us, but I understand your wanting to stay where your friends are.

Our Christmas was nice, with everyone here on Christmas Day. Eduardo and Maria came, too. We're going to miss them sorely when they go back to Mexico next month. They've been with us since the first year we bought the orchard. But Maria's mother isn't doing well and they feel they need to help her. They don't have much family left and they miss them. I certainly understand the pull of home. I sometimes wish I could split myself in two, with half of me living here and the other half in Pittsburgh with you all. Anyway, Anna's going to stay in Icicle Falls. This is where she grew up and where she wants her daughter to grow up and, of course, it's where her husband is.

I'm afraid I still don't think much of Gary as a husband, though. He's not very attentive to her. I hear rumors about him, but rumors aren't facts so I don't say anything. He's out of work again and not looking very hard for a new job, so Anna's back checking groceries at Safeway while he sits at home and lets the dirty dishes pile up. I've promised Maria I'll watch out for her. I'm not sure how I can do that, but I'm going to try.

Dylan and Colin were here by themselves. Lauren has moved out. Can you imagine leaving your child behind? Colin is the most adorable toddler. I can't begin to understand what she was thinking.

Dylan doesn't like to talk about it, but from what I can pry out of him, it sounds as if his career is the problem. Young lawyers have to work long hours and that's taken its toll on his marriage. Still, there's no excuse for this. I'm afraid Lauren is another one I never approved of. Mother, I must have some sort of second sight when it comes to people. There was something about that woman. Too self-centered? And she never liked coming over here, was always a reluctant participant in our family get-togethers. So wrong for Dylan. He barely smiled at all this visit. It breaks my heart.

I brought up the idea of him leaving Seattle

and moving back to Icicle Falls if things go south, and setting up a practice here. Of course, he won't get rich doing that but at least then Bethie and I could help him with Colin. It would be good for Bethie. We'll see what he does. One thing I know for sure, he'll never take Lauren back.

Why do young people these days have so much trouble finding the right person? That's a question I can't answer. Oh, Mother, it's so hard having grown children. Sometimes I wish I could turn back the clock to when ours were little and I could keep them safe with me here at the orchard.

Well, life goes on, and I'm going to do my best to help it go on well for those I love. Meanwhile, I'm enclosing snapshots of the family taken in front of the tree. Aren't Colin and little Mia adorable? I hope they'll grow up to be good friends.

I'd better run. I love you and miss you and can hardly wait to see you next month.

Love,
Justine

Chapter Three

It wasn't a chatty trip down the front walk. The silence felt about as comfortable as a jockstrap two sizes too small. Hardly surprising, considering how things had gone the last time Colin and Mia had seen each other. Ancient history, just like their breakup, but it sure was affecting current events.

That had been eight years ago, at Aunt Beth's surprise birthday party. By then they'd both moved on with their lives, so it shouldn't have bothered him that she was sporting a big diamond on her left hand.

It had. Even now, remembering that day still made him grind his teeth…

"Congratulations," Colin said reluctantly as he and Mia stood at the buffet table in Gram's little dining room. It was February and she was wearing jeans, sexy boots and a red sweater that for some reason reminded him of Valentines. It looked as soft as her skin and practically begged him to reach out and touch her. He didn't. The ring on her finger made her off-limits. "Is it Arthur?" *King Arthur, king of the girlfriend thieves.*

She blushed, the sure sign of a guilty conscience. "Yes. We just got engaged."

Of course it was Arthur. Colin had known there was something between them when he'd gone to visit her at school. He'd been right to break up with her, and here was the proof. A tornado of emotions swept through him—disappointment, bitterness, anger. Jealousy. He clenched his jaw in an effort to keep in the vitriol he wanted to spew.

Jaw clenching didn't work, and it spilled out. "So why are you here? Doesn't he have a family that can adopt you?"

Who said guys weren't good with words? He could tell the shot had hit home by her pained expression. She shook her head. "And to think you used to be my hero."

Okay, what he'd said had been small and mean. He wished he could take the words back. What a jerk. Did he acknowledge that he was being a jerk? Nope. Instead, he said, "I guess you were hard up for heroes."

"I guess I was."

Her dad certainly hadn't been one. Colin's family was all she'd had growing up. *Say you're sorry, fool.*

Before he could get the words out, she left with her half-filled plate and went to sit by Gram. And she stayed near either her or Aunt Beth the rest of the day, making sure Colin had no opportunity to get near her.

What did it matter, anyway? She was engaged.

Now Mia was back in Icicle Falls, this time with a naked ring finger.

His phone rang. Lorelei again. He could feel his cheeks warming as he answered, "Hey, babe."

Mia finally decided to speak. "Babe?"

He frowned and turned away.

"Are you on your way home?" Lorelei asked.

If only. "No. There's been a complication."

"What kind of complication?"

"I have to stay here a little longer."

"So you're transferring deeds."

"You said you weren't with anyone," Mia said.

"I said I wasn't engaged," he corrected her. What did she think, he'd been a monk all these years? Then, to Lorelei, "Not exactly."

"Are you with somebody?" Lorelei asked.

He wasn't sure how to classify Mia now. He opted for an answer that wouldn't piss off Lorelei. "Just an old family friend."

"Male or female?"

Why did women want to know stuff like that? "She's…" How to explain Mia to Lorelei? He couldn't even explain Mia to himself. "Someone I knew when we were kids," he said, hoping to sidestep the question.

"I don't get why you have to stay there," Lorelei said, sounding petulant.

"I have to look for something."

There was a moment's silence as she tried to translate that. "Look for something."

"What I'm inheriting. It's how the will was set up."

"Where do you have to look?"

"I don't know yet. It's like…a treasure hunt." He cringed saying the words. This was seriously whacked.

"Treasure. Like…buried treasure?"

"I don't know. This has to do with when I was a kid. My grandma always sent us looking for stuff."

"But you don't know what you're looking for now."

"Could be anything." A year's supply of coffee from Bavarian Brews, half interest in a racehorse—who knew? Whatever it was, he hoped it had more than sentimental value. Maybe, with a little bit of money...

"How long will that take?"

Lorelei's voice yanked him back into the present. "I'm not sure."

"Well, then, I should come up and keep you company."

That was all he needed, Lorelei coming to Icicle Falls and meeting Mia. She'd be bound to jump to conclusions. "No, you don't need to do that."

"I don't mind. I hear they've got some really cute shops up there."

"Yeah, but what we're doing is kind of time-consuming."

"You can't bring in outside help," Mia reminded him.

"I know," he said between gritted teeth. "I've gotta go," he told Lorelei. "I'll call you later. Okay?"

"Okay," she said, her tone of voice adding that she didn't like this new development.

"You *are* seeing someone," Mia accused as he put his cell phone in his jeans back pocket.

"So? The will didn't say I couldn't be with someone."

And Lorelei was the best someone he'd been with in a long time. Still, he wasn't ready to make a commitment, even though they'd been together for a year. She was starting to hint about rings and that made him nervous. Marriage hadn't worked so well for Dad, and the one time Colin had jumped in with a ring, it hadn't worked out well for him, either. It was a long fall once you took the big step, and whenever he peered over the edge of Cliff Matrimony, he got a good case of acrophobia.

The last thing he wanted was to discuss his love life. He turned the spotlight on Mia. "Looks like what you had wasn't so serious, after all."

"It didn't work out," she said, then picked up her pace and moved on down the street.

Yeah, good old King Arthur hadn't been much of a king. Colin fell in step beside her. "I'm sorry." Except he wasn't really. He'd never liked the guy and he'd been glad when he heard they'd broken up.

She simply nodded and the uncomfortable silence returned. Things had never been like that between them. Well, not when they were younger, anyway. The memories of their last encounter gave his conscience a sharp poke. *Apologize, fool.*

"Hey, listen, about what I said last time you were home."

She held up a hand. "Let's not go there."

"I want to go there. I'm sorry I was a shit." Eight years after the fact, but better late than never, right?

Wrong. "We all have to be good at something, don't we?" she said, clearly unwilling to forgive or forget.

Well, he had a few bruises himself. "Maybe we can

try for a cease-fire since we have to do this treasure hunt together, okay?"

"Maybe," she said, not making any promises. Then she heaved a sigh. "I'm sorry. I'm not being very nice."

No, she wasn't, and that wasn't like her, at least not the Mia he remembered. He shrugged. "No big deal."

"It was a long time ago," she added.

Yeah, it was. Old wounds shouldn't hurt. But they did. Why was that? And why, after all this time, did he still want to reach out and touch her?

Another wave of silence rolled in as they walked down the street toward Gram's house. He launched a new conversational gambit. "So, you still like Chicago?"

She nodded. "It's a great city. Lots of wonderful restaurants, theaters, museums."

Of course she'd be all over the museums, brainiac that she was.

"The botanic garden. You'd like that," she said, making an effort. Then she abruptly shifted gears. "Why'd you end up in Seattle?"

"I don't know. Inertia, I guess."

She frowned.

Yes, I am a loser.

"Aunt Beth says you're working in a warehouse."

She made it sound as if he was the world's biggest underachiever. "There's nothing wrong with working in a warehouse." Good, honest work as Gramps would have said. Except it was a far cry from what he'd wanted to do.

"No, of course not," she hurried to agree. "I'm just

surprised you ended up there. I would never have left Icicle Falls."

"Yeah? Well, you did."

Her cheeks turned red. "I mean, if I were you."

Now his cheeks felt a little warm. He'd started out with the best of intentions. After what had happened with them, he'd buckled down and finished his two-year degree, coming out with straight As. Then he'd shocked everyone by going on to Washington State University and getting a degree in horticulture, specializing in fruit and vegetable management. Yeah, he'd had dreams.

But after that he got off track somehow, wound up following a college buddy to Seattle on the spur of the moment and taking a job in a warehouse. Good money and all that.

He was still at the warehouse, and the good money never seemed to be enough. Living in the city was expensive. So was having a girlfriend.

He kept talking about returning to Icicle Falls or somewhere in Eastern Washington and buying himself a small orchard. He had that hard-won degree from WSU, but the money he needed kept evading him. Dad had helped him get through school, but contrary to popular belief, not all lawyers were rich, and it wouldn't have felt right to hit his father up for a loan. He had to lasso his dream by himself. Anyway, Dad had done enough.

It was probably too much to hope that this treasure of Gram's would turn out to be *real* treasure, like more stock options or bearer bonds. A few gold coins would be nice, or a couple thousand bucks. That would be a start.

"I'll get back someday," he said. When the time was right. He pushed away the question of what if the time was never right.

They reached the house, and a flood of memories whooshed out at him—mowing the lawn for Gram, sitting on the front porch step drinking her homemade lemonade, picking apples from the tree in the backyard. Even though she'd downsized, she'd still managed to find a house with an apple tree.

Gram had moved here after she'd sold the orchard to pay for Gramps's long-term care. It must have killed her to let it go, but when he'd asked her if she was okay, she'd put a smile on her face and said, "Home is where the heart is." She'd proceeded to prove it by gathering her family for Sunday dinners and her famous homemade pies—cherry, banana cream, blackberry. And of course, apple. Blackberry with homemade ice cream was Colin's favorite, and she always made one for the Fourth of July. Pie and ice cream and Sunday afternoons at Gram's, the best.

Colin remembered those Sundays, so full of innocent fun—trying to beat Uncle Mark at badminton, slurping root beer floats on the porch, sitting around the kitchen table, drinking hot cider and playing cards with his family on a snowy afternoon, grinning across the table at Mia like a fool.

Like a fool. Boy, that was about it.

They stepped inside, and he swore he could smell

cinnamon from Gram's apple crisp. He looked at Mia and saw that she was caught in the same memory trap.

"I can still feel her here," Mia said softly. She walked into the living room and ran a hand over the blue velvet couch that had been Gram's pride and joy. "I can't believe she's gone."

"Eighty-six is a long time to live," Colin said, trying to console both of them.

"It is. I just wish she could've lived to see…" The sentence trailed off.

"To see what?" Colin prompted.

"Nothing." She walked over to the bookcase that held Gram's scrapbooks and photo albums.

They'd spent a fair number of wintry Sunday afternoons going through those scrapbooks when they were kids, laughing at pictures of Aunt Beth as a pudgy, bespectacled tween, and then, as an adult, with her big eighties hair. Uncle Mark's Mohawk had cracked them up, too. Colin had especially liked the shot of Dad with his Datsun 280Z. He was smiling, something he didn't do a lot. Colin had also been fascinated by the pictures of Gramps, young and tough looking, wearing jeans and a white T-shirt with a pack of cigarettes rolled up in one sleeve, and of Gram, slim and pretty, posing in the apple orchard. Then there'd been the pictures of her at the town's information booth, passing out leaflets advertising the new and improved Icicle Falls to tourists, pictures of her holding a pie and a blue ribbon at the county fair, pictures of her with various foster kids. And of course, pictures of the old orchard and farmhouse, starting from when Gram and Gramps first bought it back in 1960.

The collection of scrapbooks had grown over the years, adding memory after memory—Colin and Mia waving from the tree house Dad and Uncle Mark had helped them build in the old maple at the orchard house. Pictures of them in front of Gram's Christmas tree, and out in the backyard at that same house with their Easter baskets. He knew there'd also be an album filled with shots of them when they were older—high school dances, parties, Mia's graduation when he gave her the promise ring. He hoped Gram hadn't hidden a clue in that photo album.

Mia took one of her favorite albums and settled on the couch with it. This one chronicled Colin's and her grade-school years. She opened it and there they were, dressed up for Halloween, him as an eight-year-old superhero, her as a seven-year-old princess. Colin as a superhero summed up how she viewed him back then. He'd been her hero ever since he punched Billy Williams in the eye after Billy called her a dumb girl.

"She's not dumb. She's smart, smarter than you," Colin had said.

"You like her," Billy had taunted, and Colin had socked him.

Mia had translated that as true love. Looking back, she knew it was more a case of true embarrassment, but at the time it had seemed very heroic. And maybe it was a little, since the dispute had started over whether or not to allow her into the newly constructed tree house.

"Boys only," Billy had insisted.

"She helped build it. That makes her a boy," Colin had reasoned.

Mia's heart had swelled with pride at the compliment. Oh, yes. Colin had been a true hero. They'd been so close as kids, best buddies. Now here they were, barely speaking. All thanks to Colin being such a quick-tempered skunkball. How many times had she told herself she was well rid of him after he'd broken up with her? Not enough, because now as he sat next to her with another album, here she was, feeling all tingly, just like she'd felt the first time he kissed her. *No tingles. Stop that right now.*

The tingles were obviously hard of hearing.

"This could take hours," he grumbled.

What a poor sport. "Oh, yeah, *babe* is waiting for you. Well, feel free to leave. I'll let you know when I find something." A noble offer that still sounded catty. *Meow.* All she needed now was a litter box and a scratching post.

What did his girlfriend look like? What did she care?

He frowned. "I didn't say I was leaving. And you can stop taking potshots about the girlfriend. It's not like you never had anyone," he added, bitterness seeping into his voice.

Oh, no. That was a card he didn't get to play. "We're not discussing that." The frown carved itself deeper into his face, but he dropped the subject.

She turned another page. "There's your tenth birthday party."

He looked over and smiled. "I remember that. Gramps gave me a jackknife."

"Grandma Justine was worried you'd cut yourself."

"I did, and it hurt like a son of a gun. Dad took the knife away and wouldn't let me have it until I was thirteen."

She glanced at his album. "Oh, my sewing club with Aunt Beth." There she was, a sixth grader, gathered with several other girls, including Bailey Sterling-Black, who'd been the youngest of the gang, all proudly displaying the quilted wall hangings Aunt Beth had helped them make.

"Someday I'll make your wedding dress for you," Aunt Beth had promised, and when Mia had gotten engaged Aunt Beth had reminded her of that promise. It had been pretty embarrassing to have to call and tell her never mind.

Colin flipped through the pages of his photo album, sending their lives flashing past—picnics, birthday parties, lost teeth—then shut the book. "Nothing in here." He set it aside and opened another and began the same quick perusal.

Following his example, Mia did a similar check. So much for the reminiscence Grandma Justine had suggested in her first clue.

She selected the next album. This new one contained pictures of the apple orchard and the farmhouse, as well as some taken at Beth's place.

There was one of her grandfather, who had helped work the orchard. He was fairly young, wearing overalls and a straw hat that covered his thick, dark hair.

She'd only been a year old when he and her grand-mother had returned to Mexico. There'd been plans for her mother to visit, but then they were killed in a car accident and that had been the end of any plans.

In spite of her loss, Mama was happy in Icicle Falls. The pictures of her grandparents, while interesting, were essentially pictures of strangers. The album containing so many snapshots of her mother was another story. She used to go to it as a child, hoping the sight of that smiling face would keep her connected. Mostly it made her cry. As she got older the crying subsided. But the ache in her chest never left, even though she tried to concentrate on the happy memories. The pictures of Mama when she was younger and so beautiful and full of life were still the hardest to look at—all those poses with happiness resting on her face, before the cancer hit, before her husband abandoned her. She'd been a Miss Icicle Falls, and when Mia was a little girl and looked at the pictures of her mother sitting on that parade float in her ice-blue evening gown, she'd been sure she was a princess.

Too bad Mia's father hadn't been a prince.

She quickly turned the page. There was a picture of Colin and her when they were kindergarten and pre-school age. It was summer, and someone had snapped a shot of them playing in a wading pool set up in Aunt Beth's backyard. Colin was splashing wildly and Mia had her head turned away, her eyes shut, her hands held up in a feeble attempt to shield herself from the water. She recognized Aunt Beth's printing on the edge of the picture. *Bold and Bashful*. Yep, that about summed them up.

Another snapshot showed Mia on Grandma Justine's front porch, her arms around another little girl. Bella, one of Grandma Justine's many foster kids. She and Bella had been BFFs, sworn lasting allegiance to each other. But then Bella had moved away, back to her parents in Yakima. And that had been that. There'd always been friends to make at Grandma Justine's. And friends to lose.

She had just closed the album and was contemplating this when a knock on the front door startled her.

"What the heck?" Colin muttered. He opened the front door and there stood one of Icicle Falls's finest, looking buff in her cop uniform. "Tilda?"

They'd both known Tilda Morrison for years. Mia remembered when Tilda had first started out as a police cadet in high school. Nobody had messed with her even back then, and nobody had teased her. Except Colin, who'd nicknamed her Dirty Harriet.

But what was this? Mia wondered as she stood beside Colin at the door. There was a diamond ring on Tilda's left hand.

"We had a call about a break-in here," Tilda said.

"When?" Colin asked.

Tilda half smiled. "Now."

"Oh, yeah. Funny," he said.

Another voice joined in. "I told you someone was in the house, and with that poor woman hardly in her grave. What kind of high-crime neighborhood have I moved into, anyway?"

Mia glanced around Tilda to see a thin, older woman with gray hair, glasses and a slouch marching up the sidewalk. She wore a black jogging outfit, and between that and her sharp nose, Mia couldn't help but think of crows.

"Go home, Mrs. Beecham. Everything's fine," Tilda said firmly.

Tilda the cop was tougher than jerky. Nobody talked back to her.

Apparently, Mrs. Beecham never got the memo. "Well, who are they?" she demanded.

Judging by the expression on Tilda's face, Mrs. Beecham was one question away from getting arrested for being irritating. Mia leaned around Tilda and called, "We're family."

Mrs. Beecham marched up onto the front porch. "Family?" She peered past Tilda, taking in Colin and Mia with eager, squinty eyes. "Are you her grandchildren?"

"I am," Colin said. "We're here looking for something."

"Well, I can't imagine what you hope to find," Mrs. Beecham said. "I don't think that little old lady had much."

"Let's let them get back to what they were doing," Tilda said, barring the door. This was probably a good thing, since the new neighbor looked ready to come in and see exactly what the little old lady did have.

"All right," Mrs. Beecham said. Then to Colin, "Don't you worry. I'm keeping an eye on the place."

"And every other place on the block," Colin murmured as the woman went back down the front walk.

"She's starting a neighborhood watch," Tilda said.

"Oh, yeah. We need that in Icicle Falls."

"Even small towns have problems," Tilda informed him. "Great to see you guys, by the way. Sorry about Grandma J. I'm gonna miss those ginger cookies she used to bring by the station."

"Tell Aunt Beth," Colin suggested. "She'll keep it going."

Tilda smiled at that. "Great idea."

"What's with the ring?" Colin asked. "Who'd you sucker into a life sentence?"

To Mia's surprise, Tilda actually blushed. But she still managed to shoot back, "How do you know it wasn't me who got suckered?"

"Touché," Mia said approvingly. "Seriously, is it anyone we've met?"

"Devon Black, Todd's brother."

"So you'll be related to Bailey," Mia said. "Lucky you."

"Yeah. The way she bakes, you won't have to worry about not getting any cookies," Colin added.

"When's the wedding?" Mia asked.

"December. Maddy Donaldson practically had a fit when she heard we wanted to have it at the station. She's determined to dress the place up like something out of a frickin' Martha Stewart magazine."

Mia giggled, envisioning ribbons wrapped around the cell bars and the chief's desk awash in flowers. "What does your mom say to that?"

Tilda rolled her eyes. "She's almost as bad. She's already talked about hiring that wedding planner who bought a cabin up here, and she wants to invite the whole damn town."

"Why not? You've given traffic tickets to the whole damn town," Colin teased.

Tilda pointed a warning finger at him. "Don't get on my bad side. I'll give you a ticket just for being ugly."

Since he was gorgeous and they all knew it, he merely grinned.

"Okay, I've got better things to do than stand around talking to you two fake burglars," Tilda said and turned to go down the front steps.

Colin laughed. "Yeah, it's probably time for a doughnut break."

She kept walking, saying goodbye with a raised middle finger.

"Man, that guy's in for a ride," Colin said, smiling and shaking his head as they returned to the photo albums. "You wouldn't catch me marrying the Iron Maiden."

Who would *I catch you marrying?* Mia stopped the words before they could escape. *Who cares? Who cares, who cares, who cares, who cares?*

She picked up a new photo album and began to leaf through it. She didn't have to go very far before she came across another piece of pink paper, folded in thirds and wedged between pages displaying pictures of the orchard. One photograph in particular had captured the beauty of the orchard in spring. The photographer, likely Grandma Justine, had gotten a long shot of two rows of trees in full, elegant bloom, their branches a froth of white and sunshine. It brought back memories of playing hide-and-seek and of running from row to row, searching for Easter baskets.

And now she'd found what they were seeking. "Got it."

Colin tossed aside his album. "Nice work. What does it say?"

She opened it and read, "'You two need to take a walk down Memory Lane and this is a good place to start.'"

His brow furrowed. "What kind of clue is that?"

"A cryptic one."

"I thought we were going down Memory Lane, looking through these albums."

"It would appear that she wants us to actually go somewhere."

He considered that for a moment and then bounded across the living room. "It's gotta be the attic."

"Don't worry about putting these back," Mia muttered.

Of course he didn't hear her. He was already on his way upstairs. Leaving behind a mess. What was this, a race?

But that had always been Colin, running ahead to the next clue, often jumping to conclusions. He'd loved the obvious ones in their childhood treasure hunts, ones that involved counting out paces or dashing to a specified spot, while Mia had enjoyed the challenge of riddles they had to puzzle out.

She put away the albums and then followed him up

to the attic. It was huge and filled with everything from a steamer trunk to antique dolls and old percolators and furniture that needed to be reupholstered. Colin was busy pawing around in a bunch of old wicker baskets.

"Bet it's in here," he said, opening a picnic basket.

"Bet it's not," she joked, watching his face fall as he came up empty. "What about the trunk?"

He opened the trunk and pulled out a pink envelope with a crow of triumph. She hurried over as he tore it open, then she looked over his shoulder.

You're getting colder.

She couldn't help chuckling as he crumpled the paper with a scowl and shut the taunting nonclue back in the trunk. "What's that supposed to mean?"

"I think it means that this isn't really the Memory Lane she's talking about," Mia replied. "It's got to be something physical, some kind of real lane."

"Lavender Lane," he said. "Maybe it's in that tea shop of Bailey's."

"The tea shop's too new. We don't have any memories there."

"Well, then, where?" he asked, impatient as usual. Then, "Wait a minute. You don't think…"

Memory Lane was the nickname for a little dirt road outside town that led to the river. It had no official name and, along with the parking area at the trailhead to Lost Bride Falls, it had been a favorite make-out spot for generations.

"But Gram wouldn't know about that," Mia protested.

"Gram knew about everything and everybody," Colin argued. "Come on. Let's go."

They hurried down the street and around the corner, back to Dylan's office, where they'd left their cars. "We can take my car," Colin said, unlocking the passenger door.

Getting in his car was like stepping back in time. "I can't believe you've still got this."

"She's a gas hog but she's well made. I'll keep her forever," he said.

It was more than he'd done for her.

Memory Lane was pretty much overgrown, and they wound up driving over all manner of ferns and flowers, with tree branches reaching out to scrape the car. They hadn't gone far before Colin decided to get out and walk rather than expose his baby to damage.

"I don't think this is what she meant," Mia said, looking around as they started toward the river. "This isn't someplace Gram and Aunt Beth would come to hide a clue."

"Oh, yeah?" He pointed off in the distance to a piece of paper caught in some blackberry brambles.

"That's not a pink envelope," she said.

"Well, it's some kind of paper. She probably didn't use the same paper for every clue."

"I'm sure it's something that just blew there and got caught in the blackberries," Mia surmised. "Aunt Beth wouldn't go stomping through all that just to hide a clue."

"Uncle Mark would. I bet Gram got him to help," Colin said, and charged into the underbrush.

She was in shorts; he was in jeans. She let him go in on his own.

He'd only taken a few steps when he brushed at his neck. "Crap."

She couldn't resist saying, "Told you."

He wasn't interested in either her I-told-you-so or the scrap of paper in the blackberries. Something else had his attention. He whirled sideways and waved his hands in front of his face like the Karate Kid practicing wax on, wax off in fast motion. "Crap!"

Then he began running in her direction, crashing back through the underbrush, hands waving every which way. "Bees! Run for it."

July 14, 1993

Dear Mother,
As you can see by the enclosed picture, we've had quite the building project going on around here. Mark and Dylan did the sawing and heavy lifting but Colin and Mia did all the nailing. They love their new tree fort and we can hardly get them out of it.

The other child in the picture is Jimmy Conner, our new foster child. He's going to be with us until his mother can get her life straightened out. Only six and he's already been through so much! He's a sweet boy and a little shy, but Colin has taken him under his wing and I think he's going to do well here. When he's not following Colin and Mia around, he likes being in the kitchen with me. The child is always hungry. I can't help wondering if he's ever gotten enough to eat. It makes me sad to think about how many other little Jimmys are out there in need of love. Gerald reminds me that we can't save them all. I wish we could!

Let's see, what other news is there? The annual church picnic was a huge success. My friend Sarah and I baked twenty-five pies for the pie-eating contest. I won the ladies' shoe kick, beating several of the younger women. Coach Armstrong said I'd be great at kicking field goals and asked if I'd like to try out for the high school football team. Colin and Mia won the three-legged race, and Dylan and Mark's team won the tug-of-war. So you might say the Wright family swept the games.

Gerald tried to keep up with the younger men playing softball and pulled a calf muscle, and now he's limping around. Other than that, we're all fine.

I'd better run. Jimmy and I are going to pick blackberries as I promised him a pie.

Love,
Justine

Chapter Four

Mia felt a sharp sting on her neck. Yikes! Bees! No, not bees. These were yellow jackets, a type of wasp, meanest of the mean, especially when some clueless human disturbed their nest.

She'd never been much of an athlete, but with Colin about to trample her and an angry buzz in her ears, she set a world record in her dash back to the car. She yanked open the door and threw herself onto the passenger seat, pulling the door shut behind her. Colin did the same on his side, sealing them in with an angry insect.

A decision had to be made. Stay inside and deal with Betty Bee or hop back out and risk encountering more of the family. Mia chose option one. Sort of.

"It's in the car," she shrieked, and crumpled into a ball, her arms over her head.

Colin was obviously swatting at it because the whole car was rocking like an amusement park ride. *The Towering Beehive*. The bee *zzzed* past her head. "Eeek!"

"Shit!" Colin yelped. "Shit! Crap!" Meanwhile, he

was slapping windows, the dashboard and finally her as the bee tried for a landing on her arm.

"Hey!" she protested.

"Sorry. Ow!" She heard another slapping noise. "Got it," he announced.

She uncurled herself to see that their common enemy had been vanquished. But Colin wasn't without his battle scars. His arms and neck all had waspish love bites.

"You're a mess," she informed him.

He scowled. "These hurt like the devil."

"Let's go back to Aunt Beth's. She'll get us fixed up."

"What's this *us*?" he grumped as he started the car. "You didn't get stung."

She pointed to her neck. "I guess I'm hallucinating this pain. Jeez, Colin, I told you that paper wasn't anything."

"We don't know that."

"I know it. But if you don't believe me, you're welcome to go back out there."

He frowned and backed down the road. "Never mind. You're probably right."

"I can see how you might think that paper was a clue," Mia said after a moment, trying to turn the conversation in a more positive direction. In fairness to Colin, the treasure hunts Grandma Justine concocted for them when they were young had often involved clues in obvious places—propped in front of her sheet music on the old player piano or sitting on the kitchen table. Except the ones in plain sight outdoors had also been carefully anchored.

"I jumped to conclusions," he admitted, rubbing his arm.

Typical, she thought, but kept it to herself. "This is her last treasure hunt. I suspect all our clues will be elaborate and carefully planned. But easily accessible, either by her or your aunt."

"Or Uncle Mark," Colin insisted. "I bet they suckered him into helping them."

"True," Mia agreed. Uncle Mark was easygoing and fun loving, and he'd always gotten a kick out of giving Gram and Beth a hand.

"Still, none of them would've gone stomping into the underbrush, stirring up a yellow jackets' nest."

"You wouldn't have, either, normally," she said, ready to be magnanimous.

"It's this whole weird situation. It's… I don't know," he finished lamely as they pulled up in front of Beth's house.

It *was* weird, being thrown together like this, and it was hard work dragging around their complicated past. What had Grandma Justine been thinking, anyway?

"What on earth?" Aunt Beth greeted them.

"We encountered a slight setback," Mia said.

"Yellow jackets," Colin put in.

"So I see," his aunt murmured, taking in his neck and arms. "Good thing you're not allergic. Ibuprofen is in the medicine cabinet," she told Mia. "Come on out to the kitchen," she said to Colin. "Let's get you fixed up."

By the time Mia returned with the pain reliever,

Aunt Beth had made a baking soda paste and was applying it to Colin's wounds while he sat at the kitchen table, an ice pack pressed to his neck. "Where were you two?" she asked.

"Memory Lane," Colin answered.

"Obviously not the right one," Aunt Beth said with a smile.

"Obviously. You want to give us a hint?"

"Tsk, tsk." She shook a playful finger at him. "You know the rules. No outside help."

"You're not outside help. You're family." This was accompanied by the charming smile no woman in Icicle Falls could resist, especially Colin's aunt.

Still, she managed. "Between the two of you, you should be able to figure this out." She handed the paste to Mia. "I'll leave you to finish up your treatment. I'm busy altering a wedding gown for a wedding at Primrose Haus next month," she said, and left the room.

Colin cleared his throat. "So what should we try next?"

Mia handed him the bottle of pain pills. "Obviously, we have to go back to thinking symbolically."

"Not the attic."

"No, not the attic," she agreed.

He filled a glass of water and washed down a pill, then stood looking out the kitchen window. "Well, duh."

"What?" she prompted.

"If we're going to go down Memory Lane and it's not in the photo albums and it's not in the attic…"

"The tree house?"

"We've got a lot of memories there."

"I think that's it," she said.

"Good. Let's go."

"Maybe we should find out who owns the apple orchard now, call and see if it's okay if we come over," Mia suggested.

"We'll explain who we are when we get there, and it'll be fine." Then, without waiting for any further argument, Colin was out the door and on his way down the walk.

Mia hurried after him, hoping he was right. Not that she hadn't enjoyed seeing Tilda, but two visits from the police in one day would be overkill.

It didn't take long to drive to his grandparents' old place on Apple Blossom Road, which was just as well. The sooner they were done with this treasure hunt, the better Colin would like it. Being around Mia was downright uncomfortable, the emotional equivalent of what he'd experienced with the yellow jackets. Memories both good and bad swarmed him, and their sting was ten times worse than what the wasps had delivered. Yeah, the sooner they found whatever Gram had left them and divided the spoils, the better. Then they could go their separate ways. He'd move on, take whatever he got and maybe finally get to start that sustainable orchard he'd envisioned about a million years ago.

That took care of the business dreams. The dreams of the heart were a different matter. Well, he wasn't in any hurry to rush into anything when it came to a binding relationship with someone of the opposite sex.

He'd learned his lesson. True love and fool's gold had a lot in common.

"There it is," Mia said.

The orchard. Seeing those rows of trees growing Gala apples was enough to put a lump in Colin's throat. For years his family's life had centered on that orchard. It was more than a source of income; it was part of the fabric of their lives. Gram had a million apple recipes for everything from pies and fresh apple cake to apple crisp, which she made in the fall, to mulligatawny soup, a winter staple. No Halloween party was complete without bobbing for apples or trying to grab a bite from one dangling from a string in Aunt Beth's basement, which often served as Party Central. Colin had had many conversations about school and sports and life in general with Gramps in that orchard.

He could still see himself working side by side with Gramps and his pickers, harvesting those Galas at the end of August, carefully putting them into fruit bins. At the end of the harvest, the apples had gone to the warehouse where they'd be stored in a temperature-controlled environment, then packed and shipped to buyers. Harvest was a busy time and everybody worked. The men picked while the women sold fruit at the fruit stand. In addition to apples, they'd also grown cherries and pears, and plenty of people drove over from the western side of the state to enjoy freshly harvested fruit and a mountain getaway.

Colin had earned money to pay for gas and car insurance by picking apples. He and Mia had chased each other in and out of all those rows of trees. He'd kissed her in the orchard—and they'd almost gone all the way…

Their whole history after puberty seemed to be one of almosts. He sneaked a look at Mia to see if her first glimpse of the old place was having the same effect on her. She was wiping at her eyes. Yep, it was. They passed the old dirt road that ran through the orchard and kept going, finally turning down the drive that led to the farmhouse.

Apple trees laden with fruit lined one side of the road. The misters were on, keeping the apples from getting sunburned. In another three weeks it would be harvest time. Colin wondered who did the harvesting now.

A minute later the old house itself came into view, a two-story structure painted yellow with white trim. The porch was surrounded by flower beds filled with shrubs and Shasta daisies. The battered old truck parked in front of the house made the place look like one of those paintings that hung in the windows of antiques shops in Eastern Washington. There was the old red barn, and there was the vegetable garden, still growing veggies, and the raspberry patch. And the yard with the old maple still holding their childhood tree house. Who did own the place now? Whoever it was had done a good job of maintaining it. The house had been freshly painted and the lawn mowed. The only thing showing its age was the tree house.

"I don't know," Mia said dubiously, looking at it. "The wood's probably rotten."

"Uncle Mark would still find a way to hide a clue there, no problem," Colin said.

No problem with the tree, but what was this? A German shepherd had just run around the corner of the house, barking, and that brought someone out the front door—a heavyset middle-aged man with a scruffy beard and thinning hair, wearing faded jeans, a T-shirt and cowboy boots.

"Uh-oh," Mia said. "I think we should've called before we came."

"It's okay. His tail's wagging."

"Not the man's," Mia said, pointing.

The guy didn't exactly look friendly. Neither did the shotgun Colin noticed leaning against the doorway. But nobody in Icicle Falls would shoot someone for dropping by.

Colin got out of the car and bent to pet the dog that was happy to lick his hand. He hoped the man would be as easily won over.

"Can I help you?" he called as he picked up the gun.

"Yeah," Colin called back. "My grandma used to own this place."

The man leaned the gun back against the house and started down the front porch steps. "Was your grandma Justine Wright?"

Colin nodded.

The man smiled, showing a missing incisor. "Great lady."

Mia had now decided it was safe to come out. She joined them and received some doggy kisses, as well.

"Beth told me you'd be coming by," said the man. He held out a hand. "Butch Garvey."

"Colin Wright. This is Mia Blair."

"I know all about you kids. I've been expecting you."

"So our next clue's here?" Colin asked.

Garvey nodded then spat a stream of tobacco juice. "Oh, yeah. It's around here somewhere. I helped her with it. That's some treasure your grandma has you looking for. Make yourselves at home," he added, and walked off across the yard.

Some treasure. What did that mean? It was all Colin could do not to go after Butch Garvey and ask. "So," he said as he and Mia crossed the yard, the dog dancing alongside them, "if he helped Gram, the clue could easily be in the tree house."

"You're liable to fall through the floor," she cautioned.

"Nah," he said, and began climbing up the tree.

The tree house was nothing more than a rotting four-by-six platform surrounded by equally decayed plywood walls, one with a door and another with a small window cut in it. Looking in, Colin could see all the bent nails testifying to his childish lack of carpentry skills. He remembered when this was his fortress. He could still see the dent in the wall where he'd kicked it with his foot that late June night. And there, still tacked to the wall, was the old, faded photo of him and Prince. He remembered the last time he'd been in this tree house...

Colin gave the plywood wall of the tree house an angry kick. And then another. He swiped at the tears coursing down his cheeks. Twelve was too old to cry, but he couldn't help it. Prince was dead, and he shouldn't be. Yeah, he'd gotten banged up real bad when Gramps accidentally backed over him with the truck, but he could have been fixed. Dad had no right to let the vet put him down. They'd had him since Colin was four and, next to Mia, Prince was his best friend. He kicked the wall again, denting the wood.

"Colin?"

He jumped at the sound of Mia's voice. Crap. He was crying. He couldn't be caught crying. "Go away," he said, his voice breaking. He'd come here to be alone and that meant even from her.

She didn't leave. Instead, she came in and he turned his face so she couldn't see the shameful tears.

"I didn't want you to be alone. I won't tell anybody you're crying. Cross my heart and hope to kiss a pig."

He hugged his knees and buried his face in his arms and just let go.

She scooted next to him and put an arm around his shoulders. "I'll miss him, too."

"It's not right. Dad shouldn't have had him put down. They could have operated. They should have. I don't care how much it cost!"

"I'm real sorry," she said. And then scooted to the opposite wall. That was when he saw she had something in her hand. It was a picture of him and Prince, his handsome German shepherd, on the front porch of Gram's farmhouse. He was grinning and it looked as if Prince was, too.

He wiped away tears and watched as she stuck the picture in the wall with a thumbtack. "Thanks," he said.

"Prince was a good dog."

He sat a moment, staring at the picture, then at Mia, trying to sort through all the feelings he was experiencing. Humiliation took top priority. "You really won't tell?"

She shook her head.

He nodded and focused on the picture again. "Thanks."

She leaned back against the wall and sat there with him, looking at Prince.

Mia had stayed in this tree house, keeping him company until it got dark and the adults found them and made them come inside. That had been the last time they'd gone in it. School had started shortly after, and Colin had gotten involved with the new adventure of middle school.

It was too bad that the day of Prince's death was his last memory of this kid haven, because there'd been plenty of good ones, too. Eating snickerdoodles, the first cookies Mia ever made—she'd put in too much sugar and they were great—and pretending that they were marooned on a desert island with nothing else to eat, hiding from pesky little Tommy Watkins, spying on Gram as she weeded the flower bed, working their way through a book of hidden-object games.

Since the tree house had played such a big part in their childhood, he was surprised there was no clue here.

"Find anything?" Mia called from down below.

"Nope."

"I've got another idea," she said. "Come on."

He started making his way back down. Just like the tree house, some of the branches were getting old and brittle. One protested the burden of his weight, snapping under his foot. He grabbed for another to catch himself, but that one, too, let him down, breaking in half. He lost his balance and fell, crashing into Mia in the process and bringing them both to the ground, him on top of her.

The Urge to Merge Control Center in his brain went into action, putting every bit of testosterone in his body on full alert. There were those lips of hers, soft and begging to be kissed.

"Get off," said the lips.

Colin's face caught fire. His gram had obviously designed this treasure hunt to make a fool of him. "Sorry," he mumbled, scrambling off her. "Are you okay?" he asked as he helped her up.

She rubbed an elbow. "I think so. Come on."

She hurried across the yard, walking in the direction of the orchard. He fell in step with her. "The orchard?"

"Yes. Remember that picture in the photo album?"

"We looked at a lot of pictures in a lot of photo albums."

"There was one of the orchard."

"So?"

"So, you'll see," she said.

Another few minutes, and they stood at the edge of the orchard, by a row of trees.

"Okay," he said, "what am I looking at?"

"The same thing that was in the picture," she said, pointing.

"Trees."

"No."

And then he saw it. "A lane."

"Memory Lane."

It did look like a shady lane between those trees. But with rows and rows of them, how many lanes were there? They'd be here forever, and if they didn't find anything they'd have wasted the rest of the day. Still, he didn't have any better ideas.

"Well, let's start at the road and work our way down," he said. "I'll take one end and you take the other, and we'll meet in the middle. Yell if you find anything."

An hour later he heard her calling his name. He jogged down the dirt path for a couple of rows and found her looking up into a tree.

"Got it," she said, and pointed to a branch where a Mason jar hung suspended. Sure enough, inside it was a pink paper, folded into a small square.

"All right! Way to go," he said, and started to climb the tree.

"Maybe I should do that," she suggested.

"I can handle it," he assured her.

This time he was more careful, hanging on the bough like some kind of jungle snake and inching out to where the jar hung. It had been secured with wire and required some fiddling to free it, but he finally succeeded.

Since she'd been the one to spot it, he gave her the honor of pulling out the clue. She unfolded it and there was Gram's spidery writing.

I hope you've enjoyed your walk in the orchard.
Did it bring back any memories?

Did it ever. There was something enchanted about this orchard. A guy could imagine he'd stepped back in time. Colin could still see the flash of long dark hair as Mia ducked behind a tree when they were playing tag, could see himself helping Gramps and his hired workers with the harvest. And then there was the day he and Mia had come so close to teen heaven. He could still remember the smell of her hair, the feel of her lips under his, how perfect she'd felt in his arms. The sun had been warm on his back, the warmth spreading through his whole body. It had been just the two of them, caught up in their own world.

He looked at her. Her cheeks were suddenly pink.

He moved closer and breathed in a fresh whiff of her perfume. Oh, yeah. Perfume was such a turn-on. "What are you remembering?" he asked softly.

"Playing hide-and-seek out here."

That wasn't what had made her blush. "What else?"

She leaned toward him. Subtle, just an inch, but he noticed it. They could relive that moment when everything had been so close to perfect, and this time there was no one to stop them. With one kiss they could turn back the clock…

His cell phone rang, breaking the spell.

October 6, 1993

Dear Mother,
Thank you for sending your recipe for apple cake. I made it for our family at Sunday dinner and it was a great hit. Jimmy ate two slices. He'll be with us through November and then he'll probably be going back to his mother. I'm certainly going to miss that little boy! You'll get to meet him when you come.

Everyone is excited about you and Emmaline and her family coming out for Thanksgiving. And how lovely that Emmaline and Joey's J.J. has finally found someone. I'm glad he and his intended will be joining us, too. It looks like we'll have a house full.

Now, let me tell you about my fifteen minutes of fame. I was proclaimed this year's Lady of the Autumn Leaves, a title awarded to a woman who has contributed in some significant way to the community. I was honored at a luncheon with the mayor, the city council members and the members of the Chamber of Commerce, and given a framed certificate of appreciation for my years of community service. I was also given a lovely bouquet of autumn flowers. A picture of me in my dirndl will hang in City Hall, along with the portraits of the other ladies who've received this honor over the past six years. I'm enclosing the

*newspaper article so you can read all about it.
The picture in the paper is of our Oktoberfest
parade on Saturday and yes, that's me on the
Autumn Leaves float. Did you ever think you'd
see your daughter riding on a float in a parade?
And at sixty-three, no less!*

*After the parade and festival, the family took
me to Schwangau, our town's most elegant restaurant, to celebrate. Such a day! I'll spend the
rest of the year attending various festivals as an
ambassador for Icicle Falls and riding on our
float in their parades, including Seattle's Sea-
fair parade, a very big one, indeed. It just goes
to show, a woman is never obsolete, no matter
what her age.*

*We're having another beautiful fall, as col-
orful as a paint box with the vine maples and
larches in all their red-and-gold glory. Of course,
the children can think of nothing but Halloween,
and Beth is sewing elaborate costumes for them.
Colin wants to be the Phantom of the Opera,
Jimmy wants to be a pirate and Mia wants to be
a fairy. You should see the fairy wings Bethie's
made for her. They're simply astonishing. I'll be
sure to take pictures of them in their costumes
and send them to you. In addition to sewing the
costumes, Bethie is planning a Halloween party
for the children and their friends with bobbing
for apples and a scavenger hunt. All this on top
of running her business and taking classes at
the local community college! She wants to get a*

two-year degree so she can say she accomplished something. If you ask me, she's already accomplished plenty. She's now not only doing alterations, she's making wedding gowns for some of our local brides. I'm so proud of her.

One sad note is Anna's health. The poor girl has been through so much—losing her parents in that terrible car accident in Mexico when Mia was barely two, then the cancer and her horrible husband abandoning her. And now the cancer is back. The prognosis for this latest recurrence isn't good, and I think we have some dark days looming in the New Year. But we're going to do all we can to make the holidays wonderful for both her and Mia. Having you all with us for Thanksgiving will be a huge bonus.

Must close now. I need to get over to Mountain Memories Photography to have my Lady of the Autumn Leaves portrait taken.

Love,
Justine

Chapter Five

Mia stepped away from Colin. Thank God his phone had rung. For a moment there, her common sense had taken a vacation.

She watched as he checked caller ID, then answered, "Hey, what's up?"

"Babe again?" Colin had said he wasn't engaged, but was he close to it? And if he was, what was he doing looking at her the way he'd looked at her just now, leaning kissing close, resurrecting the tingles?

The corners of his mouth pulled down and he turned his back. "No, we're still working at this. It's gonna take a while. I don't know. I'll call you tonight, okay? Same here."

Same here. What did that mean? Had *babe* said she loved him? If so, why hadn't he said the words back to her? How serious was his relationship with the mysterious *babe* if he was too embarrassed to tell her he loved her in front of someone, especially when that someone was an ex whom he could make jealous? Not that she was jealous. And Colin's love life was no business of hers. What they'd once had was long gone. It had been nothing more than young, stupid love.

Except those old feelings seemed to resurface pretty easily.

"What else does the letter say?" Colin asked, bringing their mission back into focus.

She read, "'Family is important. You can learn so much from those who have loved well and lived longer than you.'"

His brows drew together. "So, where's the clue?"

"I think that was the clue."

"Well, that leaves us with Dad, Uncle Mark or Aunt Beth," he said.

"Probably not your dad or Uncle Mark." Uncle Mark was a great guy, but most of his knowledge came from ESPN, which hardly qualified him as a sage. And Dylan wasn't likely to get philosophical and dole out advice, especially to her. Besides, she doubted he was the person Grandma Justine would've had in mind when she talked about having loved well.

"Yeah, you're right. So, back to Aunt Beth."

"Back to Aunt Beth," she agreed and started making her way out of the orchard. And the past.

It was hard to do, though. So many memories haunted this place.

Of course, there was that embarrassing one of the time Colin's dad had caught the two of them in the middle of teen passion, her out of half her clothes, him struggling into a condom. That had been the ultimate buzzkill.

Still, it hadn't ended the relationship. Oh, no. Pure

stupidity had done that. But while it lasted, it had been wonderful. She remembered a conversation they'd had in this very orchard, one of many on the subject of her going away to college.

"I'm going to miss you so much," she'd said.

He'd pulled her to him. "Then stay here and go to school. Washington State accepted you. So did the University of Washington. Don't go away."

She hadn't wanted to, but she had to go away to attend NYU business school. It was one of the oldest, most prestigious business schools in the world, and she'd been accepted there, as well. She'd worked hard to cobble together enough scholarship and loan money, and she was locked in on her target. A degree from that school would impress like no other and prove her worthy to marry into the Wright family. The only way to really get Colin's dad to accept her was to make a success of herself, so she'd graduate cum laude and return with a four-year business degree. Then no one could accuse her of being the little hanger-on, out to use Colin.

Yes, she'd had everything planned. Sadly, things hadn't gone according to plan. Life had conspired against her and Colin, untying the close knot of friendship and love that had once held them so tightly together.

Sometimes it seemed as if life was still conspiring against her. Here she was, thirty, with no husband, not even a boyfriend. No prospects anywhere. But she had her career, and she could at least hang on to that.

Alone. Her life felt like one long string of people leaving her.

Fast as she was walking, she couldn't out-walk Colin, who was a foot taller. "So how come you aren't with someone?" he asked, walking beside her.

She wanted to retort, "So how come *you* are?" Mr. I'll-Love-You-Forever, Mr. As-Soon-As-You-Graduate-We'll-Get-Married. How differently their lives would have turned out if he'd trusted her more. If she'd refused to let him break up with her instead of getting on her high horse and riding off into the sunset with the wrong man.

She shrugged. "What about you? How come *babe* doesn't have a ring yet?"

"The time's not right."

Those didn't sound like the words of a man who was passionately in love, and they sure didn't sound like the old Colin.

The two of them walked on in silence for a while, then he asked, "Do you ever miss Icicle Falls?"

"How could you not miss Icicle Falls? Sometimes I wish I'd never left."

"But you did."

The bitterness in his voice made her want to smack him. "You know why."

He waved away her reasons. "You never needed to prove yourself, not to me."

"I did to your dad. And to myself."

"Well, all you proved was that you didn't care."

She'd never done any such thing! That was all on Colin. She'd loved him her whole life, and he should've trusted her when she went away to school. "You're so full of it," she said hotly. "You and that stupid temper of yours and your dumb insecurity." What did *he* have to feel insecure about, anyway? Well, okay, so his mom had left when he was too little to understand what a mom was. She'd still stayed on the edges of his life. And he'd had a whole family besides. Plus, he'd had her, darn it all.

"You gave me plenty of reason to feel insecure," he muttered.

"I'm not to blame for everything that hasn't worked out in your life. If you want to see the real problem, look in the mirror."

"Oh, yeah. You're not to blame for anything, Ms. Perfect," he retorted.

"I'm not to blame for our breakup, that's for sure."

"Okay, let's drop it," he said with a scowl. "It was a long time ago."

"Yes, it was, so I don't know why you're holding a grudge. Because you shouldn't."

They were back at the car now. He leaned on the roof and pointed a finger at her. "I'm not having this conversation with you." Then he got in and slammed the door.

She got in on her side and slammed her door, too. "Fine."

That was the end of the trip down Memory Lane. The car turned into the ice mobile, and they were both scowling when they got back to Aunt Beth's house.

She started to get out but he caught her arm. "I'm being an ass. I guess this whole treasure hunt has stirred up some shit. Anyway, I'm sorry."

His words and penitent expression cooled her anger.

"Me, too," she said. "I don't want to fight with you." In fact, all she wanted to do was kiss him and make up for the past eight years. There was way too much water under the bridge for that, though. In fact, there wasn't even a bridge anymore.

He looked out the window at the quiet street lined with maples. "I guess Dad was right."

About her?

"We were too young," Colin said, climbing out of the car.

Yep, that bridge had washed away long ago. She got out and shut the car door as she barred the door of her heart against any sentimental thoughts. She was here to find her inheritance, that was all. And that was for the best. At least they'd cleared the air. The rest of the treasure hunt would be easier—no more awkwardness, no recriminations. No more thinking about kissing and making up.

Beth wasn't working on her alteration anymore. Now she was in the kitchen mixing up some lemonade. "Did you find what you were looking for?"

"Yes," Colin said. "You've got our next clue, don't you?"

"Did you figure that out all by yourself, Colin Cootie?" Beth teased.

"Of course not," he said. "Is that lemonade up for grabs?"

"Absolutely." She pulled two glasses from the cupboard and filled them with ice. "I haven't set foot in that house since the day your grandmother had her heart attack. I know I've got to go through her things and get the place ready to sell but…" Her sentence trailed off and she concentrated on pouring lemonade.

Mia came to her side and put an arm around her. "I'm so sorry. Would you like me to help you?"

Beth shook her head. "No. You've got your hands full with your search. This is something that's going to take a while. It's going to take a while for it to sink in—the fact that Mom's really gone." She managed a smile. "It's hard to let go, but at least I don't have to let go of all the happy memories. Anyway, that's enough about me. How about you two? Did the orchard bring back happy memories?"

"It brought back a lot," Colin answered vaguely.

And the memories were still coming, Mia thought, not all of them good. Sitting here at Beth's kitchen table was like climbing into H. G. Wells's time machine. Set the dial for 1993.

Mia and Colin were playing spy, one of their favorite rainy-day games. They'd slithered around the couch, dashed behind Uncle Mark's La-Z-Boy and were now under the dining room table, where they had a clear view of the kitchen.

All the men were still at work, and dinner was an hour away. Mama was too tired to cook—that happened a lot—and she and Mia had been invited to Aunt Beth's house for dinner. Fried chicken, mashed potatoes and gravy, cherry pie for dessert—all Mia's favorites.

She loved coming to Aunt Beth's to play. Aunt Beth worked at home, sewing pretty clothes for people, but when she wasn't doing that, she'd whip up some clay for Mia and Colin to play with or make taffy for them to pull. Most often, though, they watched afternoon cartoons on TV or played marbles. Colin always won at marbles. Spying was much more fun.

Usually they got caught. If Uncle Mark was home and caught them, he pretended they were cockroaches and chased them around with his rolled-up newspaper, taking playful potshots at their behinds. If Aunt Beth caught them she'd cry, "Spies! We have ways of making you talk." And then she'd chase them and tickle them. Of course, getting caught was an adventure. But successful spying was an accomplishment.

Today nobody noticed a seven-year-old girl and an eight-year-old boy slipping out from under the dining room table to peer around the kitchen doorway.

"I'm not going to make it to spring, Beth," Mama said.

Not make it to spring? What was Mama saying?

"I don't know if I'll even make it to the New Year."

"Don't talk about dying," begged Aunt Beth.

Dying? Mia suddenly felt very scared. Her only experience with death was her goldfish that suddenly stopped swimming last summer and just floated at the top of the fish bowl on its side. Mama had flushed it down the toilet.

"I have to," Mama said. "You've got to ask Dylan if he can draw up some papers to make this legal. In case Gary comes back."

"Gary won't do that." Aunt Beth shook her head.

"That would be too much responsibility, and he's already shown what he does when things get tough."

"Still, I don't want him taking her away from here," Mama said.

Taking who?

"We won't let that happen," said Grandma Justine, who was sitting at the table, drinking a cup of tea.

"Not that he would, the bum," Aunt Beth added. "Mia's my godchild. I feel she's as much my daughter as yours. You know I'll watch out for her."

"I know. I just don't want to have to worry."

Mia forgot all about being a spy and stepped into the kitchen. "Mama?"

Grandma Justine gave a start. Aunt Beth nearly dropped the pie she was taking out of the oven.

Mama looked scared. "Come here, baby," she said, and held out an arm to Mia.

Mia ran to her mother, sat on her lap and locked both arms around Mama's neck. She knew Mama was sick. She'd already had one of her boobies cut off. But she was going to be okay. That was what she'd always said.

"Baby, I'm not doing well."

"No!" She was going to be okay.

"You know I'm sick again, baby."

"But you'll get better," Mia told her.

"I don't think so."

Mamas *always* got better. They had to. Their little girls needed them, especially when their daddies were gone. Mia clung tighter to her mother. "No, Mama." Death took things away and they never came back.

"You remember we've talked about heaven and what a special place it is?"

Mia pulled away from her mother and scowled. "I don't want you to go to heaven."

"But I'm going to have to," Mama said. "Not right now, but soon."

Mia pressed her face to her mother's shoulder and hung on tight. She wasn't going to let go. If she hung on, Mama couldn't leave her.

Her mother began to rock her back and forth. "It's okay, baby girl. Because you know what? You're very lucky. You'll always have Aunt Beth and Grandma Justine here, to play with you and teach you how to cook and bake pies."

"I'll be here, too," Colin said. He'd followed her into the room and was standing nearby.

"There, see? It'll be all right," Mama said. "You'll always have a family."

Still, after her mother died in January it was as if she'd lost her footing and was falling off a mountain. The night of the funeral she dreamed she was alone in the dark on a winding road edged with brambles and barren trees with branches like giant claws. A horrible green fog swirled around her with all kinds of things floating in it. There was her dead goldfish, there went a skull, and here came a witch, cackling and ugly, reaching for her with bony fingers. She'd been sleeping in a big bed under a homemade quilt in Aunt Beth's house, when her own screams awakened her. Finding herself in new surroundings, she'd begun to cry. Aunt Beth had rushed into the room and held her and rocked her and told her everything was going to be okay.

But there was still the green fog.

"Don't you worry about that," Aunt Beth had said. "I happen to be the Queen of Dreamland, and what I say goes. Green fog, I command you to go away and stay away."

Amazingly, it had.

That took care of night, but days were another story. Days were harder than nights because you couldn't wake up from them. Sadness and loneliness lurked, looking for a chance to make her cry.

She became shy and timid, nervous in new situations. The first day of school was no longer an adventure but something to worry about, to tie her tummy up in knots. Would her new teacher like her? Would her best friend be in her class or would she have to start over and find new friends to play with at recess? Would the kids tease her? She knew she wasn't like the other little girls. Her mommy was in heaven and she had no idea where her daddy was. Why hadn't he come for her when Mommy went to heaven?

She asked Aunt Beth once and her question made Aunt Beth frown. "Some daddies don't deserve to be daddies. You just think of Uncle Mark as your daddy, sweetie."

Uncle Mark was a nice man, and he laughed a lot. But he wasn't really her daddy. She supposed she could pretend.

Pretending worked sometimes. She'd sit on his lap when they watched TV, and hold his hand when they walked to church. But deep down she knew it wasn't the same as having her real daddy with her.

When she was ten, her real daddy came back into her life. He got a job at Swede's garage and talked about the future. He'd buy a house in Icicle Falls. She could come and live with him. They'd make up for lost time.

He started out with the best of intentions, taking her to Italian Alps for pizza. "We'll go every week, just the two of us," he promised.

Every week turned into every other week or whenever he could "find the time," which became a rare occurrence.

"He can always find time to go to that tavern in Wenatchee," she once heard Aunt Beth say to Uncle Mark. She'd tried not to let it bother her, but those words sat at the back of her mind like a sore that never quite went away.

Aunt Beth was wrong, she decided, when Daddy got back on track and came to take her out to eat. Aunt Beth frowned at him, but Mia didn't care. Her daddy was back and he loved her. She hung on to his arm with great pride as they walked into the pizzeria.

Her father was such a handsome man, tall and lean with a big smile and muscled arms. She saw how ladies looked at him, the same way girls at school looked at boys they liked. Sometimes, he smiled at them or stopped to talk. Until Mia would tug on his arm. Then he'd say, "I'd better pay attention to my date," and the ladies would smile and talk about seeing him later.

This particular night they ordered their usual Cokes and a pepperoni pizza and settled at a corner table covered with a red-checked tablecloth. He asked about school, asked how many boys were chasing her.

"Daddy, I'm only ten," she said with a giggle.

"But you're a pretty girl, just like your mother was. I bet boys are following you all around," he added with a wink.

Boys didn't follow her. And when one did speak to her she'd get tongue-tied. The only boy she was comfortable talking to was Colin.

Their pizza arrived and they each took a slice. All that cheese and spicy pepperoni—yum!

She was starting on her second piece when he cleared his throat. "Mia, I'm not working at Swede's anymore."

"Are you going to work at the chocolate place?" If he did, maybe he'd bring her chocolates.

He shook his head. "No. I'm afraid I'm going to have to move."

"Can I move with you?"

"Not yet. I have to find a good job."

"Here in Icicle Falls, right?"

"Probably not, but don't worry. I'll write."

The pepperoni pizza wasn't sitting well in her tummy now, and she pushed away her plate. "You never wrote before."

"Things happen, Mia. You're just a kid. You don't understand."

She understood that he'd left her and her mother when Mama was sick and they needed him most. She understood that he was leaving again. She scowled at the half-eaten pizza sitting between them.

"Come on, now, don't be like that," he coaxed. "Finish your pizza."

"I'm not hungry."

"Mia, I can't help it if I have to go look for work."

"Why don't you work at the chocolate place?" she begged.

"Now, don't worry. I'll find something. I'm going down to California. I'll send for you, take you to Disneyland."

She'd rather he stayed here and took her out for pizza. "Don't go, please."

But his mind was made up. By the next week he was gone, leaving behind the promise to call her as soon as he got settled.

At least he'd kept his promise to call. For a while he checked in regularly, telling her all about San Diego and the zoo he'd take her to when he could afford to bring her down for a visit, but after a couple of months, the phone calls tapered off. Then he disappeared from her life once more.

Still, she'd been so sure he'd remember to send her a present for her thirteenth birthday. After all, it was a very important birthday, not like the last one, which he'd forgotten. She'd written him a letter reminding him. He hadn't written, back but that didn't mean he wouldn't call or send a present. Maybe earrings. Aunt Beth had promised she could get her ears pierced when she turned thirteen and she'd told him all about that, too.

She'd checked the mailbox as soon as she got home from school on the big day. There was no present there, no card. Aunt Beth must have brought the mail in. That was it. There'd be a card waiting for Mia on the kitchen counter.

There hadn't been.

Grandma Justine had baked her a German chocolate cake and given her the latest Harry Potter book, and Aunt Beth had bought her makeup and promised a trip to Gilded Lily's the following day after school for the rite-of-passage ear piercing. And there'd been a pretty pair of earrings shaped like butterflies from Colin and Dylan. None of those treats, no matter how wonderful, could make up for the fact that there was nothing from her father.

She'd left Grandma Justine's dinner table in tears and run to the orchard. Colin had followed her and found her under one of the apple trees, her knees pulled up to her chest, sobbing.

"I'm sorry your dad forgot your birthday," he'd said.

"He's left me again. I hate him!"

"You don't need him, anyway," Colin had said, putting an arm around her shoulders. "You've got us."

You'll always have a family. Her mother's prediction had come true. The Wrights had been her family all those years, helping her eventually find her footing, giving her a safe place to stretch and grow and work on climbing out of her shell.

Except now Grandma Justine was gone and all she had left were Aunt Beth and Uncle Mark. She didn't count Colin's dad. He'd never been a warm, fuzzy guy, and as she'd gotten older and more perceptive, she'd had the distinct impression that he didn't care for her. The time he'd caught her and Colin together in the orchard had confirmed it with mortifying clarity.

Colin, on the other hand, had been her best friend and loyal defender and her true love...until he wasn't.

"I bought some peaches while you were out," Beth was saying, her words yanking Mia back into the present. "I thought it would be fun if we made peach upside-down cake for dinner."

"I haven't made that in years," Mia said. "I'd love to."

"And how does fried chicken and potato salad sound?" Aunt Beth asked, smiling at Colin. Of course, she'd make his favorites.

"Sounds good," he said.

"I can help you with that, too," Mia offered.

"Except we need to get this next clue," Colin said.

"You also need to eat," his aunt informed him. "I bet you didn't even have lunch. Let's have some dinner and then I'll give you your clue."

His phone signaled a new text message.

"Babe?" Mia guessed mockingly.

"Babe?" Aunt Beth echoed and cocked an eyebrow. "You said you weren't with anyone."

"I said I wasn't engaged."

"Then who are you texting?" Aunt Beth demanded.

He scowled. "Aunt Beth, do you mind?" he said irritably, thumbing his cell phone.

His aunt's eyes narrowed. "As a matter of fact, I do. This is supposed to be family time."

"I think you guys can manage making dessert without me." Another text came in and he started replying.

"If you don't lose that phone I swear I'm going to shove it in the oven along with the cake," Aunt Beth threatened.

"Okay, okay," he muttered. The phone alerted him to yet another text. "I'll be back."

"Don't go far," Aunt Beth called after him as he ducked out of the kitchen. "Whoever he's with, it's not serious," she said to Mia.

"It doesn't matter to me," Mia said. Who was she trying to convince, Aunt Beth or herself?

April 9, 1996

Dear Mother,
I hope you enjoyed the Sweet Dreams bunny-shaped truffles. Gerald bought me a box, too, which I'm savoring. I'm only allowing myself one a day. That way they'll last longer.

Our Easter was lovely. After church we had our usual Easter dinner with ham and garlic mashed potatoes. I also made that lovely Peach Bavarian salad, which used up the last of my canned peaches. I'll have to can more next time. In honor of Anna, Bethie baked our traditional bunny cake, which we've been making since she and Anna were girls. It gave us a few tearful moments, but I'm still glad she did it. It's one more way we can keep our Anna with us.

Even though the ground was soggy, we still had our Easter basket hunt. As the children have gotten older, we've made the hunt bigger. This year we sent them all over the place looking for clues—the yard, the garden, the tree house, even the henhouse. Mia took a spill and muddied her dress, and Colin very chivalrously postponed the search while Bethie ran her home to change.

By the way, that living arrangement is working very well. Mia's irresponsible father has no problem whatsoever with Bethie taking care of his daughter. And yes, I know what you're going to tell me. I should try for more charity toward the man. But honestly, I can't find anything about him to like. I worry that he'll end up hurting little Mia just like he did her mother. I guess all I can do is pray and try to be a good grandma to her and Colin. I do so love those children.

Oh, and speaking of children, we got a sweet Easter card from little Jimmy Conner and his mommy. They're doing well and want to come out and visit us this summer.

That's all the news for now. Kiss Emmaline for me.

Love,
Justine

Chapter Six

Colin finally turned off his phone and went for a walk. His steps took him to the downtown area. New shops had been added since he was a kid, as well as the skating rink, but the flavor of the place was exactly the same. A lot more people, though, that was for sure.

Of course, that was what Gram and all the other movers and shakers who'd reinvented the town over fifty years ago had wanted. They'd saved it from extinction, turning it into the American equivalent of a Bavarian village. With the mountains serving as a backdrop, the Maypole in the middle of town, all the murals and flower boxes on the buildings, it looked like something lifted right out of the Bavarian Alps. Between the German costumes the shop owners wore and the oompah bands playing in the gazebo, plus the yodeling and people playing alpenhorns every time there was a festival, Icicle Falls was probably more German than half the towns in Germany. Every year the place seemed to get more popular with tourists.

And newcomers kept moving in. You always used

to see people you knew on the street. Not today. There were no old-timers in the throng of new faces.

Oh, here was someone he recognized, Hildy Johnson, coming out of Johnson's Drugs. Getting stuck talking with the town gossip was the last thing he wanted to do. He ducked around a corner and jogged across the street, making his way to Bavarian Brews. He hadn't had a Blended Bavarian since he hit town and was suddenly craving one, a drink featuring bits of chocolate and caramel swirls.

He'd barely gotten in line when Cecily, one of the Sterling sisters and part of the Sweet Dreams Chocolate Company empire, joined him. Except she wasn't Cecily Sterling anymore. Now she was Cecily Goodman.

"Welcome home," she said.

He'd always liked Cecily. She had a kind smile and a kind heart to go with it. She'd owned some kind of matchmaking service down in LA before she moved back to town. Hardly surprising since she'd had a rep as a matchmaking genius back when they were all teenagers. Not that he'd needed her help; he'd known who he belonged with. Or so he'd thought.

"Hey, how's it going? I heard you had a kid," he said.

She beamed. "Luke Junior. He's adorable."

That was hardly surprising, either, considering how gorgeous Cecily was.

"I'm sorry about your grandma," she said.

His appetite for a Blended Bavarian died. "Thanks."

Sensing his need to move away from that particular pain, she hurried on. "So, when are you moving back to Icicle Falls?"

At the rate he was going, never. "Good question."

"You will come back, you know," she teased. "We all do."

"Yeah?" What would it be like if he did manage to come back? He'd heard the saying that you can't go home again. Even if he did, he'd never be able to recapture what he'd had growing up.

"Oh, yeah. And, speaking of coming back, I had a chance to catch up with Mia at the memorial service."

Oh, boy, here was a conversational land mine Colin didn't want to step on. Never have conversations about an ex-girlfriend with a matchmaker. He pulled out his phone. "Sorry. I, uh, need to make a phone call."

She nodded and gave him one of those knowing smiles women were so good at. "Sure you do."

He beat it out of there and checked for texts. None from Lorelei. That was surprising. And a relief, actually. He was in no mood for another barrage of questions.

Before returning to the house, he stopped in at Lupine Floral. He always brought Aunt Beth and Gram flowers when he came to visit. This time he'd been too distracted. But hey, it was never too late to flower up.

"Oh, dear boy, how are you?" Heinrich, one of the owners, greeted him.

"I'm okay," he lied. "How about bundling me up a bouquet for my aunt?"

"I have just what she'll like in the cooler." Heinrich pulled out a fat bouquet of orange, yellow and red flowers, all his aunt's favorite colors. "We're going to miss your grandmother," he said as he rang up the sale. "She was one of a kind. Your poor aunt. This is going to be especially hard on her. You really should move back."

Yep, that was the curse of a small town. People not only knew your business, they also felt entitled to run it. Colin decided he'd had enough of wandering around town. This killing time was killing him. He paid Heinrich and got out of there.

Back at Aunt Beth's, dinner preparation was under way and all kinds of great smells greeted him. He came into the kitchen to see Mia taking the peach upside-down cake from the oven. Aunt Beth was at the stove, frying chicken.

"Oh, flowers. Thanks, Colin Cootie. Mia, put those in a vase, will you? And Colin, you're just in time to set the table."

Colin handed over the flowers, then started counting silverware. Once—when he was about ten—he'd argued that setting the table was girls' work. "We don't discriminate in this family," his aunt had informed him. "Everyone pitches in where he's needed, and right now you're needed to set the table." And that had been that.

Over the years he'd been needed for everything from taking out the compost to picking peas. He'd raked brush, driven the tractor, picked apples and helped Gramps plant new trees. All those country chores had woven themselves deeply into his psyche.

So what the heck was he doing still working at a grocery warehouse in Seattle and living in a pricey apartment where the closest he got to dumping compost was sending a bag of garbage down a chute? If he was going to work in a warehouse the rest of his life, he could just as easily work at Sweet Dreams. Or he could get a job with one of the fruit packers in Wenatchee. What was there in the city to hold him?

Oh, yeah. Lorelei.

He'd met Lorelei at the gym. He'd seen her training other guys, smiling and laughing with them, making their training session look like a real party. "Okay, now, give me twenty more sit-ups. Show me that six-pack."

Then one day he found himself on a treadmill next to her. Her red hair was gathered into a ponytail that swung back and forth when she ran. She kept checking him out; he kept checking her out. He'd already run two miles before she came over, but he stayed on until she stopped, logging in five more. She toweled off, grabbed a bottle of water and smiled at him. "This is my laid-back day. How about you?"

"I'm a wimp," he'd said.

She'd smiled some more. "Stick with me and I'll get you buff. Although you look pretty buff. I think you'd make my job easy."

A little flattery, that was all it took. Next thing he knew, he was working out under her careful supervision. Then he was running his first marathon and training to do the Seattle to Portland bike ride, along with ten thousand other participants. It felt great. Suddenly, his life had meaning. Well, sort of. Not on a par with being a doctor or missionary or something, but he was doing more than punching the clock at work and then going out for a beer with the guys or to the occasional

Mariners game. Now he had a girlfriend who might just be a keeper, and he had lots to do.

So much to do that he began to find himself having, well, almost too much of a good thing. Lorelei liked to keep busy, which meant that Colin now liked to keep busy. Workouts, marathons, bike rides, restaurants, clubs, dancing, more workouts, not to mention a workout between the sheets. By Fridays he'd been starting to drag. By Sundays he'd been wishing it was Friday, so he wouldn't have to go in to work. He began to wonder if he was running low on testosterone.

"You need iron," Lorelei informed him one day when she was towing him around the mall. So into the health store they went, where they stocked up not only on iron but also on protein powder and pills guaranteed to give him adrenal support.

After a week of taking all that, plus an expensive multivitamin she'd recommended, he did feel better. It also helped that she caught a cold and was stuck at home sick for a couple of days, and he got a chance to recharge.

"I'm sorry we can't be at the gym together," she'd croaked.

"Me, too," he'd said. He never told her that he'd skipped the gym.

Other than running him ragged, Lorelei was good for him. She inspired him. Yeah, they were pretty good together…when he didn't need a break.

Wanting a break from your girlfriend. Was that normal?

Uncle Mark was home now, a big bear of a guy who

wore jeans to work and covered his bald spot with a Mariners baseball cap.

"The women got you setting the table again?" he asked Colin with a grin.

"Don't you be giving him a hard time," scolded Aunt Beth from her post at the stove, "or I'll tell him about those chocolate-cherry cupcakes you baked last month."

Uncle Mark made a face and went to the fridge. "I'm starving. When's dinner?"

"As soon as Dylan gets here. And if you're going to drink all the lemonade, you'd better make some more."

"I'm already on it," Mark said, and took a can of frozen lemonade from the freezer.

By the time Dad wandered in, dinner was ready and everyone sat down at the table, taking the same places they had for years when they were together. Well, almost. There was no Gramps and now there was no Gram. Uncle Mark said grace and Aunt Beth, Mia and Colin echoed, "Amen" when he was done. Dad didn't say anything. He and God hadn't been on speaking terms in years. The only time Gram ever got him to church was Christmas Eve.

After some of his own disappointments, Colin understood how his dad felt. He'd said as much to his grandma once; she'd merely shaken her head and said, "God gives the same free will to everyone. Your father can't blame Him when people misspend it and end up hurting others."

Probably not. People did a good job of screwing up

their lives without any help from God. Colin was a perfect example of that.

He took a chicken leg, even though he suddenly didn't have much of an appetite.

"Have some potato salad," Aunt Beth urged, passing him the bowl.

Nobody made potato salad like Aunt Beth. Colin took some and wished he felt more like eating.

Dinner was far from comfortable. There was Uncle Mark, who kept the conversation limping along with his running commentary on dinner. "Great chicken, Bethie." "Hey, guys, these beans are straight from the garden." And Dad, eating in silence. And Mia, not contributing much to the conversation, just picking at her food.

Uncle Mark was saying, "I'm ready for some of that peach upside-down cake," when Colin's cell phone rang.

"Don't tell me, let me guess," murmured Mia.

Yes, it was Lorelei again.

"If that's the same person who's been texting you all day, tell her you're busy," Aunt Beth said.

Colin ignored her and ducked away from the table. "Hey, what's up?" he answered as he made his way through the living room.

"Surprise! I'm here."

"Here." Here? *As in...here? In Icicle Falls?*

"I know you said I didn't have to come, Col, but I think you need me."

Like he needed a nail driven into his eye. "Where are you right now?"

"Colin, we're dishing up dessert," called Aunt Beth.

And meanwhile, Lorelei was dishing up a mess. He slipped out onto the front porch, half expecting to see her Kia sitting at the curb. Of course it wasn't. She didn't have Aunt Beth's address. And she wasn't tracking him, for crying out loud. Except that was what it felt like.

"I'm in the town square by that cute gazebo. So, where should I come?"

Not here! "Uh."

"Colin, Aunt Beth says to get back to the kitchen or she's going to give Uncle Mark your piece of cake."

He whirled around to see Mia standing at the screen door.

"I'll be there in a minute." Sheesh.

"All right," said Lorelei.

"No, not there."

"What?"

"I was talking to someone else."

"That *friend*?"

Colin's head hurt. "Let's get you settled someplace."

"Where are you staying?"

"With my dad. But you can't stay there."

"Gee, thanks." Okay, that hadn't come out right.

"No, I don't mean it like that. It's in the will." Well, sort of. This was hard to explain.

"In the will," she repeated slowly.

Yeah, that sounded nuts. This whole thing was nuts.

"Tell you what, go to Gerhardt's Gasthaus and check in. It's three blocks off the main street on Pine. I'll come see you as soon as I can." And the way his aunt was nagging him, that was going to be sooner rather than later.

"Okay." Lorelei sounded a lot less happy than when she'd first called. "Then let's meet up for dinner."

Crap. "Sorry, I just ate. I didn't know you were coming."

She sighed. "Okay, I guess I'll get something to eat. By myself."

Even though he wasn't responsible for the fact that she was having to eat alone, he still felt as though he was. Lorelei didn't cook, but the one dish she sure could serve up was guilt.

"I'll see you in a little while," he promised.

"If you want to go hang out with your girlfriend, I can take over," Mia said as he ended the call.

Yeah, no ulterior motive there. She'd probably be happy to cut him out of his grandmother's will, just like she'd been happy to cut him out of her life. "I don't think so," he said. "We're in this together."

"Suit yourself."

"Colin, this friend of yours is becoming a nuisance," Aunt Beth said as he and Mia came back to the kitchen table. "You know the conditions of the will."

"I do, don't worry," he said.

His aunt didn't say anything else, but she was frowning as she set a slice of cake in front of him.

Cake with a topping of peaches, melted brown sugar and butter, all smothered in whipped cream—it landed on his taste buds like some kind of magic potion, transporting him to happier times when Sunday supper always ended in some fabulous dessert. After dessert it was cards or, in the summer, croquet or badminton on the lawn or sitting on the front porch with Mia and his dog while the grown-ups visited with passing neighbors. When he hit adulthood, he'd envisioned himself with a family, enjoying apple crisp or peach upside-down cake, sitting on his own front porch or playing games with his kids. So far, he had no family and no front porch, only an apartment with a balcony and a barbecue. What the heck was he doing with his life?

"So," Aunt Beth said, "are you two ready for your next clue?"

It was about time. Colin nodded and shoved away his empty plate. "Bring it on."

Aunt Beth produced a pink envelope from her kitchen junk drawer and laid it on the table. Colin and Mia both reached for it. Remembering her earlier comment, he pulled away his hand and let her open it.

She didn't read it out loud so he prompted, "What does it say?"

"'Go to your favorite haunt and ask for a…'" Her brows knit.

"A what?"

She passed the stationery over. "It's a word scramble."

"I should've known she'd slip one in," he grumbled. Sure enough. *Ask for a Nitesuj Grerub.* "Okay, you're the smart one," he said to Mia. "What's this supposed to be?"

She shook her head.

"Great."

"Guess you two will have to put your heads together," Aunt Beth said with a smirk.

"Or bang them on the table," Colin muttered. "Come on, let's go out on the porch."

"I hope you're enjoying this," Dylan said to Beth as the two disappeared.

"Immensely." She grinned and took another bite of her dessert.

"I don't know," Mark said. "It's all pretty…"

"Unorthodox," supplied Dylan. "Sending these two on a scavenger hunt isn't going to make them fall in love and live happily ever after."

Beth pointed her spoon at him. "That's where you're wrong. You've been wrong about those two ever since that incident in the orchard. In fact, if it wasn't for you, they'd probably be married by now and have a couple of kids."

"Oh, fine. I'm the destroyer of happiness," Dylan said sourly, pushing aside his plate.

"I'll admit they played their own parts in that, but you scripted your share of the mess. You're a cynic when it comes to relationships. And you know why?"

"Please don't tell me."

"Well, I'm going to. It's because you're a wounded romantic. What you need is…"

"Oh, no. No advice from my sister," he said, holding up a hand.

"It's not too late," she told him. "You could get your own happily-ever-after."

"I'm perfectly happy, thank you," he said. "And don't worry about me. You've got your hands full bossing Mark around."

"I'll share the wealth," Mark offered.

"That's okay," said Dylan. He kissed his sister on the cheek and left.

"He's hopeless." Beth finished the last bite of her cake.

"Sorry," Mark said. "I'm with Dylan on this one."

"That's because you're a man, and what do you know about love?"

He grinned. "I picked you, didn't I?"

She smiled at that and kissed him. "Yes, you did, you lucky boy." She'd barely finished speaking when they heard the sound of a car starting. "Looks like they figured out their clue."

"Since when is there such a thing as a Justine Burger?" Colin said as he and Mia drove down Center Street.

"Since your grandma and Aunt Beth designed this hunt," Mia replied.

"Let's hope the servers at Herman's were told about it," he said as they pulled into the parking lot.

The only thing that had changed about Herman's Hamburgers was the model and year of the cars parked outside. They walked past the same life-size wooden figure of a woman in a German dirndl holding a platter with a hamburger. The little sign hanging from her neck still said Willkommen in Herman's. The place was packed with young families crowded into booths for a Friday-night treat, devouring burgers and shakes and, same as when Colin and Mia were young, teens hanging out and flirting. It smelled like fried onions, and even though Colin had just had dinner, his mouth watered.

"This place never changes," Mia observed as they got in line behind a half dozen teenagers. "Even the menu's still the same."

"Except for the garlic fries," he said, pointing at a high school boy walking by with a huge serving of them.

"An excellent addition." Mia sighed. "I wish I had room for a chocolate-dipped cone."

How many of those had they ordered over the years? Enough to stock a hundred ice cream trucks, probably.

"Colin."

The voice behind him cracked like a whip and made him jump. He turned to see a petite redhead wearing shorts and a top that showed off a perfectly toned body. Her lips, a little thin to begin with, were now an angry, red line. And the green eyes were narrowed to slits.

"Lorelei," he stammered. "What are you doing here?" She didn't eat beef. Why had she picked tonight to start?

"What do you think I'm doing here?" she snapped. "I was trying to find someplace to eat and saw your car pull in."

"Uh, good choice for dinner. They've got great burgers." Oh, boy, was that the best he could do? Under the circumstances, yeah.

Lorelei looked as if she'd rather bite his head off than eat a burger. "Are you taking a break from your... whatever?"

"Treasure hunt," Mia said. "Hi. I'm Mia."

Lorelei looked at Mia as if she might just bite her head off, too. "I'm Lorelei, Colin's girlfriend. I came up here to help him."

"That was nice of you," Mia said sweetly.

Colin was beginning to sweat. They needed to turn up the AC in here. "Lorelei, I'm sorry, but I can't bring in outside help. It's a stipulation in the will."

Lorelei glanced suspiciously at Mia.

"We're inheriting something together," Colin explained as the line moved up.

"Together." Lorelei repeated the word like a student learning a foreign language. "And you're looking for it at a burger place." She sounded beyond skeptical.

Not surprising. This was really weird. "One of our clues is here."

A carefully penciled eyebrow shot up. "Written in French fries?"

And Gram had thought this would be fun? Now it was their turn to order. "We want a Justine burger," he told the skinny kid taking orders.

The kid scratched his nose, inadvertently drawing attention to a zit growing near one nostril. "A what?"

"A Justine burger," Colin repeated.

The kid gaped in confusion then called to the girl at the drive-up window. "Hey, Carly, have we got a Justine burger?"

"A what?" she called back.

"A Justine burger."

"Nope."

"Nope," the kid echoed. "Sorry."

"Maybe we got the clue wrong," Colin said to Mia.

Mia shook her head vehemently. "No way. Is your manager here?"

"Yeah, I'll get him." The kid took off.

"You're looking for a *burger*?" Lorelei sounded incredulous.

"It has our next clue," Colin explained.

"You expect me to believe that?" she said in disgust.

"Yeah, I do. Why would I lie?"

Again, Lorelei checked out Mia. "I don't know. You tell me."

Oh, boy.

Now the night manager, who didn't seem much older than the kid taking orders, appeared. "Hey, you guys wanting the Justine burger?"

"Yes," said both Colin and Mia.

"I think Evan knows about that."

Of course. It made sense that Gram would have talked to the current owner of Herman's. "Thanks," Colin said. "Where is he?"

"He's not here. But he'll be in tomorrow when we open at eleven."

"Looks like that's it for tonight, then," Mia said, and Lorelei smiled.

"I guess so. I'll take you back to Aunt Beth's."

"Hey, what about me?" Lorelei asked.

"I can walk back," Mia said. "It's not that far."

"I don't mind taking you," Colin told her. It was tacky to make her walk home. "I'll be right back," he promised Lorelei, who'd already slipped her arm through his.

She frowned.

He pulled a twenty from his wallet. "Order whatever you want and a huckleberry shake for me."

The frown didn't leave, but she took his money and said, "Okay."

He gave her a quick kiss and that was embarrassing. It shouldn't have been. She was his girlfriend, after all. But with Mia standing right there…

As if she cared. She'd moved on years ago, so what did it matter if he kissed another woman in front of her?

"You could've stayed," she said as they got back in the car.

"Hey, I'm not such a bum that I'm going to leave you to walk home."

"Like I said, it's not far."

"It's the principle of the thing."

"You always were chivalrous," she said softly. "You remember punching Billy Williams in the eye?"

He snickered. "Poor, old Bill Will."

Then there'd been the other time, with Adrian Malk, but neither brought that up. Too humiliating for both of them. Silence entered the car like a big old rhino and camped between them for the rest of the ride.

The car had hardly come to a stop when she hopped out. "Thanks."

"I'll come by tomorrow at ten to."

She nodded, then ran up the walk to Aunt Beth's.

He watched her go, thinking what a great ass she had. Heck, she had great everything. The woman looked good from every angle. Why wasn't she with someone?

His cell phone let him know that Lorelei was waiting.

And that brought up a whole new question. Why was he with someone who wasn't Mia? Oh, yeah, because Mia hadn't wanted him. Anyway, he was happy with Lorelei. She was great. *They* were great. Yep, great.

"We finally get to hang out?" she greeted him when he sat down next to her in the booth at Herman's.

"Sorry," he said, and kissed her. Not so embarrassing this time.

"Well, I did come all this way," she reminded him.

That irritated him. Who'd asked her to? "I told you that you didn't need to. I don't know how long it's going to take."

"That's okay. I've got all weekend." She slid a burger his way. "Here. I ordered us veggie burgers."

Veggie burgers? He hadn't noticed that on the menu. When did Herman's start serving veggie burgers? And, "Where's my huckleberry shake?"

"All that fat," she said, wincing. "I got us water instead."

Water? At Herman's? "I don't think so," he said, and went and ordered himself a shake. Large.

She frowned when he returned with it. "You're clogging your arteries."

"Hey, you told me yourself that we need some fat in our diets."

"Not a boatload in one serving," she said. "Do you want to die young?"

He shrugged and took a guzzle. Oh, yeah. That was what good tasted like. "I'll die with a smile on my face." He offered her the glass. "Try some."

"No, thanks," she said, wrinkling her nose.

"Suit yourself." He took a bite of his veggie burger. "Yummy, isn't it?"

Not compared to a cheeseburger with grilled onions. He wrapped it back up and shoved it toward her. "I'll pass."

Lorelei gave up on the subject of nutrition. "Your old friend is pretty."

Colin found himself wishing they'd kept talking about fat and fake meat. "Uh, yeah."

"How long have you known each other?"

"Since we were kids. We grew up together."

"But you're not related."

"No. My family took her in when she was seven."

"So, she's adopted?"

"More or less. Her mom and my aunt were best friends. Her mom died of cancer."

"Gosh, that's sad," Lorelei said, and took a big drink of her water. "But you're both inheriting something?"

He shrugged. "My grandma loved her."

"I guess." Lorelei seemed shocked that Gram could leave something to someone who wasn't a blood relative.

Maybe that was unusual. Colin didn't know. All he knew was how his family operated, and that was with open arms. Well, except his dad, who was more of an arms crossed kind of guy.

"What do you think she left you?"

"I have no idea."

"Was she rich?"

He hadn't thought she was. Maybe he'd thought wrong. But where had she gotten the money for stocks and savings? She'd had to sell the orchard to pay for Gramps's stay in the care facility. All Colin could figure was that Gram hadn't used it all up before he died. Still, she'd lived so frugally, as if she was just managing on Social Security. He'd always tried to get her extravagant gifts for Christmas and birthdays to make up for it—two-pound boxes of chocolates from Sweet Dreams; gift certificates to Schwangau, the fanciest restaurant in town; hardcover copies of books by her favorite authors. She had the complete collection of Vanessa Valentine novels.

"Maybe she was like those millionaires you read about," Lorelei mused. "They're eating dog food and they have millions in the bank."

Colin frowned at her. "My gram never had to eat dog food." No one would have let that happen.

"Not her, but you know what I mean."

Discussing his grandmother's finances with Lorelei felt wrong. "Can we not talk about this?"

She blinked. "Oh, well. Sure." She wadded up her hamburger wrapper. "Why don't we pick up some wine and go back to that B and B where I'm staying. The view is gorgeous."

He knew what the view was. He'd seen it most of his life. But he said, "Okay."

They got a bottle of local wine, and he followed Lorelei back to Gerhardt's Gasthaus, where they sat out on the balcony of her room, taking in the evening glow as the sun set over the mountains.

Lorelei oohed and aahed for a couple of minutes and then returned to the topic of Colin's inheritance. "It's really kind of cool, this whole treasure-hunt thing," she said, and took a sip of her Gewürztraminer.

It would've been cool if Gram was still alive. And if he wasn't having to do it with Mia. *Do it…* No, no, don't be thinking like that.

"If it's money, you should invest it. We could invest it in something together. Did I tell you? Lenny might be selling the gym."

"What?" Colin tried to pull his wandering thoughts back to the conversation at hand.

"Now that would be a great business to invest in."

Suddenly, he felt like a buzzard. Colin and Lorelei, Mr. and Mrs. Buzzard. "I really don't want to talk about stuff like that now."

"I was just trying to be helpful."

"Well, you're not."

She sniffed. "You don't have to get snotty."

"Sorry," he said with a sigh. "It's been a long couple of days."

"Of course it has," she said, and poured him some more wine. "It's hard to lose someone you love."

"Have you?"

"Oh, yeah. I still miss poor Georgie." She shook her head. "He was such a sweet little dog."

She was comparing his grandmother to a dog? "Lorelei."

"I know. You don't want to talk about it. Men are from Mars. I get it. My mom has that book."

He felt as though he was on Mars right now. No, make that Planet Strange.

"Let's talk about something else," she said brightly.

Finally. Better yet, he thought, let's not talk at all. He looked at the giant mountains looming over them, and then his gaze drifted up to where the sun was leaving behind a bleeding sky. Was Gram up there somewhere, looking down on them?

"It's beautiful," Lorelei said. "And so romantic." She smiled at him, and placed a foot on his thigh. "Isn't it?"

"Uh, yeah." *So, do something about it*, came the message from the Urge to Merge Control Center. Instead of following orders, he tossed down the last of his wine and stood up. "But I should get going. I've got an early day tomorrow."

"Since when is eleven in the morning early?"

Good point. And what was his problem, anyway? "I've got to go do some stuff with my dad," he lied. He could *find* something to do with Dad. There was still Scotch left in that bottle.

He bent and gave Lorelei a kiss and she wrapped her arms around him and hung on like a limpet, making the kiss worth his while. Lorelei knew how to make a kiss worthwhile.

Mr. and Mrs. Buzzard get it on. He broke away. "I'll catch up with you tomorrow."

"When?"

He shrugged. "I don't know how many more clues we have to work through."

"Fine. I'll go shopping."

Her tone of voice implied punishment, but that was fine with him. It would keep her busy and out of his hair.

Out of his hair. Hmm. A guy shouldn't feel like that about his girlfriend.

"Okay, I'll talk to you later," he said, and scrammed.

Something is wrong with this picture, he concluded as he got in his car. But when it came to love he was no artist, and he had no idea how to fix it.

May 25, 2002

Dear Emmaline,

I'm taking advantage of a lull at the information booth to write you a line. We'll see how long it lasts. We're always busy on a holiday weekend. In fact, we're busy most weekends. We've had a record number of visitors this year. More and more people are discovering Icicle Falls, and we have quite the team of volunteers now. Isn't this note card, with our little downtown all dressed up for spring, pretty? What a change from what the town looked like when Gerald and I first moved here!

It was lovely to chat with you on Mother's Day. The day certainly didn't feel the same without Mother, though. To live to be ninety-two, with all her faculties intact, was remarkable, and I'm grateful we had her for so long. Still, I miss her.

After our phone chat, Gerald and Adrian and I went over to Bethie's for dinner. I told her I didn't want her cooking on Mother's Day, but she insisted. Mia made a special cake shaped like a hat, and Colin gave Bethie and me Sweet Dreams chocolates. Gerald was not happy that Adrian didn't use any of his allowance to purchase a card for the mothers, but honestly, the boy's spent the past six years bouncing from foster home to foster home. I don't blame him for *wanting to hoard every penny. Besides, he's only been with us a few months, which, in my opinion, hardly makes either Beth or me eligible for a Mother's Day card. Considering the fact that his birth mother abandoned him when he was three, it's no wonder that Mother's Day doesn't mean much to him.*

Having said all that, I must admit I'm finding this boy a challenge. He's the oldest child we've ever taken in, and I'm afraid his character is already formed. We keep trying with him, though, and let me tell you it's exhausting. Or maybe it's simply that taking in children at seventy-two is exhausting. I think, perhaps, our days of foster-parenting may be coming to an end.

Well, dear, I can see a car pulling up, which means we have more visitors looking for a map and some brochures. I'll drop this in the mailbox on my way home. Give my love to Joey.

Love,
Justine

Chapter Seven

Colin showed up at Beth's house the next morning ten minutes before eleven. Beth was working on an alteration and had left Mia to enjoy a second cup of coffee and the morning sunshine out on the porch swing.

"You ready?" he called to her as he came up the front walk.

"Yeah, I'll get my purse." She went inside and put her mug in the dishwasher, then grabbed her purse and hurried back out the door. She found Colin perched on the railing, the morning sunshine glinting in his hair, and her heart did a flip. She half wanted to ask him what he and Lorelei had done the night before, but the answer to that was obvious, so instead she said, "I sure hope Evan has our clue."

"If he doesn't, we're gonna have to come back and ask Aunt Beth to give us a hint."

"What's *babe* doing while you're clue-hunting?" she asked as they walked to the car. Okay, that was mature. *Honestly, Mia, how old are you, fourteen?*

"Shopping."

"Icicle Falls is a great place for that."

"It's a great place for everything," he said, and opened the car door for her.

"Yes, it is," she had to agree.

"Not as great as Chicago, though," he added as he got behind the wheel.

"Oh, I don't know."

"I thought you liked it."

"I did. I do."

"What did I just hear, a Freudian slip?"

"No, and since when do you know about Freud?" she retorted.

"Hey, I went to college, too. You getting tired of hanging out with movers and shakers?" he mocked.

"Of course not." She'd worked too hard to prove herself these past few years to be tired of her corporate world. She was making decent money and now she was promoting a good product. "There's nothing wrong with being a mover and shaker."

"There are a lot of ways to be one," he said.

"True." Grandma Justine was proof of that. She'd never left this small town, but what a big difference she'd made. "Brighten the corner where you are," she used to say.

So, Mia asked herself, *what corner are you brightening?* The answer evaded her. But hey, she was just getting started. Give her time. Soon she'd be making boatloads of money and she'd attend charity balls and donate small fortunes to the Red Cross and the Humane Society.

Herman's was a few minutes away from opening to the public, but they went to the entrance, anyway, and Colin knocked on the glass door. A couple of high school kids were setting up behind the counter. One, a pretty girl with curly blond hair, came to the door and opened it.

"It's almost eleven, so I guess I can let you in," she said with a smile.

"We're actually here to see Evan," Colin explained. "Is he around?"

"Sure, I'll get him." Colin and Mia followed her to the counter, then waited as she disappeared into the nether regions of the kitchen, yelling, "Evan! Somebody here to see you."

A moment later Evan himself, a skinny fortysomething guy sporting glasses and a beard, came into sight. "Hi, what can I do you for?"

"We're here for a Justine burger," Mia said.

"Wow, she pulled it off, huh? I told her this was some crazy idea, but she thought you guys would like it." He reached beneath the counter and removed what looked like a hamburger wrapped in a yellow, black and red wrapper—the colors of Germany's flag. "Here ya go."

Colin took it and said thanks. Then they turned their backs on Evan, who was leaning on the counter, enjoying the show, and opened it. The Justine burger consisted of two stale hamburger buns with a folded piece of the now-familiar pink stationery between them.

"Pretty damned clever, huh?" Evan commented.

"Yeah, clever," Colin said. Then to Mia, "Let's go back to the car."

Once in the car, he handed the paper over to her and they read it together.

My darlings, I think you should go to watch the river rush by. It's just like time. You probably haven't come to realize yet how precious that time is and how quickly it carries you along. We can't afford to waste it on the wrong person.

Mia had already come to realize that. She felt sad whenever she thought about her father and what a waste of time he'd been. He still contacted her every once in a while, mostly to hit her up for money—"Just a loan," he'd always said—which he never paid back.

He wasn't the only person she'd wasted time on. Adrian Malk, the last foster kid Grandma Justine ever took in, was far worse than a waste of time. He was a nightmare. Before Adrian, Mia had never swerved in her undying devotion to Colin.

They parked the car and got out. Somewhere downriver, campers were cooking lunch over a fire. The smell of wood smoke hit her with an ugly memory, taking her back to that summer when she was sixteen and oh, so foolish.

He was almost seventeen, an older man. He had dark hair and eyes, and an Adam's apple that bobbed up and down when he talked. Mia found it fascinating. She found everything about Adrian Malk fascinating. He wore his jeans halfway down his butt and walked with a swagger. And he swore. Swore! Not in front of

Grandma Justine or Aunt Beth, but when he was out of earshot he used words that made Mia blush. He always beat Colin and her at video games when the families were all at Grandma Justine's. The aura of cool that surrounded him made it easy to excuse the fact that he mocked everything and everyone, and ducked out of chores whenever possible. When you were so cool, chores were beneath you.

"Who invited him, anyway?" Colin grumbled as he and Mia drove to the river for the big end-of-school party. "The guy's a loser."

"I did," Mia said, "and he's not a loser."

"He doesn't even have a driver's license," Colin continued scornfully. Colin had gotten his the second he turned sixteen. Dylan had bought him an old Corvette that he'd worked on for months with his grandpa, but made him pay for his own gas and insurance. He proudly drove it everywhere and never complained about having to work part-time at Swede's garage on Saturdays, in addition to the work he did around the orchard.

"How's he supposed to get a car when he's stuck in foster care?" Mia argued.

"Gram said he could use hers, and she said she'd pay for driver's ed if he'd bring up his grades. He didn't. The guy cuts more classes than he goes to."

Mia shrugged. "So, he's not into school."

Colin took his eyes off the road long enough to gape at her. "You're kidding, right? You've got straight As. Since when do you stick up for a moron who's going to fail his junior year?"

"Not everyone's good in school." She'd said as much to Colin after his dad had reamed him out for barely passing English last semester. After all, not everyone was a Geek Girl. She couldn't help smiling at Adrian's fond nickname for her.

"Just because he flirts with you and tells you you're cute doesn't make him cool."

Mia thought it did. Only the day before she'd stopped by Adrian's locker and told him about the end-of-school party. He'd run a hand up her arm, shooting an electric current through her whole body. "You gonna be there?"

"Of course," she'd said. "Everybody goes."

He'd cocked his head and studied her. "I may have to check it out. Got any places down by the river where we can go have our own party?"

Her heart rate picked up. There was something dangerous about Adrian Malk, something that made her pulse jump. He scared the sensible part of her, but the sixteen-year-old besotted girl part of her had no intention of listening to her sensible side.

"Maybe," she'd said coyly.

"Then maybe I'll come," he'd said and tapped her playfully on the nose.

He was going to be there, she knew it. They'd take a romantic stroll and then he'd kiss her. It would be like the kiss in the classic movie *The Princess Bride*. This would be a kiss to leave all other kisses in the history of kisses behind.

"Don't you be hanging around him tonight," Colin warned as he drove them to the party.

And miss the kiss of a lifetime? No way. "Don't tell me what I can and can't do," she fired back.

"I mean it, Mia," he said sternly. "You stick with me."

Not so long ago she'd have liked nothing better. But where was that getting her? Colin was not more than a big brother to her. He'd never run his hand up her arm, tapped her on the nose or promised romantic adventures and excitement.

"Don't worry about me. I can take care of myself," she informed him.

"He's twice your size."

"So?"

"So stay away from him."

"You're not my dad!"

"Your dad? Like *he* cares?"

True, but the words still hurt. She pressed her lips together and glared out the window.

"Jeez, Mia, I just don't want to see you get hurt. Is that so bad?"

"I'm not going to get hurt and I can look after myself."

"Fine," he snapped. "Be stupid if that's what you want."

And to show her how little he cared, he ignored her the minute they got to the river, ambling off toward Bill Will, Neal Barrows and David Simpson, who were already boasting about being seniors, even though their junior year had just ended. A bunch of kids had started a fire in the picnic-area fire pit. Coolers lay scattered around, filled with soda pop and hot dogs. Some, of course, held contraband—beer. Boom boxes were blasting, kids stood or sat in clumps, laughing and eating chips. A few were at the riverbank, dangling their feet in the water. And there, at the edge of the crowd, sat Adrian Malk, nursing a beer. He'd attracted a couple of other guys who were trying to be just as cool, and they sat on fallen log benches, looking down on their more innocent counterparts, who were happy dancing or tossing a football.

Tammy Granger and Jenny Hook, the two loosest girls in school, were with them, flipping their hair and flirting. Mia had no intention of lowering herself to their level, so she joined Bailey Sterling at one of the coolers and helped herself to a Diet Pepsi.

"Those two," Bailey said, following Mia's gaze, "I don't think there's a single guy at school they haven't done it with."

Did one of them want to do it with Adrian? Mia wasn't ready to give up her virginity, but she found she was jealous all the same. The idea of Adrian kissing some other girl, telling her she was cute, made her frown. Adrian didn't seem all that interested in them, though. He just sat there wearing a superior smirk. Then he saw her and the smirk turned into a smile. He nodded, acknowledging her presence.

Feeling both self-conscious and elated, she gave him a brief smile and then focused her attention on her can of pop.

"Oh, my gosh," said Bailey. "Is Adrian checking you out?" Then, without waiting for an answer, she came to her own conclusion. "He is! You should go talk to him. Don't let the slut sisters get him."

Mia saw him at school all the time and at Grandma Justine's, but she suddenly felt shy, incapable of moving. "Maybe later," she said, digging into another cooler and pulling out a package of hot dogs. "I'm starving."

They joined some other kids at the fire, and Mia tried to concentrate on eating her hot dog and visiting with her friends, but it was hard to concentrate when she knew Adrian was watching her. And Colin was ignoring her.

The night danced on, bringing dusk and then darkness. More contraband appeared, and the scent of marijuana joined the smell of the wood fire. The revelers got noisier and the music got turned up. This wasn't really Mia's thing. Adrian was still at the edge of the party and she couldn't bring herself to make the first move. So what was the sense in staying any longer?

She looked around to see where Colin was, but couldn't spot him in the growing crowd of kids. Well, she didn't need to wait for him to give her a ride. She could walk home. Icicle Falls was the safest place on the planet.

She'd almost gotten to the walkway leading out of the park when someone grabbed her arm. "Where are you off to?"

Adrian. Her mouth felt dry. "I'm going home."

"Don't go. The party's just starting," he said. "Come on." And before she knew it, he was leading her away from the other kids, down a path and over a bridge that led to Bluebird Island, a nature preserve with a cozy spot complete with a carved wooden bench where nature lovers could enjoy the peace and quiet. During the day it was a restful getaway. Tonight it was a different kind of getaway.

Her heart began to beat faster. This was it. She finally had Adrian all to herself and he'd picked such a romantic place to kiss her.

He sat on the bench and pulled her down beside him. This was what she wanted, right? To be alone with the handsome Adrian Malk? Except suddenly she was nervous. She'd hadn't really dated. Most of the kids went out in packs until two broke off here or there to become a couple. She hadn't done that, and now here she was, alone with a boy. What if she wasn't a good enough kisser?

And what was that she heard? It sounded like snickering somewhere off in the bushes.

"Are you scared?"

"No," she lied.

"Well, you don't need to be. I know what to do."

And he didn't waste any time waiting to show her. Before she could say anything he was kissing her, and his hand was inside her top, yanking her bra down over one breast. This wasn't the romantic kiss she'd been dreaming of. It was raw and savage. And scary.

She pulled back. "Adrian, don't."

"Come on," he said. "You've been wanting this ever since I got here." He pushed her down on the bench, holding both her arms above her head, and leered at her.

She tried to squirm away. If she could get her hands free, she'd punch him. "Let me go!"

"Don't fight it. You're gonna love this. I promise," he said, and unsnapped her jeans.

That was when she screamed.

It brought people running, but not anyone she wanted to see. Here were his two buddies.

"Hold her down," Adrian commanded.

No! "Colin!"

Adrian's face was in front of hers and now he wasn't smiling. "Scream again and I'll hit you, bitch. And you'd better not tell anyone about this."

Colin had been right. Adrian Malk was no one she wanted to be with. She should have listened to him. Where was he when she needed him? Humiliation and terror gripped her, and tears streamed down her face as she tried to free herself. This couldn't be happening. Not to her, not in Icicle Falls.

And then she heard it, a thrashing in the underbrush, and Colin calling her name.

"I'm here!" she cried.

He burst onto the scene like some sort of superhero. A superhero who was at least six inches shorter than Adrian. And there was only one of him.

He seemed oblivious to all that. "Let her go."

"Who's gonna make me?" Adrian retorted, tightening his hold on Mia.

His two friends advanced on Colin. Oh, they were both in trouble now. Mia's tears came in a torrent. Sure enough, the two boys began pummeling him. She struggled to get free of Adrian so she could help Colin. He was fighting back but not successfully. She cried out and struggled even harder as he doubled over from a punch to the stomach.

Now there was more noise in the bushes. "Col!" somebody called. "Did you find her?"

"Let's get out of here," Adrian said to his friends. Then to Mia. "You tell anybody about this and you're dead. So's he."

He ran off, melting into the darkness along with his pals, leaving Mia sobbing on the bench, hurrying to pull her pants back up and adjust her torn top.

Colin staggered over and put his arms around her. "Are you all right?"

She nodded and wiped her runny nose. "You saved me." She couldn't even say those three simple words without crying again.

"Saved you? I got the crap beaten out of me."

"If you hadn't come…" She couldn't finish the sentence. All she could do was hang on to him and cry.

"I'm here now," he said, and she felt the feather touch of his lips on her hair.

Now Bill Will, Neal and David arrived on the scene. "Are you guys okay?" Neal asked.

Mia clutched at her torn top and buried her face in Colin's shoulder. She wanted to curl into a ball and roll away, become invisible.

"Yeah," Colin said. "But when I find Adrian Malk, I'm gonna kill him."

"We need to go to the cops," David said.

"No!" No way was Mia going to tell anyone what had happened to her.

"Mia, you can't let him get away with this," Colin said sternly.

She shook her head violently.

"Okay, then. We'll tell Aunt Beth. She'll know what to do."

She especially didn't want to tell Aunt Beth. The idea of telling her was even more humiliating than telling the police.

"Colin's right. You can't let him get away with that shit," said Neal. "He'll turn around and do it to someone else. And she might not be so lucky."

"Come on." Colin stood and held out his hand to her. "I'll take you home."

She tried to stand, but her legs were rubbery.

He put an arm around her and helped her up. "Come on, Mia. It's okay. I'm with you."

"We'll go, too," said Bill Will. "In case those guys come back."

Colin nodded, and they left the river, taking a path that would skirt the party scene and save Mia any embarrassment. "Don't be telling anybody about this," Colin warned them.

"What kind of shits do you think we are?" David demanded. "Don't worry, Mia. We won't tell anyone."

But Colin did tell Aunt Beth, who told Grandma Justine, who called the police. Adrian Malk was taken away and logged into a juvenile detention center, and Mia lived in terror that he and his henchmen would somehow escape and kill both her and Colin. But his crime wasn't treated lightly. He was soon bound over to Superior Court and tried as an adult for what he'd done. Having to recount everything that had happened to the prosecutor was mortifying and brought back the whole experience. The court appearances were scary and humiliating, but she got through them. Then it was all over and, as quickly as he'd crashed into their lives, Adrian Malk was gone, sent to prison. He was the last foster kid Grandma Justine ever took in.

And almost the last man Mia wasted time on.

"What else does it say?" Colin prompted.

Mia shook off the awful memories and gave their clue her full attention.

"'Look and you'll see where you need to go on the other side,'" she read.

"Seriously? And where at the river?"

"Let's start with the park," she suggested, and reminded herself that the river held more good memories than bad. She had enjoyed plenty of picnics down there with the Wrights. Colin's grandpa had taken her and Colin fishing on this river, and they'd spent plenty of time fishing on their own, too. They'd skipped rocks and when the water was low, jumped from boulder to boulder, crossing to the other side to explore winding hiking trails.

Once at the riverbank, Colin didn't turn toward the area where all the kids had partied. Instead, he went farther downstream to where they used to go fishing. The sun was doing its magic act on the water, making it sparkle as if it was covered with fairy dust.

He sat down on the bank and took in the view of evergreens and ferns and wildflowers crowding the opposite bank. "I remember fishing here with Gramps."

"We had a great childhood," Mia said, sitting down next to him.

"Yeah, we did," he agreed.

She looked at their latest clue again.

"I wish Gram would just get to it," he said, sounding disgusted.

"Maybe she wants us to think about our lives."

"I don't want to think about my life," he muttered.

There were parts she didn't want to remember, either, but these clues made it impossible to ignore the past. At least for her. "So, how many people have you wasted time on since…" Here she stumbled. When he tallied the numbers, did he include her? "Since I saw you last," she amended.

"I don't know."

"Liar."

"Everybody wastes time on the wrong person at some point. Look at my dad. He's proof of that."

"Thanks for not using me as an example," she said, and gave him a shoulder bump.

He picked up a rock and threw it in the river.

She sat for a moment, watching him. Then she couldn't resist asking, "Do you think you've got this relationship thing figured out?"

His only answer was a shrug. If all he could do was shrug, maybe he still wasn't with the right person. And if Lorelei wasn't the right person… *Oh, no. You're going someplace you shouldn't go.* But she kind of wanted to go there, anyway.

Why was it so hard to sort out your love life? The river had no answer.

But as she stared across it, she saw the answer to this latest riddle. "That's it!"

December 26, 2002

Dear Emmaline,
*Thank you for the lovely lavender soap. I will
enjoy that so much! I was glad to hear that the
gingerbread house we had shipped to you made it
in one piece. Cass Wilkes is such a lovely young
woman and I enjoy giving her business whenever
I can. Of course, that's no sacrifice, considering how much we all enjoy her gingerbread cre-
ations. She now ships those houses all over the
world! I ordered her largest one this year, but it
still didn't last long, not with Colin and Mia nibbling away at it like mice. My Christmas cookies
disappeared in a blink, too. Dylan devours the
spritz, and Mark loves the gumdrop cookies. As
for Colin, he never met a cookie he didn't like.*

*Bethie and Mia are out today enjoying the
after-Christmas sales in town, but I decided I'd
rather stay home and relax with the new Vanessa
Valentine novel Colin gave me, which I'm going
to do as soon as I finish this letter. Christmas
wore me out.*

*In fact, this year has worn me out. Between
the horrible experience with our last foster child
and our disappointing harvest, I'm ready to wipe
the slate clean and start new. And to write a little less on that slate! Honestly, Emmaline, for
the first time in my life, I'm actually starting to*

feel the years. I look in the mirror and see the gray hair and wrinkles and ask myself, who is that old woman?

Of course, by today's standards seventy-two isn't that old, and my friend Sarah White—you remember Sarah; she owns the Sleeping Lady Salon—keeps trying to talk me into coloring my hair. Maybe I will.

Well, dear, that's all for now. I hope you and Joey have a happy New Year.

Love,
Justine

Chapter Eight

Colin looked across the river, where Mia was pointing, and all he saw was a riverbank packed with trees. What was she seeing that he wasn't? "What is it?"

"Don't you remember?"

"Remember what?"

She shook her head. "The trail to the Indian petroglyphs. Part of it runs alongside the river. Remember Uncle Mark taking us up there and how cool we thought they were and how we tried to draw them on rocks around the orchard? I'll bet Grandma Justine sent him there with our next clue."

So far they'd found clues hanging from trees and inside hamburger buns. Why not in the crevice of those boulders with the petroglyphs? "You might be right," he said and started down the bank.

"We could drive down the highway to the bridge, come at them that way," she suggested.

"Where's the fun in that? Anyway, it'll take an extra twenty minutes. Look how low that spot in the river is. We can get across it in under five."

"Okay," she said, and kicked off her sandals.

Colin led the way, jumping from rock to rock. This was like being a kid again. So fun, so freeing, so… slippery. One minute he was flying along like a mountain goat, the next he was knee-deep in the river. And his shoe was floating off down the river. And Mia was doubled over laughing.

"Very funny," he said, and waded off to get it, slipping on river rocks as he went. The shoe raced on ahead like a small canoe shooting rapids. He finally plunged in after it and caught the thing. Of course, now he was completely drenched. Oh, yeah, he was having fun now.

They made it to the other side, her perfectly dry, him dripping wet with his jeans stiff and his pride bruised. "If you say we should've driven over the bridge, I'm gonna throw you in the water," he warned.

"I wouldn't dream of it," she said, and managed to keep a straight face for all of two seconds before she started giggling.

Then he had to smile. She laughed. He did, too. "I think I've lost my edge," he said, and sat down to put on his runaway shoe.

"You're going to squish all the way up the trail," she said, giggling again.

He did.

It took them about forty minutes to get to the rock outcropping where the petroglyphs were. It was a narrow trail, a shelf high above the river. A sign warned hikers to watch their step in case they fell into the river and got swept away.

"There they are," Mia said.

Walking up to their long-ago discovery, Colin could remember how seeing that primitive artwork had stirred a hardly recognizable yearning deep in his young-boy soul to create something equally lasting, to make his own mark on the world. So far he hadn't made any mark at all. "I'm always surprised that these are still here," Mia said.

He nodded agreement. How many hundreds of years had passed since someone made these stick-figure selfies?

"I think I see an envelope," she said, peering into a tiny crevice.

He could see it, too, encased in a zippered plastic food storage bag and wedged in there. He reached in and pulled it out, disturbing a small lizard in the process.

The thing darted out, and Mia gave a yelp and jumped, nearly losing her footing.

Colin caught her and pulled her to him, leaning back against the rock to secure their balance. Mia in his arms again. It felt so right. So did the way she was looking up at him. Oh, man. Did temptation get any more appealing than this? Every nerve in his body was suddenly on high alert, and his blood was flowing south.

His cell phone rang. It wasn't hard to guess who was calling.

"You'd better answer that," Mia said, stepping away.

Yeah, he'd better. He'd better get his head on straight, too. He and Mia were history.

"How about a lunch break?" Lorelei said.

"Don't tell me—she wants to meet you for lunch."

Was Mia psychic? "How'd you know that?"

"It's got to be past noon by now."

"You go ahead and eat," he told Lorelei. "I'll catch up with you when I can."

"I can wait," she said.

At the rate they were going, she'd starve. "You could be waiting a long time. We're in the middle of something." They sure had been. He felt a guilty flush creep up his neck.

"We?" There was a whole sentence of ragging on him packed into that one word.

"Me and Mia. It's going to take a while to get back."

"Where are you? This town isn't that big."

"We're not in town. We're in the woods."

"In the woods." Lorelei would have made a great lawyer. She was really good at repeating innocuous testimony and twisting it to sound suspicious. *In the woods? A likely story. And what, pray tell, Mr. Wright, were you doing in the woods?*

"For crying out loud, Lorelei, give me a break. It's where one of our clues was." *I never pulled the trigger, Judge. I'm innocent.*

"This is all pretty dumb if you ask me," Lorelei grumbled.

Nobody had. Fortunately, he stopped the words before they escaped his big mouth.

"If you don't want to meet me for lunch, just say so," she huffed.

Actually, he didn't, not when he was busy trying to solve a very important puzzle.

That's all? Look a little deeper, said his conscience.

"I do," he insisted to both her and his pesky conscience. "It's just that I don't know how long I'm gonna be."

That was true. Man, all this wandering around town with Mia was making him crazy. They had to hurry up and finish their treasure hunt.

But part of him didn't want it to end. The stupid part. *Don't screw up*, he warned himself. *Don't try to haul the past into the present*.

Yeah, right. It was impossible not to with all the places Gram was sending them.

"I guess I'll do some more shopping," Lorelei said. "Call me when you're back in town."

"Okay," he said, resigned.

"You guys seem to fight a lot," Mia observed as he ended the call.

"No, we don't. Not usually. She's having a hard time with this. So am I." Okay, why had he said that?

"How?"

"It's just weird, is all, you and me hanging out together again. And... Never mind. Read the clue," he finished and shoved the envelope at her.

She took it from the plastic and read, "'Run, run, as fast as you can. To the place you can buy a gingerbread man.'"

"Well, that one's easy. Let's stop by Gingerbread Haus on our way to the restaurant."

Mia raised an eyebrow. "Oh. Am I invited?"

"We're in this together," he said, and started back down the trail, wondering if Lorelei would have read some hidden meaning in that remark.

They made it across the river without either of them

falling in and drove to Gingerbread Haus to see if Cass Wilkes had a pink envelope kicking around.

"As a matter of fact, I do," she said when they came in. "I've been waiting for you two to show up." She took in Colin's wet clothes. "You guys having fun with this treasure hunt?"

So far he'd been stung by wasps, fallen from a tree, soaked himself in the river, had some uncomfortable moments with his libido, and some equally uncomfortable moments with his girlfriend and his conscience. *Define fun.*

"We are," Mia answered for both of them.

"Justine sure enjoyed putting it together for you. I'm surprised your dad went along with it, though," Cass said to Colin.

"I don't think he was happy about it."

"He can be a stick in the mud sometimes," Cass said, "but someday someone's going to come along and unstick him."

Colin doubted that. And he didn't really want to stand around discussing his dad's love life. "Uh, how about that clue?"

"Sure. It'll take me a minute to put it together."

Colin and Mia exchanged glances. "Put it together?"

"What do you suppose she meant by that?" Colin asked as Cass disappeared into the kitchen area.

"I have no idea," Mia said. She drifted along the display case, eyeing the various offerings.

"I must've bought a hundred gingerbread boys in here," Colin said.

"I always loved those cream-puff swans. I haven't had one in years," Mia added with a sigh.

"I'll get you one." He reached into his back pocket for his wallet.

"Oh, no. Those things are deadly. I think I already gained a pound just looking at them."

"You don't need to worry about that. You look great." *Should you be saying that to your first love when you have a girlfriend?* scolded his conscience. Probably not, but it wasn't a lie. She did. "Give us two of the swans," he told the girl behind the counter.

"No, really, I'd better not." Mia's protest was half-hearted.

"You know you want one," he teased as the girl boxed up two.

He handed over a ten-dollar bill and received change and the box with the cream puffs. He opened it and held one out to Mia.

"Get thee behind me, Satan," she said, raising a hand and turning her head away.

That didn't stop him. He brought it up to her mouth. "One bite. Just take one bite."

She did, getting whipped cream on her upper lip and chin. He watched as she closed her eyes and gave a little groan, and he almost groaned, too.

"Mmm," she said. "Delicious."

And how delicious would it be to lick the whipped cream off her lip and then...

Stick with the cream puffs, he told himself and took a bite. "Oh, man, that is good." She reached for it and he moved it away from her. "You said you only wanted one bite."

"I changed my mind."

She reached for it and he turned, holding it high. "We're gonna have lunch. You'll spoil your appetite."

"Life's uncertain. Eat dessert first."

"You'll gain a pound," he joked.

"I don't care," she said, jumping for it. "Give that to me."

He held it higher. "Say *please*."

"Give me that cream puff," she growled. She was practically climbing up him now. Oh, yeah, this was fun.

She suddenly stopped, as if sensing how very close their bodies were. She frowned and stepped back.

Reality had set in and the fun was over. "Okay. Here you go," he said and passed the rest to her.

"Thanks," she murmured, pink cheeked, and took it.

He pulled out the other cream puff and chewed on that, a much wiser choice than nibbling Mia's lip.

They were just finishing when Cass returned, carrying a large bakery box.

"Oh, yeah," he said as she handed it to Mia. "She put our clue inside something to eat."

"Not exactly." Cass winked. "There *is* something edible in here, but it's not your clue."

"Not our clue," he repeated.

"It's what you have to do to get your clue," Cass told him.

Now what sort of posthumous trick was Gram up to?

Mia opened the box and they looked inside. All it held was pieces of gingerbread.

"What's that?" Colin asked.

"A gingerbread house," Cass answered.

"It's pieces of cookie."

"Everything you need to assemble a house. No frosting, though."

"Where's that?" Colin asked.

"Your grandma wants you to make it yourself."

"Seriously?" he said in frustration. This game of Gram's was never ending.

"And she wants you to pick out the decorations, too," Cass went on to say. "It shouldn't take you more than an hour. When you get done, bring it back and I'll give you your next clue."

"Okay," Colin said to Mia, "let's get going."

"What about Lorelei?"

"She'll be fine."

"You should call her."

Probably good advice. He called Lorelei. "We're out of the woods but we have one more thing to do."

"What?"

"Just… I'll tell you later, babe," he said and pushed End before Lorelei could demand that he explain further. "Okay, we're fine," he lied.

"Sure you are."

"Like Cass said, it shouldn't take that long to put together a few pieces of cookie."

"You go have lunch. I'll do it," Mia offered.

It was a sincere offer, not something born of one-upmanship. And decorating gingerbread houses was sure more up her alley than his, but he realized he didn't want to miss out on this.

"No, I'm in," he said, and that made him think of Gram.

"In for a penny, in for a pound," she used to say.

"What does that mean?" he'd asked her once.

"It means if you're going to do something you may as well jump in and do it with your whole heart," she'd replied. "I think you kids would say go big or go home," she'd added with a grin.

Well, he wasn't going home until he found what Gram had for him, no matter what. He was going for it—but only the treasure, not the woman. He already had a woman.

They stopped by his dad's house and Mia waited in the car while he changed into dry clothes. Then they went to the grocery store to load up on gumdrops and peppermint discs. "And M&M's," Colin said. "You gotta have M&M's."

"Okay, that should do it, then."

"What about frosting? That stuff comes in a can, doesn't it?"

"Frosting in a can won't hold everything together. We need to make royal icing."

"What the heck is royal icing?"

"It's this frosting you make that pretty much turns to cement once it dries."

"Cement, that sounds good."

"It's not bad. Anyway, it doesn't have to taste good since we're not keeping the gingerbread house."

"Oh. Yeah." That was kind of disappointing. He'd

been looking forward to eating a gingerbread wall lined with M&M's.

Mia shook her head. "I swear you've got the worst sweet tooth. Why aren't you fat?"

"Clean living."

By unspoken consent, they went to Aunt Beth's kitchen to work on their project. They could have gone to Dad's, but he didn't have much of a functioning kitchen. Other than making a sandwich or having a bowl of cereal, neither Dad nor Colin had spent much time in there. What was the point when there was always something good getting served up at Gram's or Aunt Beth's? Anyway, Colin knew Mia had never felt comfortable in Dad's house, especially after the fiasco in the orchard.

Aunt Beth and Uncle Mark were nowhere to be seen when they got to the house. "They're probably out running errands," Mia said. "It is Saturday, after all."

Saturday. Normally, Colin would be at the climbing gym with some of his buddies, or riding bikes onto the ferry to Bainbridge Island with Lorelei. Or filling the day with any number of physical activities, like working out at the gym or going hiking. It was all fun, but in the end, looking at his life in light of the ones his grandparents had lived, it could hardly qualify as meaningful. Aunt Beth had raised Mia and helped raise him. Dad did pro bono stuff. What was *he* doing? No one ever came right out and said it, but he suspected his family was disappointed in how little he'd accomplished so far.

Assembling the gingerbread house was tricky. Who

knew it would be so hard to get those walls to stick together? And after the house collapsed, they had to start over putting on the roof, and that had him holding his breath.

"This is hard," he said. "No wonder Cass charges so much for these things."

"I think we've got it, though," Mia said and stepped back to admire their handiwork. She cocked her head. "Well, it's a little sloppy. Maybe I should scrape off some of the frosting."

"No, let's not do anything that might make it collapse again."

"All right, then, I guess we can decorate."

"Sounds good to me." He ripped open the M&M's bag, poured out a handful and popped them in his mouth.

"They're for the house, remember?"

"Sure, I remember," he said, and stuck one along the roofline. "Hey, Christmas lights," he said after he'd added a few more.

"Not bad," she agreed, lining gumdrops along the base of the house.

"Not bad? It's downright artistic," he said, and tossed an M&M at her.

"Hey," she protested, and retaliated with a gumdrop.

Which of course, called for another M&M assault.

She giggled and threw a second gumdrop.

Somehow, those opening volleys devolved into an outright candy war, and soon Colin had her cornered with what was left of the royal icing.

"Don't," she warned. "That'll make a mess of my hair.

"All right." He set it on the counter.

The moment he did, she dipped into it and got him in the face, and then they were off and running again.

Finally, with candy everywhere and royal icing on their clothes and faces, they called a truce.

"We'd better get this cleaned up before Aunt Beth comes back," Mia said and grabbed a dishcloth.

Colin fetched the broom and dustpan and got to work sweeping. "When was the last time we had a food fight?"

"Thanksgiving weekend, your senior year. With the whipped cream."

He remembered. He'd just wanted to see if she did. That had ended with a mess in the kitchen, too. And a kiss. He missed those days. Did she?

He dumped the candy and walked over to where she stood at the counter, suddenly very busy mopping up icing. "Mia."

She stopped scrubbing and looked out the kitchen window. "Sometimes I really miss our old life. I miss Grandma Justine."

"I know," he said, and put an arm around her. "I do, too."

She turned into him and he hugged her. It still felt so right. They should've been together. He should never have let her go, should have fought for her.

Before he could say as much, his cell phone demanded his attention, bringing him back to his senses. Lorelei was the present. Mia was the past.

She stepped away. "I bet that's Lorelei. She's probably starving," he said and answered. "Hey, babe."

"Okay, I'm at some place called Zelda's," Lorelei informed him. "Are you done yet?"

"Almost," he assured her.

"Great! I'll get us a table. For two."

"Make it for three," he told her and she hung up on him.

No more was said about Lorelei as he and Mia cleaned up and then drove back to Gingerbread Haus. No more was said, period.

"That's quite the creation." Cass smiled, checking out their slightly lopsided gingerbread house.

"Right up there with the Charlie Brown ugly Christmas tree," Mia said. "I don't think either of us is going into the gingerbread house business anytime soon."

"Good. I don't want any competition," Cass joked.

"No worries there. Nobody can compete with you," Colin told her.

"What a flatterer you've become," she said, waving away his compliment. "Now I'll get your clue. You can keep the house, by the way."

"Hey, thanks," Colin said, and broke off a piece of the roof. Gentleman that he was, he offered it to Mia first.

She shook her head.

"Fine. More for me." He took a bite. "Mmm."

"Stop that." She broke off a piece for herself. "You're a bad influence," she said and stuffed it in her mouth.

He wouldn't mind being a bad influence. *Earth to Colin. You have a girlfriend waiting for you at Zelda's.*

Man, he was screwed up.

February 16, 2003

Dear Emmaline,

I hope your knee is healing well. I've heard knee replacements are painful, but in the long run I'm sure you'll be glad you had it done. It was so nice of Joey to call and let us know you came through the surgery okay. I have a little something from Sweet Dreams coming your way. It may not speed your recovery, but I promise it will make you feel better.

I was sorry to hear about J.J. losing his job. How awful to get laid off after fifteen years with the same company! I hope he'll find a new job soon.

We all had a lovely Valentine's Day here. Gerald took me to Schwangau for a candlelight dinner. It's such an expensive restaurant. I always feel a little guilty about spending that much money on a meal. Gerald told me he'd spend ten times that to give me a romantic dinner. Wasn't that sweet? I swear I love that man even more than I did when we were teenagers. Bethie and Mark spent the night at a fancy hotel in Seattle, and our Colin and Mia went to Herman's Hamburgers and a movie. She made him Valentine cookies, and he bought her a long-stemmed pink rose. They're such a cute pair and so enamored of each other. I'm sure it would have pleased

Anna no end to see them together. Who knows? Maybe this will turn into a lifelong love like Gerald and I have enjoyed. Dylan has been in Seattle all week. On business, he claimed, but I wonder if there's a lady over there. I don't ask anymore. He seems happy as a bachelor so there's no sense in worrying about him.

Well, dear, there's not much else going on here to report. I do hope you're up and around again soon.

Love,
Justine

Chapter Nine

Cass returned with another pink envelope. "Good luck," she said, and handed it to Mia.

They left, taking their culinary creation with them. Colin put it in the backseat, leaving Mia to read their next clue. "Okay, what does it say?" he asked as he started the engine.

"'What's sweet and flat and round? For your next clue, go where it's found,'" Mia read. She tapped her chin. "Sweet and flat and round?"

"Elephant ears," Colin said. "Except you can only get those at the street dance or on the Fourth of July."

"Sweet and round, sweet and round," she mused. This wasn't that hard a clue. Was her brain getting worn out?

"Pancakes," Colin said suddenly.

"Of course." It stood to reason that one of their clues would bc at Pancake Haus. Mia had worked there part-time when she was in high school, and once she and Colin got together, he'd come in every Saturday for breakfast.

He shook his head. "Trust Gram to send us there."

Mia blushed.

"Not one of your finer moments," he teased, making her face burn even hotter.

Her behavior *had* been a little out of character. Okay, a lot. But darn it all, she'd been provoked.

Mia was now a junior. The ugliness with Adrian Malk was behind her, and she and Colin were an item. The new school year was starting off great. She and Colin went to football games, ate lunch together in the cafeteria and did their homework together. In some ways nothing had changed since they still hung out like they always had. In other ways, everything had changed because now there was also the sweet thrill of holding hands and sharing kisses. Come December there'd be the Christmas Ball, then Colin's senior prom. The rest of her life was good, too. She liked all her classcs at school and she especially enjoyed the self-defense class she was taking through the Icicle Falls Parks and Recreation Department. She was in the high school equivalent of the Garden of Eden.

Then the snake arrived. Emily Green was new to Icicle Falls High. She was cute and dressed like a fashion model. And she was a flirt. Every boy in school was hot for her but who did she set her greedy little eyes on? Colin.

It seemed as if every time Mia turned around, there was Emily, flirting with him—in the lunch line, in the hall between classes, at the football games. Mia found herself wishing that Colin played football instead of baseball. At least he would've been out on the field where Emily couldn't get her hooks into him, instead of sitting in the bleachers. No matter where they sat at the games, she always seemed to find them, plunking her designer-jeans-clad bottom down on his other side and then playing dumb and asking him to explain every play to her.

"Colin, you're so smart," she'd coo, and of course he ate it up.

"You know, she's out to get him," Bailey Sterling said to Mia when some of the girls gathered in Mia's room for an impromptu slumber party.

"She's out to get every boy in town," Christie Ortega added bitterly. And Christie would know, since her breakup with Eddie Schultz was directly connected to a certain under-the-bleachers tête-à-tête between Emily and Eddie.

Eddie had dumped Christie, and then been seen at Herman's slurping milk shakes with Emily. It had been short-lived and now Eddie was moping his way down the halls to his classes, and Emily was batting her extended eyelashes at Colin.

"I think she likes taking other girls' guys," Bailey said.

"It's a power trip," Christie said. "Watch out, Mia, because the cuter the guy…"

She didn't have to finish the sentence. Colin was one of the cutest guys in school.

"She'd better not come after Colin," Mia said. Except she already had.

"Or what? You'll beat her up? Everyone knows you don't have a mean bone in your body," Christie said.

"Then we'll beat her up for you," Bailey said, which made both girls laugh.

"You might break a nail," Christie teased.

"I can be tough," Bailey insisted, and the other two laughed.

"That's the problem. We're all too nice," Christie said with a sigh.

"There's nothing wrong with being nice," Mia scolded her. "I believe in the Golden Rule, and I think in the end we all get exactly what we deserve."

Christie frowned. "I didn't deserve to get my boyfriend stolen."

"No. You deserve better than a guy who'll dump you just because some other girl comes along and flirts with him."

"And what are you going to do if Colin dumps you?" Christie asked.

"He won't. We're like Cathy and Heathcliff in *Wuthering Heights*."

"And you know how *that* turned out," Bailey said with a shake of her head. "I never did get that book."

"It's about undying love," Mia explained.

"Yeah, but she married someone else," Bailey protested.

"Okay, then, we're like Buttercup and Westley in *The Princess Bride*," Mia amended. And they were. Colin had proved that when he rescued her from Adrian Malk.

"Or Leonardo and Rosamunde in *Forever Love*," Christie suggested. "I loved that book," she said. "But then I love all of Vanessa Valentine's books. Those heroes never go off and sleep with other women."

"You don't really think Emily did it under the bleachers with Eddie, do you?" Bailey asked, wide-eyed. "I mean, I know they were under there for a while but still... It was cold out. And people were all around."

"There weren't any people under the bleachers," Christie said with a scowl. "Anyway, I don't know and I don't care. All I'm saying," she said to Mia, "is you'd better watch your back."

"I think you need to tell Emily what's what," said Bailey. "Be..." She scrunched up her face, looking for the right word.

"Proactive?" Mia guessed.

"Yep, that's it."

"I agree with Bailey. We should beat her up. Let's grab her in the locker room after PE," Christie said, obviously relishing the thought.

"We're not going to beat anyone up," Mia said firmly.

"Well, you should at least threaten her," Christie advised.

"I don't need to. I trust Colin."

"Yeah, well, I trusted Eddie and look where it got me," Christie said resentfully.

Good point. Mia decided it couldn't hurt to have a little talk with the newcomer. Maybe they did things differently in Portland where Emily came from, but here in Icicle Falls, girls didn't poach.

Mia finally worked up the nerve when they were walking out of the locker room after PE. She started out with a diplomatic, "So, how are you liking it here?"

"It's okay, I guess," Emily said. "You guys need a mall."

Everyone was doing fine shopping in the local stores or going to nearby Wenatchee. "We kind of like it the way it is."

Emily shrugged. "I guess. The boys are cute," she added, and gave Mia a superior smirk.

"Um, about that. We have sort of an unwritten rule about boys."

Emily's only answer was to cock an eyebrow.

"We, um, well, if someone's with someone, we don't go after that guy."

"If someone's with someone, he doesn't go after another girl," Emily shot back with a toss of her blond hair. "And I'm new here, so I don't know who's with who."

"Well, Colin's with me. Now you know."

For such a pretty girl, Emily sure had an ugly smile. "Yeah? Then how come he flirts with me?"

Mia blinked. Colin didn't flirt with her, did he? "I think you're the one doing all the flirting."

"Am I? Well, if he's really into you, you don't have anything to worry about, do you?" Emily retorted and turned down the hall to go to her next class, leaving Mia standing in the stream of students, gaping after her.

She chewed on Emily's words for the rest of the school day, barely paying attention in geometry or US history. And the next Friday night at the football game, she watched carefully as Colin explained yet again the concept of first, second, third and fourth downs to Emily. Didn't they have football in Oregon?

"What's wrong?" he asked later as they drove to Herman's for postgame burgers with the gang.

"Nothing." He shouldn't have to ask. If he had to ask, she certainly wasn't going to tell him.

"Well, something's wrong."

Okay, she *would* tell him. "Emily. You were flirting with Emily."

"You're jealous?"

"No. I don't think you should pay so much attention to her when you're with me, that's all."

"I wasn't paying attention. I was just being polite."

"Do you have to be so polite?"

He grinned. "You're cute when you're jealous."

"I'm not jealous."

"Sure you're not," he said and tugged on a lock of her hair.

Well, okay, so what if she was? Colin was special and she didn't want to share.

It seemed as though ever since their talk, Emily was even more determined to steal him, and the Saturday morning she showed up at Pancake Haus for breakfast, Mia was convinced she was stalking him. Colin and Andy Forrester and Billy Williams always came in for breakfast before heading off to their Saturday jobs—Andy to Mountain Escape Books, Bill Will to the nearby guest ranch where he mucked out stalls and took city slickers on trail rides, and Colin to Swede's garage, where he did oil changes on cars and rang up gas purchases. The three of them always took a booth together, but today here was Emily, squeezed in on the end, right next to Colin. What was she doing here?

"Emily, you're up early," she greeted the interloper as she handed out menus.

"The boys told me you guys have really good pancakes," Emily replied and smiled at Colin.

Mia frowned and Colin looked uncomfortable. Andy and Bill Will just sat there, clueless and grinning.

"So, the usual for you guys?" Mia asked.

"Yep," Bill Will replied.

"What will you have, Emily?" Mia asked Emily. *A punch in the nose?*

"Should I have the pancakes?" Mia asked Colin. What, she couldn't make up her own mind?

"I don't know. Get what you like," he said.

"Get the pancakes," urged Andy.

"Okay," she said. "And could you warm the syrup? I like warm syrup on my pancakes." Then she turned her back on Mia as if she was some lowly serving wench and asked Colin what he was doing after work.

Mia stormed off to the kitchen to put in the order. She served two other tables and wrote up the bill for a third. Finally, she fetched the order for Colin's table.

"Where's my warm syrup?" Emily asked.

"It's coming," Mia said through gritted teeth.

She snagged a little glass pitcher from another table and gave it a quick zap in the microwave then started to put its metal lid on. Inspiration stopped her. She wouldn't be needing the lid.

"What took you so long?" Emily said when she returned. "I had to get it just right," Mia replied. "I hope this is warm enough." And she tipped the pitcher over Emily's head.

Emily let out a shriek and jumped from the booth, syrup dripping down her hair.

"Oh, my gosh, I'm so sorry," Mia said as the boys laughed uproariously.

Emily glared at her. "You did that on purpose!"

Well, duh. "Maybe I did. Just like you've been running around stealing other girls' boyfriends on purpose. I already told you we don't do that here and if you want to have a single friend in this town, you'd better stop." Whoa, had she just said all that? And in a public place? She was suddenly aware of several pairs of eyes on her. She wanted to run away.

So did Emily. She burst into tears and rushed from the restaurant.

Oh, boy, here came Dot Morrison, the owner. And she wasn't smiling. "Mia, can I see you in my office?"

It wasn't a request. Mia followed her, feeling like a prisoner on the way to her trial. This would be her last day of work, not only here but anywhere. Dot would certainly never give her a reference. *Don't hire Mia. She assaults customers. Syrup is her weapon of choice, but she's probably equally good with a snow globe or a can of peas.*

They went into the little office off one corner of the kitchen and Dot shut the door. "Sit down," she said, and pulled a cigarette out of the half-used pack sitting on her desk.

Mia squirmed in her seat while Dot lit her cigarette, inhaled and blew out a cloud of smoke.

"You want to tell me what that was all about?" Dot

took another drag on her cigarette and studied Mia through the haze of smoke.

Mia bit her lip.

"Never mind. I can guess. You have a rival."

"She's stealing everyone's boyfriends," Mia blurted.

"Breaking the girlfriend code."

She understood. Mia nodded, relieved.

"And your boyfriend was next on the list."

"I told her we were together."

"Obviously, she needed to be taught a lesson."

Exactly. Mia nodded again.

Dot's eyes narrowed. "But not in my restaurant. There's another code you may not be aware of, Mia, and that's the good-employee code."

Mia's face burned and she felt sick. Dot was definitely going to fire her.

"You made quite a scene out there."

Now Mia was close to tears. She hung her head. "I'm sorry, Mrs. Morrison."

"You should be. Not for teaching that little stinker a lesson, but for wasting quality syrup on her. Don't you be doing that again. Next time you have a problem, tell me. I'll take the kid outside and give her what for. But let's save the syrup for the pancakes. Okay?"

Mia stared at her. "You're not going to fire me?"

"Only if you pull a stunt like that again."

Relief washed over Mia. "I won't. I promise."

Dot stubbed out her cigarette in an ashtray brimming with butts. "See that you don't. Now, get out there and keep my customers happy."

Mia practically bolted for the door.

"And Mia."

She stopped with her hand on the doorknob and turned.

"Good for you," Dot said with a wink. "Don't take any crap from anybody and you'll be fine. One more thing. You don't have to worry about Colin. I've seen the way that boy looks at you. He's yours, heart and soul."

Until Arthur had come along. Then everything had blown up. And she'd let it blow. How stupid they'd both been!

April 22, 2003

Dear Emmaline,

Another Easter has come and gone in a blink! Where does the time go? Our day was lovely and the Easter treasure hunt kept Colin and Mia busy for a good hour. Bethie and I made this one as hard as we could, sending them back and forth between our houses and the orchard. We probably won't have many more in the future, as the children will soon be moving on with their lives. In fact, I need to stop referring to them as children, don't I? Colin will graduate this year, and next year Mia will be done with high school.

It's been a joy to watch them grow up into such fine young people. Colin is so good with his hands. He loves working on cars and he's a big help to Gerald in the orchard. He's always reading up on ways we can improve the quality of our fruit and increase our harvest. He's a smart boy, but he'd rather be outdoors fishing or working on his car than inside doing schoolwork. His father is insisting he get a college education, but we all know he won't be following in Dylan's footsteps. Colin wants to work the land like his grandfather. Mia is our little schoolbook smartie. She's doing so well in school, getting straight As.

As for the rest of the family, Dylan's practice continues to grow. Bethie is up to her neck in *tulle and satin, working on wedding gowns for three June brides, and Mark is thinking of running for the city council come fall. Goodness, what a bunch of overachievers we have in this family!*

I should bring this letter to a close. I'm making split pea soup with my leftover ham bone and I need to get started.

Don't you and Joey worry about J.J. I'm sure he'll find another job soon.

Love,
Justine

Chapter Ten

"I wonder what ever happened to Emily," Colin said as he and Mia walked into Pancake Haus.

"She moved to Wenatchee. Christie heard that her husband left her for another woman." In a way, Mia felt sorry for Emily. She was probably reaping exactly what she'd sowed all those years she lived in Icicle Falls, but heartbreak was a crummy crop, even when you deserved it.

"Leave it to the women to have all the dirt," Colin said.

"You asked."

"It was just an idle comment. I don't really care what happened to her. I've stayed in touch with everyone I wanted to." Almost everyone. He'd started to call Mia countless times after they split, only to abort the attempt.

The breakfast crowd was long gone. A few people lingered over late brunches and the small selection of lunch items Dot kept on the menu. They walked past a booth where a couple of women sat enjoying lattes and Belgian waffles, and made their way to the counter, where Dot herself was filling plastic tubs with clean coffee cups, a carrot stick dangling from her mouth. Been There, Done That, Don't Ask, said the slogan on her sweatshirt under a picture of the cartoon character Maxine, to whom Dot bore a strong resemblance.

"About time you two got here," she said after they'd exchanged greetings. "I've been expecting you for hours. Justine must really be putting you kids through your paces."

"She definitely is," Mia said.

Colin pointed to the carrot. "Getting your beta carotene for the day, Dot?"

She took a chomp and shook her head. "Tilda made me quit smoking. Every time I want a ciggy I shove a carrot stick in my mouth. Let me tell you, it's not the same. I think I'm going to try e-cigarettes."

"Yeah, Tilda's gonna be impressed with *that*," Colin said sardonically.

Dot gave a long-suffering sigh. "Well, let's get to your clue. I've got it in my office. Come on back."

Dot's office was small and cramped, with paperwork piled everywhere.

"This looks the same as when I was working here," Mia said.

"Yeah, a mess. A messy desk is the sign of an orderly mind." Dot pawed around under the piles of papers and finally came up with the pink envelope. "I'm dying to hear what your clue is. Justine was very mysterious." She passed it to Colin, and he pulled out the pink paper and read, "'Roses are red, violets are blue. Someone has a clue for you.'"

Dot chortled. "Ha! That Justine was a clever one."

"You know what it means?" Colin asked.

"Well, I can guess. Can't you?"

"Lupine Floral," said Mia.

Dot chomped off another bite of carrot and nodded in Colin's direction. "Make him buy you some flowers when you're there."

"You'd better take that lunch break now," Mia told Colin as they left.

"Let's hit Lupine Floral first," he said. "There can't be that many clues still to go."

"Okay, if you want to be in trouble with your girlfriend, it's your funeral."

"Order roses for my grave," he cracked. "One more stop, and then we'll get lunch. I've gotta admit, I'm ready to eat."

Yet again, Lorelei summoned him on his cell phone. "Okay, I'm still at this place called Zelda's and I'm really getting hungry."

"Me, too, but we have one more stop."

"How about we make it just you and me for lunch?" Lorelei suggested.

"Can't. Mia and I have another clue to work on."

"You couldn't take an hour off?"

"The sooner we solve this, the sooner you and I can go back to Seattle." And that was what he wanted, to finish with this whole schizoid mess. He was having these crazy thoughts about Mia because Gram's hunt was making him sentimental. You couldn't recreate the past, and that was all they had. She was a hotshot at her big company in Chicago now, and he was... living in Seattle.

"Okay, fine," Lorelei said. "I'm starting without you. They've got a drink called a Chocolate Kiss. A chocolate kiss is better than none."

"Well, you like chocolate, babe," he said. Lame.

Mia cocked an eyebrow as he ended the call and shoved his phone back in his pants pocket. "Don't ask," he said.

Heinrich was nowhere to be seen when they walked in, but his partner Kevin was manning the floor. He was in the process of helping Gerhardt Geissel, who owned Gerhardt's Gasthaus, choose some flowers.

"I'll lay you odds he's buying a Deep Shit bouquet," Colin said to Mia.

"Deep Shit bouquet?"

"Yeah, as in he's in deep shit with his wife and trying to get out."

"When she sees these, she'll fall into your arms and beg you to take her to bed," Kevin predicted. "Or maybe to the kitchen table."

"The only thing we've done on our kitchen table for the last thirty years is eat," Gerhardt said with a solemn shake of his head. "And Ingrid's already made the bed. Once the bed is made for the day…" he added with another head shake.

Kevin gave him a consoling pat on the arm. "Well, this will at least get you out of trouble."

"Oh, yeah. Deep Shit bouquet," Mia whispered.

"One of the only things a guy stands a chance of getting right," he whispered back.

"Was that said with some bitterness?" Mia teased.

He shrugged. "More like regret. What would you have done if I'd sent you flowers after we broke up?"

"The same thing I would've done if only you'd believed me."

If only. Those two words summed it all up. Too late now.

Colin walked over to where Gerhardt was paying for a King Kong–size bouquet with enough roses to fill the White House rose garden. "That's a serious bundle of flowers, Gerhardt."

"Needs to be," Gerhardt muttered as he gathered it up. "So how are you two doing on your treasure hunt?"

"Is there anyone in town who doesn't know about this?" Colin asked.

"Oh, come on now," Kevin said. "This is better than any of those Real Housewives' shows on TV. We're one of the clues," he told Gerhardt. "Heinrich was beside himself. He's such a romantic. Heinrich," he called in the general direction of the back room. "Guess who's here."

Heinrich was already on his way out. "Dear boy, I knew you'd be back," he said to Colin. "It was all I could do not to say something when you were here earlier."

"But he can keep a secret when he needs to," put in Kevin. "So can I," he added, then turned to Gerhardt. "So if you and Ingrid wind up on the kitchen table…"

Gerhardt merely shook his head. "I'd like to stand here all day listening to your *Quatsch*, but I have work to do. And believe me, after what I said about Ingrid's useless brother, getting her to forgive me is going to be hard work, even with the flowers."

"Especially if you use the word *useless*," Heinrich warned.

Gerhardt took his out-of-control bouquet and left, and Heinrich turned his full attention to Mia and Colin. "Now, what can I do for you two? As if I couldn't guess."

"You can give us our next clue," Colin said.

Heinrich was about to retrieve it, but Kevin said, "Wait. Make him show you the proof."

"Yeah." Heinrich crossed his arms and frowned. "Prove it."

"You guys have way too much time on your hands," Colin said and produced the pink stationery.

Heinrich unfolded it and read with Kevin peering over his shoulder. "That is so cute. A little obvious but cute."

"The next clue?" Colin nudged.

"Such impatience," Heinrich said, and went back to his workroom to fetch it.

"While you're waiting, how about some flowers?" Kevin suggested. "Our Stargazer lilies have a lovely fragrance. Or you could go with the classic single long-stemmed rose, the sure way to a woman's heart," he said, smiling at Mia.

Mia blushed. "That's okay."

"No, it's a good idea," Colin said. "But it has to be pink. That's her favorite color."

"No problemo," Kevin said and went to select a pink rose from the cooler.

Meanwhile, Heinrich was back with their next clue. "Here you go," he said and handed it to Mia.

"What does it say?" asked Kevin, who was now wrapping Mia's rose with some baby's breath and a fern.

She opened it and announced, "It's driving instructions."

Now this was the kind of clue Colin enjoyed. "All right!"

"Like pirates on a desert island walking off paces. I love it," said Kevin.

"Oh, I wish we could help you. Such fun!" Heinrich declared as Kevin gave Mia the rose. "Enjoy the rest of your hunt."

"And the rose," said Kevin, who was making change for a ten. "Nothing says love like flowers."

"Or 'I'm sorry,'" Colin murmured. Which was he saying to Mia? Never mind!

"Does it sound like it's far?" he asked as they walked to the car. "Maybe we can stop there before we go to Zelda's."

Lorelei's ringtone called out from the back pocket of his jeans.

"Gee, I wonder who that is," Mia said.

"We're on our way," he answered. It looked as if there'd be no more stops.

"Hurry up," Lorelei said. "These kisses are grrreat but I need food."

He could tell. "I think she's getting bombed," he said to Mia after he ended the call. "She's not a big drinker. Empty calories," he added.

"I'm sure you'll find a way to help her work them off later."

"Is that a little bit of snark I detect?"

"No," Mia said airily and got into the car.

Was she jealous? "How come you don't like her?" he asked as they drove toward Zelda's.

"I never said I didn't like her. I hardly know her."

"Then maybe you're jealous." If she was…

"And maybe you're delusional."

Yeah, he probably was.

"So, are you in trouble?" Mia asked.

He shrugged."Want the rose?" she offered.

"No, that's yours." But he hoped to heaven she'd leave it in the car.

She did, God bless her, even though she must have realized it would wilt in there.

Lorelei was ensconced in a booth with her drink. She had her hair down and wore a tight black top, sleeveless and low cut, over her jeans. The outfit's hot factor was considerably diminished by the frown. "Where have you been?" she greeted Colin.

As if she didn't know. "Trying to figure out where my inheritance is," he said, sliding in next to her.

She eyed Mia suspiciously. "All this time?"

"Yeah, all this time," he said, and now he was frowning, too. "You don't have to stay here."

"I want to," she insisted. "I want to help you."

"But you can't," Mia said sweetly.

Lorelei squinted as if she was having trouble bringing Mia into focus. "Nobody asked…you," she said, and downed the last of her drink.

"Babe, how many of those have you had?"

"Two," Lorelei said, and held up three fingers.

"Have you eaten anything yet?"

"No. I was waiting for you."

Their waitress arrived. "Let's order," he said.

Lorelei picked up her menu. "I haven't decided what I want."

"You've had at least an hour to make up your mind," he said.

"I…know."

"How many drinks has she had?" he asked the waitress.

"Three. She's done."

"She'll take the Northwest salad," Colin said.

"No, I want a veggie burger," Lorelei declared.

"You had that last night," he reminded her. "Don't you want something with no carbs?"

"I'll work them off when we get back to Seattle," Lorelei said. "Or later tonight." She laid her hand on his thigh, making him think of Mia's earlier snarky comment. Normally, he would've been happy to help his girlfriend work off some calories. Instead, here he was, wishing she'd go back home. Multiple personalities, that was it. He had multiple personalities.

"I'll have the Northwest salad, too," Mia said. "Iced tea to drink."

"I'll have another Chocolate Kish," Lorelei slurred.

"I'm sorry," the waitress said, "but three's the limit."

"What kind of restaurant is this?"

"She'll take an iced coffee," Colin said.

"And for you, sir?" asked the waitress.

Aspirin. "Just water. And a club sandwich."

"How many more clues do you have left, anyway?" Lorelei asked as the waitress walked off.

"I have no idea," Colin replied.

She leaned an elbow on the table and gazed up at him. "I wonder what the treasure is. If it's gold we should invest in the gym. We could also cash some in and go to Hawaii. Or Peru. We could go zip-lining in Cuzco, babe."

Mia raised an eyebrow and Colin felt his face sizzling. This habit Lorelei was developing of speculating on his inheritance and how to spend it—with his grandmother barely gone—was tacky. More than that it was... He didn't want to put into words what it was, but the big one crouched there at the back of his mind. *Greedy.*

Of course, he was out looking for his inheritance. What did that say about him? *Gram, I swear I'd rather have you back than whatever you left me.* Suddenly he wasn't hungry.

When the waitress returned with their drinks, Colin nudged Lorelei's toward her. "Have some iced coffee."

She took a quick sip and then started talking again. "I don't understand why it's taking you so long to find this...whatever." She waved her drink, sloshing it on him.

"It's just the way the clues are coming," he said, grabbing a napkin.

"You should take a break," she said. "Let's spend a little time wandering around town. Give your mind a rest."

"Lorelei, I really want to get this done," he said.

"Fine. Suit yourself."

Okay, Lorelei was not showing well. There was more to her than shopping and getting tipsy and talking about trips. He wouldn't pick such a loser girl-friend. She recycled and did the Susan G. Komen Race for the Cure every year. She ran marathons and half marathons and…spent money like it was water, nagged him every time he ordered dessert when they went out to eat. Which they did a lot. Lorelei was into fitness, but she was also into expensive restaurants and fine wine. Clothes. Jewelry. Yeah, the simple life.

Their lunch arrived, and Lorelei decided she needed to remove the top bun from her veggie burger. He took advantage of her preoccupation to ask Mia, "So where are we supposed to start?"

She pulled out the stationery again and consulted it. "Grandma Justine's house."

He nodded. "After we eat, we should run Lorelei back to Gerhardt's."

"I don't want to go back there. I want to do some-thing," Lorelei said.

"You shouldn't drive," he told her.

"I didn't drive here. I walked. This town is so small, I bet I could walk the whole place in an hour."

"You tired of it already?" he asked.

"There's not much to do."

How the tune had changed from her earlier raving over what a cute place it was.

"I mean, what do people here do for fun?"

They went dancing at the Red Barn, came here to Zelda's for karaoke night, visited with friends at Ba-varian Brews, hiked in the mountains, fished in the river, got married, raised families, tended orchards, made wine. "There's plenty to do here."

"If you say so," she said. She stuck out her lower lip. "I guess I'm just feeling lonely."

"Lorelei, don't start." At the rate she was going, she'd have him in a straitjacket before the weekend was over. Actually, he didn't need Lorelei for that. He was doing a fine job of driving himself crazy without her assistance.

"You go off with Miss Mountain Girl and don't worry about me. Even though I came up here to help you."

Alcohol did not bring out the best in Lorelei. And Lorelei was not bringing out the best in him. "Look. I promise we'll do something tonight, okay? I'll take you dancing."

"Okay," she said, mollified.

"Can you find enough to do until then?"

Lorelei glared across the table at Mia and asked Colin, "What are you going to do for dinner?"

"I just had lunch." How the hell was he supposed to know what he was doing for dinner? He'd barely touched his sandwich, but it was definitely time to go. "Look, I'll catch up with you later. Okay?"

"You're leaving now? You're not even done eating!" Lorelei protested.

He shook his head, signaled the waitress and gave her his credit card.

"Where did you say you were from?" Lorelei asked Mia while they waited.

"I didn't," Mia said, and smiled. It wasn't a friendly smile.

Women. Life would be so much easier if men didn't need them.

September 27, 2003

Dear Emmaline,

I'm glad to hear that your first art show went so well. Maybe you'll go on to become the next Grandma Moses. Not that you're as old as her, of course, but you know what I mean.

All's quiet here on the western front these days. Mia is starting school back in New York, and Colin is busy taking classes at the local community college. He misses her terribly, but it might be good for them to have a little time apart. You've heard the saying, absence makes the heart grow fonder. Although I can't imagine Colin becoming any fonder of his Mia than he already is. Dylan is convinced they're too young to know what they're doing, but I think he's wrong. Some people are simply lucky enough to find each other at an early age, and that's what happened with these two. Watching them together reminds me so much of Gerald and me, and you and Joey, when we were all young.

I forgot to tell you the other day. I'm now offering a weekly baking class, teaching some of our younger women to bake pies. I swear, Emmaline, it's almost a lost art! Two of our local young wives and Bailey Sterling are going to be my first pupils. I was originally going to do this only for adults, but that girl loves to cook and she begged to be included. Her mother says she was thrilled when she learned I was going to let her join us. This week is our first lesson and we're making apple pie. Dylan will be especially happy about that, as apple is his favorite.

Well, dear, on that note I'm going to close. My students will be coming later this afternoon and I want to take a little rest before "school" starts. Give my best to Joey and tell J.J. congratulations on his new job.

Love,
Justine

Chapter Eleven

"Okay, now what?" Colin asked after he and Mia had driven two blocks from their starting point at Grandma Justine's and turned left.

"Go three blocks to Fir Street and take a right," Mia read. "Then left again onto Alder."

Colin steered them onto Alder. "What's next?"

"Center Street." They cruised down Center, the main street in Icicle Falls. Downtown was busy with tourists ducking in and out of shops, buying ice cream, stopping to listen to the German oompah band playing in the gazebo. It was easy to see the town's appeal. Thanks to all the window boxes blooming with summer flowers and the fancy murals painted on the buildings, Icicle Falls really had the cute vibe going strong.

This town was more than cute, though. It was a friendly town, a close-knit community, the kind of place that called you back from wherever you'd moved.

Mia felt the call growing louder by the hour. Someday, she promised herself, she'd come back with her perfect husband and her two adorable children, a boy and a girl, naturally. She'd buy one of those impressive homes overlooking the river. In addition to donating money to the Humane Society and the Red Cross, she'd also spread the love around town, giving money to the hospital and the historical society. She'd drive into town in her BMW, notice Dylan walking down the street and wave. *Look at me now.*

She could see it all so clearly. All except the perfect husband. She couldn't seem to bring him into focus.

How long had Colin and Lorelei been together? What if they suddenly weren't?

It wouldn't make any difference to her. She and Colin lived different lives on opposite coasts. They were never meant to be together. It was that simple.

Alpine Street led them to the block nicknamed Foodie Paradise, home to Gingerbread Haus, Bavarian Brews, the Spice Rack and Sweet Dreams Chocolate Company. Sweet Dreams Chocolates to most and plain old Sweet Dreams to the locals. Right around the corner on Lavender Lane was her friend Bailey's business, Tea Time Tea Shop, with its popular tearoom.

"Where now?" Colin asked.

"To Kringle Court, then go right."

He turned the car down the small street where Christmas Haus was located. "Are we anywhere near the end of this?"

"We have several more streets to go," Mia said. It did feel as though they were going nowhere, especially after a few more turns took them in a big circle around town. What was the purpose of this?

"Jump ahead a few," Colin suggested.

She did and they finally found themselves on the

edge of town at a small building not much bigger than a toolshed, made to look like a miniature chalet—the Icicle Falls Information Booth.

"This is it, one and a quarter miles from the Icicle Creek Lodge. I should've known one of the clues would be here," Colin said as they got out of the car.

Inside, the booth held a small desk and a couple of chairs, and on the wall hung racks of maps and brochures for every shop, restaurant and activity in town. Amy Appleton was running it, talking with a middle-aged couple she'd loaded up with brochures. She'd gained weight over the years, but at seventy-five her hair was the same jet-black Mia remembered. Mia had first started volunteering at that booth after leaving middle school, and Amy had been both her supervisor and her public-relations coach.

"Make sure you stop at the Sweet Dreams retail shop and get some of their wonderful chocolates," she told the couple.

"Oh, we will," said the woman. "And what's a good place for dinner?"

"It depends on what you'd like," Amy said, and then rattled off the name of every restaurant in town. Giving them all five-star ratings, of course.

Mia could see Colin getting fidgety. Grandma Justine had probably hoped they'd enjoy this treasure hunt she'd sent them on, but Mia could tell he'd just as soon be done with it and get out of town. Kind of sad, considering how much fun they used to have with the small-scale hunts Grandma Justine and Aunt Beth designed for them when they were kids.

They weren't kids anymore, though, and this was poking at a lot of old hurts. She thought of a song in one of those old musicals Aunt Beth was so fond of—"This Nearly Was Mine."

What would've happened if she'd never gone away to school? Would she and Colin be living here? Maybe he'd have his own orchard and she'd be using some of the windfall apples to make into applesauce. Maybe they'd have a couple of kids or a foster child.

Maybe she didn't want to keep thinking like this. What was her problem, anyway? She was doing fine where she was. More responsibility, more money, a nice one-bedroom apartment not far from Lincoln Park and almost enough money in savings for a down payment on a condo. Really, all that was missing in her life was a man.

When she got back home, she'd take another stab at internet dating. Every man on those sites couldn't be cheap or a fake who put up a ten-year-old picture of himself. She'd find someone with plenty of ambition who also had a sense of humor and who liked kids. Someone better than Colin. Colin 2.0.

Colin 1.0 sure made jeans and a T-shirt look good.

So what? There were hundreds of men out there. She'd find one and live happily ever after. In Chicago. And Colin could stay in Seattle with Ms. Fitness and... burn calories.

Finally, the couple took their brochures and went on their way, and Amy smiled at Colin and Mia. "Well, Mia, nice to see you again. I can remember when you first started here. You were, what, thirteen?"

"Fourteen," Mia said.

"You were such a shy little thing. Justine thought working here would help you overcome your shyness. And it did, didn't it?"

It hadn't exactly helped her overcome her nerd rep, but it *had* helped her acquire more confidence and a certain amount of poise with strangers, a skill that now served her well in the business world and got her through those presentations she hated making.

Amy turned her attention to Colin. "And Colin, I'm sorry I didn't get a chance to speak with you at the service. We were so sorry to lose your sweet grandma."

"Thanks," Colin said, his smile fading.

"We're going to miss her so much," Amy continued. "She was such a mover and shaker. She was still coming in on Saturday mornings right up until the end. I hope I have that kind of energy when I'm in my eighties."

"Did she, by any chance, leave something with you for us?" Mia asked.

Amy's smile turned sly. "Why do you ask?"

Mia could almost hear Colin grinding his teeth. Patience was not his strong suit. "She's sent us on a bit of a treasure hunt, and we think our next clue is here somewhere."

"Aren't you the smart ones? As a matter of fact, there *is* something here for you." Amy stepped over to the desk and pulled a postcard out of the top drawer, then handed it to Colin.

Mia looked over his shoulder. The picture showed Icicle Falls at its best, all lit up for the holidays.

"Isn't that the most charming picture ever?" Amy

asked. She probably wasn't expecting an answer, since she didn't leave any conversational space for one. "I love every season here in Icicle Falls, but I must say Christmas is my favorite. All the buildings decked out with lights and the caroling and the fun, and our pretty mountains—it's simply magical, isn't it?" At last she paused, allowing time for someone to agree with her.

"Yes, it is," Mia said. Christmas in Icicle Falls felt like the set of a holiday movie—beautiful and heart-warming. She'd loved going to the tree-lighting ceremony as much when she got older as she had when she was a child. Waving to Santa, singing Christmas carols in the town square with the throng of locals and tourists. Watching the giant tree in the middle of the square come to life with all those colored lights. And when it snowed, it was like living in a snow globe.

Special as all of that was, the times with the Wright family were what had made Christmas in Icicle Falls so wonderful. The huge holiday dinners, the presents under the tree, the laughter and teasing. That was something she'd been unable to duplicate living in Chicago. That was something she wasn't sure she'd ever be able to duplicate.

"But I still like summer the best—when the flowers are in bloom and we have all our summer celebrations," Amy went on. "So many lovely things happen in the summer."

Family picnics, hikes in the woods, swimming at the pool, hanging out with friends—yes, summer was a lovely time. But if anything bad was going to happen to Mia, it seemed that fate always put it on the summer calendar.

* * *

The summer after Colin graduated from high school was busy and happy. In between her working at the information booth and his being in the orchard or at Swede's garage, they'd hike or laze on the riverbank. He'd be fishing, she reading. Or they'd be hanging out with their friends at Herman's, sharing milk shakes. And kisses.

Oh, she loved kissing Colin. She could kiss him all night long and never get tired of it. She never got tired of being with him, period. Every day she'd wake up excited to see him, and every night she went to sleep dreaming of him.

Then came the annual street dance on July third, and it had been, as Amy would say, magical.

Mia and Colin had enjoyed corn dogs and shaved ice, laughed with friends and danced so close it was hard to tell where one of them began and the other left off. Colin, her knight in shining armor, was the center of her universe and she loved him with all her heart. That was the night they were finally going to do it, she just knew. He hadn't pressured her to go all the way, but she knew he wanted to, so she'd decided it was going to be that night.

But she'd chickened out at the last minute, memories of Adrian Malk's assault tainting the moment in the back of Colin's car. "It's okay," he'd said. "This is a crappy setting, anyway. We need someplace romantic."

On the afternoon of the Fourth of July, he found it. Everyone had stuffed themselves with fried chicken and potato salad at Grandma Justine's and they were sitting around the backyard, letting their food settle before starting on dessert.

"Come on," Colin said, taking Mia by the hand.

"Don't be gone long," Gram called. "We still need to crank the ice cream."

"And your dad and I aren't gonna be the only ones turning that crank," Uncle Mark added.

"Don't worry, we'll be back," Colin assured them.

They left the house and the yard and the rest of the world behind and entered the orchard, their own private world. Sunlight filtered through rows and rows of trees filled with apples, ripening for the harvest.

"It's so beautiful here," she said. A warm breeze stirred the branches, making them flutter just like Mia's heart did when Colin pulled her close.

"Yeah, it is," he said. "And so are you." He kissed her, and there went her heart again. He smiled at her, then led her down one of the rows. "I could see myself taking over for Gramps someday."

"I bet Grandma Justine would like him to get someone to take over now. She wants him to slow down."

Colin gave a snort of disgust. "If Gram had her way, he'd be sitting around the house all day shelling peas. That's not Gramps."

"She's just worried he's going to wear out. He's so tired lately." Surely Colin had noticed that. They'd all been watching a movie on TV earlier in the week and he'd fallen asleep right in the middle of it.

Colin frowned. "It's hard to imagine Gramps ever wearing out. I mean, he's always been so healthy and strong. I figure he'll be around till he's ninety. Heck, he'll probably make a hundred as long as he takes his medication."

"I think a lot of times he doesn't," Mia said.

Colin looked at her, puzzled. "Of course he does. Why wouldn't he?"

Sometimes Colin wasn't very observant. Maybe he didn't want to be, where his grandfather was concerned. So she just shrugged and settled on the grass under an apple tree.

"Do you know something I don't?" he asked, sitting down next to her.

"No," she lied.

"Yeah, you do. What?"

Mia plucked a blade of grass and studied it. "I heard Grandma and Aunt Beth talking. He thinks it's like messing with nature. Grandma has to nag him to take it."

Colin frowned again. "Well, he'd better. Now I'm gonna nag him, too."

"I feel like a tattletale," Mia confessed. "Maybe I shouldn't have said anything."

"Yeah, you should have." He placed an arm around her. "Sometimes I think you know more about what goes on in my family than I do."

"They're my family, too," she reminded him. She hadn't been born a Wright. She was connected by friendship and commitment and love, and in the end that connection could be as strong as shared DNA.

"Thanks for telling me," he said as they cuddled under the tree. "I'm glad I have you." And then to prove it, he kissed her. It was a tender kiss, his lips gentle, his hands slipping through her hair, sending tingles through her body. Colin was such a romantic guy, so sweet. There was no one else she wanted to be with. Why did she worry about sex being scary when she was with him? That didn't make sense.

Surrounded by all those trees, the dappled sunlight warm on their skin, she knew this was the perfect spot to give herself to him. "I think I'm ready," she whispered.

He looked at her, his expression a mixture of hope and concern. "Are you sure?"

She nodded. "I'm sure. We've waited long enough."

He grinned and pulled a condom out of his pants pocket. "Good thing I'm prepared."

She giggled. But then he kissed her again and she got serious. "I'm a little scared," she confessed.

"So am I. I've never done this before, either, you know, but I'm gonna try my best to make it good for you. I love you, Mia. I always have and I always will."

"Oh, Colin, I love you, too!"

With that, the kisses turned passionate, and soon Colin's shirt was off and her top and bra were discarded. And even though she felt self-conscious she wasn't scared.

"I want you so much," he murmured against her neck, and she slithered out of her shorts.

Yes, this was going to be wonderful, she thought as he started fumbling with his condom.

"Col. Where are you?"

Colin froze, half in and half out of his new fashion accessory, and Mia's eyes popped open. "Your dad!"

The romantic moment died a quick death as they scrambled for their clothes.

"There you... What the hell?" Dylan Wright stopped in midstride, his eyes narrowing to slits and his lips pressed together in an angry slash. "Get your clothes on, both of you," he growled.

He didn't have to tell Mia twice. Face flaming, she turned her back and put on her bra. This couldn't be happening.

"Jeez, Dad," Colin protested, struggling into his pants. "You could have, like, given us some notice."

"I've been calling you for the last ten minutes," Dylan snapped. "Now, come on."

Dylan grabbed his shirt and shoes.

"Mia, Beth wants you to help her slice strawberries." A simple request, a nice, friendly request. Except the words came out like chips of ice.

She nodded and pulled on her shorts then scooped up her sandals and ran for the house.

As she went she could hear Dylan scolding his son. "What the hell were you thinking? And Mia, of all people. Do you know how that could have ended?"

And Mia, of all people.

The words scalded her heart. Dylan had never been very friendly, but she'd had no idea how much he disliked her. What a fool she'd been, thinking herself worthy to someday become a real member of the Wright family. She was only the little orphan they'd taken in.

She found it hard to explain this to Colin, who later insisted that everyone loved her.

"Except your dad. I heard what he said."

"He was just pissed off. He thinks we're too young."

It was more than that, she was sure. Of course, she supposed she shouldn't have been surprised. The Wrights were well-off financially, and important. They owned an orchard, for crying out loud, and Uncle Mark had his own company. Dylan was a lawyer. Grandma Justine was one of the town's leading citizens. And who was Mia? Her mother never got more than a high school education and her father was a loser.

The only way she could prove herself worthy would be to go out and really make something of herself. She was already taking Advanced Placement classes and checking into college scholarships for state schools. Now she'd have to up her game and climb higher on the prestige ladder. Any old four-year college wouldn't cut it.

As for having sex, between Dylan's reaction to their attempted lovemaking and Aunt Beth's lecture on the sanctity of sex and how Mia should wait until she was married, she decided maybe she wasn't ready, after all. She just hoped Colin would understand.

"This is between us," he insisted the next time they were alone together. "It has nothing to do with anyone else."

"I know, but now I want to wait. Your dad's right. We're too young." *And I'm not in the same class as the rest of you.*

Colin swore. Then he pouted. Then he got over it. "I'll wait until you're ready. You're killin' me, but I'll wait."

"When we're older, when we know it's serious."

That made him angry all over again. "You think I'm not serious? I'll prove how serious I am. I'll get you a ring."

"Colin, you're just starting college and I still have to graduate from high school," she reminded him.

"Well, guess what you'll be getting for a graduation present."

True to his word, he gave her a ring. It was made of Black Hills gold and decorated with a flower that had petals of black and pink. Between the fun of her senior prom and the thrill of being class valedictorian, graduation had been an exciting event. But Colin's gift had been the biggest thrill of all.

"After I finish college and have some money, I'll get you the real thing with a big, fat diamond," he promised.

"I don't care about diamonds," she insisted. "All I care about is you."

Too bad he hadn't believed that enough to trust her when she went away to school.

"'Maybe you need to take a hike,'" Colin read, bringing Mia back into the present. His brows knit. "*Take a hike*. That narrows it down."

"Well," put in Amy, doing her information-booth volunteer duty. "Our most popular hike is still Lost Bride Trail."

"Is that the hike we're supposed to take?" Colin asked her. "Did Gram tell you?"

Amy mimed zipping her lips.

Colin turned on the charm, smiling at the older

woman and putting an arm around her. "Come on, Mrs. A., you know everything that goes on around here. Help us out. At least send us in the proper direction."

"Your grandma told me not to tell."

"Okay, how about this? If I'm right, give me a kiss," he said, leaning down and pointing to his cheek. "Are we supposed to take the Lost Bride Trail?"

The old woman blushed and smiled and gave him a peck on the cheek.

"Thanks! You made my day."

"And you made mine, you rascal. You two have fun," she said, and turned to greet a young family who had just appeared in the doorway.

Colin and Mia headed for the Lost Bride trailhead. Then, armed with bottled water, they started up the trail to Lost Bride Falls. Mia had seen the fabled lost bride back when they were first engaged. The famous ghost of Rebecca Cane, who had so mysteriously disappeared back during the mountain town's gold-rush era, was rumored to lurk behind the falls. A sighting always meant a wedding was in the future for whoever happened to see her. Mia remembered the day she'd seen the ghost, but Rebecca sure had failed her...

Aunt Beth hosted a graduation party for Mia, complete with balloons in the Icicle Falls High colors of gold and purple. The requisite Congratulations, Graduate! sign had been hung in the dining room, and the table was loaded with a huge platter of barbecued chicken, a variety of salads, chips and dip, and a fancy cake from Gingerbread Haus. Grandma Justine and Grandpa Gerald had given Mia a check for a hundred dollars. "For spending money when you get to school," Grandma said. Aunt Beth had given her a Target gift card so she could furnish her dorm room. Dylan had handed her a card, signed stiffly, "Congratulations, Dylan." He'd enclosed a check for fifty dollars. The gift felt mandatory. She would so much rather have had a genuine smile and a hug, but that would never happen.

Anyway, all the gifts paled compared to Colin's.

"I knew you two would end up together," Aunt Beth said. "Just like Uncle Mark and me. We were high school sweethearts, too."

"You're not going to do anything rash." This from Dylan, half question, half command.

"Of course not," Mia had said sternly. "We're both going to graduate from college first." Honestly, even she knew they were too young to get married.

"Let's not wait that long," Colin begged later as they walked up the trail to Lost Bride Falls.

"Col, we have to." They were going to school on two different coasts. Anyway, his roots were planted firmly in the rich soil of the Cascades. There was no reason to uproot him.

She convinced him to stick with the plan, to wait and get married after they were done with college. And he convinced her not to wait to seal their love. They were as good as engaged and that meant as good as married.

Aunt Beth's cautionary words from the last summer surfaced. *I know it's hard to wait, but marriage is the safest, best place for sex. If you make such an inti-*

mate commitment too young, you're guaranteed to get your heart broken. Now she wasn't so sure about that reasoning. Marriage was no shield against emotional wounds. Colin's dad and her mother were proof of that. And besides, Colin would never break her heart.

The falls was a beautiful setting for their love scene, and their union was as perfect as possible for a first time.

To add her blessing, the ghost of the lost bride made her appearance. "Look!" Mia cried. "I see her!"

Colin looked. "Where?"

But then, like an elusive rainbow, the bride was gone.

The ghost's disappearance had been as much an omen as seeing her. Mia just hadn't realized it at the time.

Would either of them see the bride today? She had her doubts.

October 26, 2005

Dear Emmaline,
I certainly enjoyed our chat last week. I'm so im-
pressed with all your new computer skills. Yes,
one of these days I suppose I should get a com-
puter, but this email thing sounds complicated. I
rather like communicating with cards and pretty
stationery. But you're right. Email would be so
much faster. I'll think about it. Maybe I can get
Gerald to buy me a computer for Christmas. We
could share. Dylan's been trying to convince him
for ages to start using a computer for the busi-
ness. It's hard to break old habits, though. Ger-
ald still keeps his records the old-fashioned way.
Anyway, we'll see.

Now, as for news, Colin is off to visit Mia at
school this weekend, and all of us old people
are going to Zelda's restaurant for a Halloween
party. Even Dylan is going, although he's an-
noyed about having to wear a costume. Bethie
wants to make him a Zorro cape and mask. I
think he'd be a very dashing Zorro! She's turning
Gerald and me into apples. How I'm going to be
able to sit down in an apple costume, I have no
idea, but Bethie assures me she'll make it work.

Next week is my last pie-baking class. We'll be
baking pumpkin pies to get everyone in the mood
for Thanksgiving. At my age I shouldn't be in a

hurry to get from one holiday to the next—time is flying by fast enough as it is!—but I am looking forward to Thanksgiving when our Mia will be back and we'll all be together. Of course, I'm happy to see the young ones leave the nest and spread their wings, but it's always good when they come home for a visit.

Do let me know how Joey's appointment with the cardiologist goes.

Love,
Justine

Chapter Twelve

Colin and Mia's walk up the trail to Lost Bride Falls was a quiet one, the conversation carried by the birds singing and the squirrels chattering in the trees. Colin suspected that, like him, Mia was caught in a fresh net of memories.

Eventually, he heard the thunder of the falls, and then they saw glimpses of it between the trees. Finally, they came to the scenic look-out that framed the cataract in all its glory.

Seeing the waterfall was like stepping behind the curtain of time. He found himself reliving the magical time they'd spent up here, as well as the experiences that had led to it.

Colin had accepted Mia's childhood adoration as his due, and actually considered her his best friend—although he would never have admitted that to his buddies. But then along came puberty. His body began to change. So did hers. Breasts. Mia had breasts. Whoa, they were fascinating. *But don't stare! Okay, stare, but don't let her catch you. Wait a minute, this is Mia.*

She's like your sister. What are you doing staring at your sister's boobs?

So the inner dialogue went. Colin's eyes and brain agreed that there were other breasts in Icicle Falls, other girls to ogle, even date. The dates never evolved into anything serious, though, because the one vital organ that had been left out of the equation was his heart. Mia owned it. And it seemed his friends all knew that, since none of them ever hit on her.

Then Gram took in Adrian Malk, and Colin experienced heartburn for the first time in his life. Things had started out well enough, all friendly with video games and shooting hoops at the park, but that changed once Colin saw Adrian in action, making fun of Joe Coyote, asking him why he wasn't living on the rez, taking over the lunch table and giving poor Andy Forrester a bad time because he was overweight. Colin, Neal and Bill Will switched to a different lunch table, taking Andy with them, and Adrian replaced them with guys who were losers and bullies. How soon until Adrian aged out of the foster-care program and left Icicle Falls? It couldn't happen quickly enough for Colin.

"Are you and Adrian not hitting it off?" Gram asked him once.

"Not really," he'd replied. Adrian was a shit, as slimy as an eel. And he, too, was fascinated with Mia's breasts. He didn't even care if she caught him staring. That alone made Colin hate him.

"So, have you done it with her?" Adrian asked one day late in March when he and Colin were in the orchard, raking brush. Actually, Colin was raking. Adrian was leaning on his rake, watching.

Colin frowned at him. Mia was too young to be doing it with anyone, including him.

A corner of Adrian's mouth lifted in a sneer. "Didn't think so. Bet you haven't done it with anyone, farm boy."

"Yeah? And you have?" Colin retorted.

Of course he had. Adrian Malk had probably had sex with every girl in his school in Seattle. And he'd probably been kicked out. How had he ended up all the way over here? All Colin knew was that things hadn't worked out with Adrian's last foster home. If you asked Colin, things weren't working out here, either.

"Girls are easy," Adrian said.

"Mia isn't," Colin snapped.

"Yeah? I could have her anytime I want."

Something hot and fierce raced through Colin. He pointed a warning finger at Adrian. "You stay away from her."

There went that sneer again. "You got a little crush, farm boy?"

"You touch her and I'll break your neck."

Adrian laughed. "You and who else?"

Adrian might have been a couple months older and a few inches taller, but Colin knew he'd have no trouble tearing the guy apart like a soft pretzel if he came anywhere near Mia.

He was about to say so when Gramps appeared at the end of the row, and Adrian began doing an imitation of a worker.

"How's it going, boys?" Gramps called.

"Great," Adrian called back.

Yeah, great.

After that conversation in the orchard, Adrian began to set his trap for Mia. He'd flirt with her, tugging playfully on a lock of her hair or tapping her on the nose, winking when he passed her in the hall at school. And she fell for it like a starving mouse looking for cheese.

The worst was when Gram included Adrian in their annual Easter treasure hunt. It wasn't the first time Gram or Aunt Beth had included an extra kid who was staying with them. Colin had never minded before. He sure minded this time.

"An Easter egg hunt? What are you guys, five?" Adrian mocked when it was just him and Colin. But once Mia showed up he changed his tune. "Okay, Mia, you'll have to help me out here. You're the smart one."

Not where guys are concerned, Colin thought bitterly as she blushed and smiled as if she'd won the lottery.

The Easter goodies in their baskets that year were a lot like winning the lottery—Cadbury eggs, ten-dollar bills, gift cards to a couple of shops, movie tickets, Peeps marshmallow chicks.

"Pretty cool," Adrian decided.

He gallantly gave Mia his Peeps but Colin noticed he kept the other stuff for himself. Yeah, real impressive. Colin gave Mia the chocolate eggs and promised to spend his Herman's gift certificate on her that Friday.

She thanked them both with a kiss on the cheek, but she blushed when she kissed Adrian. And Adrian sent

Colin a superior smirk. It was all Colin could do not to push his fist through that smirking face.

Adrian's presence covered Colin's spring days like a shadow, sucking the fun out of Sunday dinners and family card games. Adrian shirked chores and cheated at cards and made fun of Uncle Mark's bald spot when he was alone with Colin in the orchard, Colin working and him loafing. What a jerk.

Dad didn't much like him. Neither did Uncle Mark, and Gramps soon picked up on his slothful ways and told him off a couple of times.

"He needs love," Colin once overheard Gram say to Gramps after Gramps had reamed Adrian out.

If you asked Colin, he needed to be gone. But he stayed. Come May, rumors started flying around school that he was sleeping with a senior girl, but that didn't stop him from flirting with Mia.

Then she invited him to the end-of-school party at the river. As if he was one of them, as if he belonged. He didn't belong in Icicle Falls. He was a cancer, ready to spread.

Like Gram and Aunt Beth, Mia made excuses for him.

Okay, so he'd had it rough. So had a lot of the kids who'd come to stay with Gram, but they'd been different. They'd wanted to get their lives together. Rudy Gonzales had become a star quarterback at Icicle Falls High. He'd grown up, settled in town and was now a councilman. Shelley Burwell had discovered a flair for drama and gone to Hollywood, where she was making

TV commercials. Andy had gotten adopted and had a 3.9 grade point average.

But when it came to Gram's good influence, Malk was like Teflon. Nothing stuck.

"That kid's trouble," Dad had predicted when Adrian came on the scene. Dad had been right.

Colin had tried to explain to Mia what a loser the guy was, but would she listen? No.

"Don't worry about me. I can take care of myself," she'd insisted as they headed to the annual gathering at Riverwalk Park.

Her inviting Malk had pissed him off big-time. He'd been looking forward to the party, to horsing around with his friends, roasting hot dogs. Maybe going for a walk along the river with Mia. Maybe even kissing her. This acting like they were brother and sister thing wasn't really working anymore.

But now? He was disgusted with Mia's lack of taste. Fuming, he left her as soon as they got to the party and went to hang with the guys.

"What's with you?" Bill Will asked on seeing his glum face.

"Nothing," Colin muttered.

"Cheer up, man," David Simpson said with a grin. "We're seniors now. We rule."

If Colin was a ruler, Malk would've been banished from Icicle Falls.

The evening wore on, and he continued to ignore Mia in the misguided belief that she'd get that he was angry and come apologize for being so stupid. But once the sky turned dark, he suddenly—ironically—

saw things clearly. *He* was the one being stupid. What the heck was he doing, ignoring Mia when he wanted to be with her? Did he suppose he was punishing her? The only one he was punishing was himself. Meanwhile, Malk was probably flirting with her, buttering her up so he could…

What had he been thinking, leaving her unguarded? Colin broke off from his buddies, who were drinking beer, shooting the bull and tossing rocks in the river.

"Where are you going?" asked Neal.

"To find Mia."

"Big surprise," cracked Bill Will.

"If she's with Malk, you're out of luck," Neal warned.

"If she's with Malk, I'll kill him," Colin growled.

"Hey, dude, don't be stupid," Bill Will called after him.

On the contrary, getting Mia away from Malk would be one of the smarter things he'd done.

Mia was nowhere to be found. She wasn't farther down the river or at the bonfire with the other kids.

"I saw her go off with Malk," said Andy, pointing toward Bluebird Island.

"And you let her go?"

"What was I supposed to do?" Andy retorted. "Beat him up?"

Colin took off at a run, his heart pounding. Malk couldn't have her. He didn't deserve her.

Colin was halfway down the winding path to the nature preserve when he heard her scream. Shit!

Not wanting to waste time on the scenic path, he cut through the woods, crashing through the underbrush.

He emerged to find her pinned to a bench, Malk's idiot pals holding her down while Malk had his filthy hands on her.

Colin had enough adrenaline flowing to take on a dozen Malks. Sadly, he didn't have the size, especially with Malk's goons falling on him.

He and Mia would both have been toast if his own posse hadn't come riding in. At the sight of them, Malk and his worthless friends ran off like the gutless wonders they were.

Finding Mia in such danger had been a nightmare, and he rushed to hold her to assure both of them she was okay.

"You saved me," she said to him, as if he was some sort of superhero instead a guy who'd just about had the crap beaten out of him.

He said as much, but she didn't see it that way. She clung to him and began to cry in earnest.

"It's okay. I'm here now," he told her. And that was how it was supposed to be. He would always be there for her. They were supposed to be together. He kissed the top of her head. It was a small kiss but a big moment, one that changed everything between them. A boundary had been crossed, and they had left behind the simple friendship of childhood and moved into new territory.

"You're with me now, Mia," he informed her once they were back in his car. "That's how it oughta be."

"That's how I want it to be," she said.

And so it was.

His dad had lectured him about being rash and tying

himself and Mia down too early. "You don't know who you are yet or what you want out of life. Neither of you."

Dad was wrong. Colin knew who he was. He was a farm boy as Malk had put it. He wanted to live in Icicle Falls, and he wanted to live here with Mia. He didn't need to know anything more than that.

Once she graduated from high school he sensed another boundary about to be crossed. Mia was ready to leave home for a bigger world. That fall, she'd be attending NYU, going for a business degree. He had to make sure she didn't lose sight of the vision, had to make sure she wouldn't forget that they belonged together. So he gave her a ring. Not a diamond. He couldn't afford that. Anyway, if he gave her a diamond when she was so young, everyone in the family, not just Dad, would have a fit. The ring he found was pretty and it showed that he meant business.

After her graduation party, they went up to Lost Bride Falls on Sunday afternoon. It was a sunny June day with blue skies and warm weather, great for a hike.

And other things. Colin had his trusty condom in his pocket again. This time he was going to use it. Nobody would find them up here and start lecturing. Anyway, they were a whole year older now and as good as engaged. There was no reason to wait.

It wasn't a long hike, but it felt like a year as they wended their way up the mountain path, past firs and hemlocks and cedars, Lady's Slippers peeping out at them from beneath the underbrush.

They rounded a bend—and saw the falls in all its mountain glory, crashing over the crag, concealing the cave that lay behind the cataract. He and his dad had gone behind the waterfall once and explored that cave. He still remembered how cold and dank it was. If ever there was an ideal home for a ghost, that cave was it.

Maybe they'd see the ghost of the lost bride today. He took Mia's hand, and they stood there taking in the sight.

"Do you see the lost bride?" she asked.

All he saw was water. If he had to wait to get laid until he saw that ghost, he'd be waiting until he was ninety. He drew Mia close. "Never mind her. All I care about is seeing my own bride."

Then he kissed her. And she kissed him back, enough to encourage him to lead her off the trail, down by where Icicle Creek began, with a front-row seat to the falls. Oh, yeah, here was a nice, mossy spot, private and hidden from view. He sat down and held out a hand. "Come here, you," he said with a grin.

She cuddled up next to him and it was a perfect moment. They could have so many perfect moments if they chucked her out-of-state school plan and got married. She could go to school here in Washington.

Except she was determined to go to that university in New York, and of course, that was the practical thing to do. It was a great school and she'd worked hard to get that scholarship. It would be stupid not to take advantage of the opportunity.

But he hated to let her go. He voiced a thought he'd been kicking around ever since she got her letter of acceptance. "You know, I was thinking. I could come to New York with you, get a job out there. We could get married."

For a moment she seemed excited by the idea. Then she frowned and shook her head. "You need to at least get your associate degree. If you quit after one year, your dad will blame me."

"No, he won't," Colin insisted. Okay, maybe he would. But so what? It was his life, not Dad's. "I can finish anytime."

"Col, I want to make sure we do everything right."

He knew what that meant.

"After we're done with school, we have our whole lives to be together," she said.

"We have our whole lives right now," he told her, and kissed her neck.

She threw back her head, a sure sign that it was all systems go, and that was fine with him. So, hidden under an outcropping of rock on that bank across from the falls, she finally gave herself to him completely.

"I love you so much," she said later, tears in her eyes. "You'll come visit me at school, won't you?"

"Count on it," he answered.

"And I'll come home for holidays and for summers, so we won't really be apart that much." She looked as though she was going to cry, but then she brightened and said, "It'll all work out. You'll see."

"I guess," he said doubtfully. "I hate that you're not going to be here."

"But even if I was going to a state college, we wouldn't see that much of each other during the school year."

"Yeah, you're right…"

"Of course I'm right," she quipped and laid her head on his chest. They stayed there holding each other, her watching the falls and him watching her. Suddenly, she let out a little gasp and sat up, pointing. "Look! I see her."

He looked. All he saw was water. "Where?"

Her excited smile fell. "Oh, she's gone."

She'd probably never seen the ghost of the lost bride at all. She'd seen the play of light and shadow and taken it for the ghost. "That's okay," he said. "As long as you've seen it, we're good."

She smiled. "Now I know everything will work out."

He stared at her, puzzled. "You didn't know before?"

She failed to meet his gaze. "Your dad thinks you can do better."

Not that again. Ever since Dad had caught them in the orchard, she'd been convinced he didn't like her. "Come on, I've told you, that's not true. He likes you fine."

"No, he doesn't. But maybe once I've graduated, have a good job…"

"Once you've graduated, we'll be married." *Let's get our priorities straight here.*

Nothing had gone according to plan. So much for the idea that seeing the stupid ghost of that lost bride promised a happy ending. Sure hadn't worked for him.

Here was where Mia had given herself to the man she thought was the love of her life, where she'd seen the ghost of the lost bride and dreamed of a wedding followed by a happy life with her best friend. Boy, had things taken a wrong turn.

No ghostly bride flitted behind the violent froth of waters today. Rainbows and sunlight diamonds, but no bride.

She sneaked a glance at Colin. He was looking pensive. "What are you thinking?" she asked.

"Nothing."

"You can't think nothing."

"Sure you can. Guys do it all the time."

"Well, you weren't. You didn't have a think-nothing expression on your face."

He raised one sandy eyebrow. "There's such a thing as a think-nothing expression?"

"Yeah, there is." She let her mouth go slack and her eyes go blank. "That's a think-nothing expression. You were looking like this." She demonstrated by tightening her lips and drawing her brows together.

"Ah, well, thanks for explaining."

"So, what were you thinking?"

His brows drew together again. "Do you really want to know?"

Maybe not. "Yes," she said, and braced herself.

"I was remembering the last time we came up here and how wonderful it was."

"I was remembering that, too," she confessed, and the memory of his lips on hers sure brought back those pesky tingles.

He shook his head. "What happened to us?"

He was going to do the love forensics thing now?

Really? "You know what happened to us," she snapped, and the tingles ran for cover. "Your suspicious mind and quick temper, that's what happened. Just because I went away to school didn't mean I stopped loving you. Why couldn't you trust me?"

"I did trust you, and fat lot of good it did me. You broke my heart, Mia."

"Right," she said in disgust. "Who broke up with whom?"

"What was the point of pretending?" he demanded. "I saw how things were with you and Arthur."

She could smack him. "You *imagined* how things were."

"Yeah, and I guess I imagined that diamond ring on your finger when you came home."

"What was I supposed to do, Colin? We were through. Did you want me to wait forever for you to get over yourself and come to your senses? Well, excuse me for not wasting my life."

Except in a way she had. The life she'd wound up with hadn't been the one she'd wanted, and Arthur had been a mistake. Good old funny, clever Arthur. Tall and skinny with dimples when he smiled, curly brown hair, and a never-ending appetite, Arthur, as Mia's roommate succinctly put it, was adorable.

"I'd take him in a heartbeat," Mia's roommate, Angie, said as she and Mia walked to Starbucks in search of lattes. "If he'd even look at any girl besides you."

Mia held up her left hand, showing off her ring. "I'm taken."

"I don't see a diamond there. I bet Arthur doesn't, either."

"There will be."

"I don't know. That childhood-sweetheart thing only works in movies."

"Well, they could do a movie about Colin and me. We're like Heathcliff and Cathy. The happy-ending version," she quickly added.

"Hurry up and explain that to Arthur so I can have a crack at him."

Yes, she and Arthur needed to have a talk. Mia didn't want to lead him on. So when he suggested going for lunch after Lit class, she reminded him about Colin.

Her reminder bounced off him like raindrops off a turtle's shell. "You're not married yet. In fact—" he lifted her hand and examined it "—you're not officially engaged."

"As good as," she said, taking away her hand. "So you'd be wasting your time."

"I like wasting time," he cracked, "especially with you. Come on. Let's go get something to eat. You can explain why I should care about anything Albert Camus has to say. If you ask me, his writing is absurd."

Mia chuckled at the pun. If she hadn't already given away her heart, Arthur could probably have taken it.

Autumn turned the leaves orange and gold, and as Halloween approached, Colin planned to come visit her at school and scare away any big-city ghosts. They'd been emailing or talking on the phone every day, and she'd told him all about her classes and her new friends—Manda Jenkins, the math genius; her crazy drama-major roommate, Angie; and Arthur. Although she tried not to mention Arthur too often. Colin didn't like hearing about him, seemed to see him as a threat in spite of her assurances that she and Arthur were simply friends who happened to share a couple of classes.

It was Colin who made her heart race every time he called; Colin who turned her dreams hot and steamy on those crisp October nights. She could hardly wait to see him. Angie had promised to stay with Manda and her roommate for the weekend, so Mia and Colin could have the exclusive use of their dorm room.

"You owe me for this," she told Mia. "I'm on the floor on a blow-up mattress and I'm going to have to put up with Sherry Know-It-All."

"I'll have Colin bring some Sweet Dreams Chocolates from Icicle Falls," Mia promised. "You'll love me forever."

"They better be good. That's all I can say."

"They are. Anyway, you're getting a little dramatic here. You won't see that much of Sherry. She'll be in the library all weekend, and Saturday night's the party. So you only have to live through Sunday morning."

"Which'll be bad enough. But hey, you'd do the same for me, right?"

"Absolutely."

"I still think you should've sent him to stay with Arthur and Gregory, get to know some of the guys."

"I'm not sure Colin and Arthur are going to hit it off."

That was an understatement. Friday night, after Colin got in, they joined her friends at a local pizzeria near the college. Mia wound up with Colin on one side of her and Arthur on the other. Arthur was his usual clever, bantering self. Colin, who started out acting friendly, got quieter as the evening wore on. By the time they were done eating, he was a clam.

When the bill came, Colin dug out his wallet, but Arthur said, "No worries, I've got it," and tossed down a hundred-dollar bill.

Then Colin became a scowling clam. A Heathcliff.

"What on earth is wrong with you?" she demanded when they got back to her room.

"Nothing," he growled. "Is that Arthur rich?"

"I don't know." He always had plenty of money but so what?

"You didn't tell me he's rich."

"Does it matter?"

Colin's only response was to deepen his frown.

Mia frowned, too. "Colin, I really don't understand what's going on here. The way you were at dinner, that's not you. Everyone's going to think you're a jerk. You couldn't spare one smile?"

"I guess my lips were broken. Sorry," he added. 'I was a jerk."

"A blue-ribbon one, but I love you, anyway," she said, giving him a smile and wrapping her arms around him.

"I just don't like that guy," he muttered.

"What guy?" she teased, and kissed him.

He wasn't so easily distracted. "You know he's hot for you."

"Well, I'm not hot for him."

"You were flirting with him."

She threw up her hands and flopped on the bed. "I was laughing at his joke."

Colin frowned again. "You tossed your hair. Everyone knows when a woman tosses her hair she's flirting."

Okay, they needed to lighten up. Mia flicked back a lock of hair. "Yeah?"

That made him smile. When Colin smiled, those blue eyes of his lit up and crinkled at the corners. There was so much warmth in them. His smile set her heart on fire and made her knees go weak. It always had.

"Okay, maybe I jumped to conclusions," he admitted. He joined her on the bed and drew her to him. "And maybe we can find something better to do than talk about Arthur." Then he kissed her, proving that his lips weren't broken. Oh, no. They were in perfectly good working order.

The next day they picked up their costumes at a costume rental store, then she took him to some of the city's popular tourist attractions, hoping to make him fall in love with its energy and excitement the way she had—the Empire State Building, the Statue of Liberty, Central Park. The park took up the rest of their day. They wandered through the zoo, rode the carousel and watched the men playing chess. They went up into Belvedere Castle and enjoyed the panoramic view of the Great Lawn and Turtle Pond. Colin insisted they ride in a horse-drawn carriage. And there he told her she was the most beautiful sight in all of New York, and kissed her.

"So what do you think of the city?" she asked, as they got hot dogs from a food cart.

"I gotta say, even with all the cool stuff here, I still like Icicle Falls better."

"Me, too," she said. Three more years of school after this, and she could come back for good. She'd make sure she graduated cum laude, then she'd land a job in Icicle Falls, say at the bank. She'd work her way up to being a loan officer, and eventually manager. Or maybe she'd start her own business. Then no one would think of her as a leech, taking advantage of the Wright family.

They were hardly back in her dorm room when Colin pulled her into his arms and kissed her. "That's what I like best about New York, being here with you."

Oh, so romantic. Of course she had to fall into bed with him and reward him properly.

Later, as they lay there, him playing with her hair, he said, "Let's bag the party tonight."

Good idea.

Before she could speak, Angie called. "Hey, we're all going to get something to eat before the party."

Mia looked at Colin. "We're not sure we're going to make the party."

"You've probably been going at it like rabbits all day. Come out and be social."

Mia caved. "Well, maybe for a little while." They'd put in an appearance and then they could go do something, just the two of them.

"I guess we're going to the party," Colin said when she hung up.

She sighed. "I guess so." She didn't enjoy big, noisy parties where she barely knew anyone, but it was at Arthur's frat house. He'd be disappointed if they didn't show.

"We can leave early," she promised. The more she thought about it, the less time she wanted to spend with a bunch of other people. Especially female people. Colin was so cute, girls would be hitting on him all night.

They donned their costumes—hers a serving wench, his a pirate—and joined her friends at their favorite hole in the wall for burgers, then moved on to the frat house.

Mia had been right. It seemed they'd just gotten in the door when some girl in a scanty French maid costume was sidling up to Colin, offering to walk his plank. He turned down her offer, telling her his ship was in dry dock, earning himself major boyfriend points.

"There you are," called Arthur, who was wearing a devil costume. "You need beer," he added, leading them to where the keg was set up. "Some party, huh?" he shouted over the blasting music.

It certainly was. The place was as packed with food as it was with people—bowls of chips and popcorn, platters of sandwiches, plates piled high with store-bought cookies. Someone had brought caramel apples and there was plenty of candy corn. Beer was the main attraction, though, and a few revelers were already tipsy.

And here came the French maid again. "He's with me," Mia said, stepping in front of Colin.

Arthur laughed. "Give up, Mia. Everybody knows you can't trust a pirate."

"And everybody knows you can't trust the devil," Colin shot back, slipping an arm around Mia's shoulders. "Come on, babe, let's dance."

They found a spot in the crush of bodies and danced. Then they ate chips and drank beer and danced some more. A couple of beers later—or maybe it was three, who knew?—Mia needed to find the bathroom.

"Let's get out of here," Colin was saying.

She nodded and her head protested. *Eeew. Don't do that.* "I'll be right back."

The downstairs bathroom was occupied, so she went upstairs, where she was sure she'd find another, feeling as though her head was floating behind the rest of her. She hated feeling buzzed. No more beer. Ever. She only drank the stuff to be polite. She really wasn't fond of the taste.

After the bathroom, she started down the hall and encountered Arthur coming in the opposite direction.

"Having fun?" he greeted her.

"I think I drank too much." In fact, she was sure she'd drunk too much. It was either that or some giant was spinning the frat house.

"Whoa there," he said, putting an arm around her to steady her. "I think I need to cut off the booze."

She laid a hand on his chest and blinked at him. "We're spinning."

"We'd better call the boyfriend."

"We'd better." That was so thoughtful of Arthur to watch out for her. "Arthur, you're sweet. Has anyone ever told you that?"

He shook his head. "You shouldn't say stuff like that to a man who's in love with you." He touched a finger to her lips. "Are you sure it's serious with Colin? 'Cause if it isn't…" He didn't finish the sentence. Instead, he lowered his lips to hers. Oh, this was not a good idea.

She was about to say so when someone called her name. Colin. His angry voice broke them apart, although Arthur kept a steady hand on her arm. "I think she's had too much to drink."

Colin glared at him. "You giving her a breathalyzer test?"

"No, I just bumped into her."

"Yeah, right."

"Insecure," Arthur murmured. "I wonder why. After all, a man can trust his woman if she really loves him."

Colin grabbed Mia's hand and began towing her toward the stairs. "Come on, Mia. Let's go."

"Don't let him bully you," Arthur called after them.

He *was* bullying her, wasn't he? Acting like some kind of crazy caveman when she hadn't done anything wrong.

Outside the house revelers were standing on the porch, sitting on the steps, gathered on the lawn. Someone called Mia's name, but she couldn't tell who. Colin was leading her away so quickly she didn't dare turn her head for fear of throwing up.

Even though her head didn't seem to be attached,

her brain was working well enough for her to get angry. "I didn't do anything, you know. Why are you mad at me?"

"Didn't do anything? You were about to kiss him. What, you couldn't keep away from each other, even for one weekend? Is that it?"

"No."

"What's really going on between you two?"

Okay, Colin wasn't being rational. "How much have you had to drink?"

"No more than you, and you didn't see me groping someone the minute your back was turned."

"I wasn't groping anyone!"

"Damn it, Mia, I came all the way out here to be with you and instead of us being together, I wind up stuck at a party with a bunch of strangers while you're flirting with some other guy, the same guy I've been hearing about practically since you got here."

She hadn't talked about Arthur any more than she had Angie or anyone else. And when she'd told Colin about the party two weeks earlier, he'd said it sounded like fun.

It hadn't been. "Why are you spoiling this weekend?"

"I'm not the one spoiling it. I'm not going around kissing other people."

"We didn't kiss!" Okay, they almost had. What had she been thinking? She should've pushed Arthur away instead of standing there like a wench in the headlights. Oh, she didn't feel well. "I don't want to talk about this." She just wanted to find some bushes and barf.

Colin sighed. "Aw, Mia." He reached for her.

But she had more pressing needs than making up. She waved him away and staggered off. "Leave me alone." *Let me go puke in private.*

"Fine," she heard him snap.

"Fine," she echoed. What a silly argument. Of course they'd make up in the morning. But tonight... Oooh, she didn't feel well.

She found the requisite bushes and upchucked. Then she staggered back to the frat house, plunked down on one of the front steps and put her head in her hands, trying to anchor it back on her neck.

"There you are," said Angie, sitting down next to her. "Hey, you don't look so good. Where's Colin?"

"I don't know," Mia muttered. "He's off having a tantrum."

"Lovers' quarrel, huh?"

"He doesn't need to be jealous. Arthur and I are just friends. I wasn't going to kiss him."

"Uh-oh. What happened?"

"Nothing. I don't feel good. Where's Arthur?"

"Stay right there," Angie said and disappeared.

"Stay right here," Mia agreed. Except she should go find Colin. Where was he? Could he make his way back to the dorm?

A moment later Arthur was beside her on the steps. "I thought you'd gone."

"We had a fight." She and Colin never fought. They shouldn't have fought tonight. She could feel her lower lip wobbling and the tears spilling from her eyes.

"Hey, now," Arthur said, wiping away the tears. "Don't cry."

His words had the opposite effect. Another tear dripped down Mia's cheek. And since Arthur's shoulder was so conveniently there, she used it to cry on.

"I'm sorry," he said, and put an arm around her.

"I've loved him all my life."

"I don't know why," Arthur said. "He seems like kind of a jerk."

A jerk wouldn't have picked her for his softball team when they were kids, even though everyone knew she couldn't catch and she couldn't hit a beach ball, let alone a softball. A jerk wouldn't spend his allowance getting her penny candy from Johnson's Drugs. A jerk wouldn't be there for her when her dad left. Wouldn't save her from the likes of Adrian Malk. Wouldn't send her candy from home her first week away at school.

"You have to come with me and explain that we're just friends," she insisted.

"He doesn't deserve you."

"Arthur, please."

"Okay, okay. Come on."

But Colin wasn't at the dorm. Had he gotten lost?

"Don't worry. I'll wait for him," Arthur promised.

"Thank you, Arthur," she said. "You're the best." She threw her arms around him and kissed him on the cheek. And now she needed to go ride the porcelain bus. She staggered back to her dorm room, leaving Arthur downstairs to watch for her lost boyfriend. Yes, Arthur was the best.

Somewhere she could hear voices, male voices, angry male voices. But she had an important appointment in her bathroom. And after that she had to lie down on her spinning bed. She'd just lie here and wait for Colin to get back. But shortly into her wait, someone pulled the curtain of sleep and she was gone.

The next morning she was alone in her dorm room. The only proof that Colin had, indeed, found his way back was the piece of paper lying on Angie's bed that said, "We're done."

December 27, 2005

Dear Emmaline,
Thank you for the lovely presents. Gerald enjoyed his cheese and sausage, and I very much appreciated the dusting powder. Chantilly is still my favorite fragrance. Gerald did get me that computer, and Colin has promised to turn me into a computer genius. Who knows? Maybe the next missive you get from me will be electronic.

Our Christmas was a little subdued this year. We missed Mia. Colin smiled and joked with Gerald, but there was such sadness in his eyes. So different from last year when he and Mia were kissing under the mistletoe! It reminded me of how sad Dylan was after Lauren left. Dylan still maintains that this is a case of two young people growing up and growing apart. I find that hard to believe. Colin and Mia have always been special to each other. I'm sure they'll sort things out.

Meanwhile, poor Bethie is not at all happy. Mia has been like a daughter to her all these years and not seeing her either at Thanksgiving or Christmas was hard. Mia sent presents and she called both of us on Christmas morning, but it's not the same. There's talk of Bethie flying out to see her next month, though, so that will be good.

On a brighter note, Gerald and I have big

plans for New Year's Eve. We're having a party. Amy and Edgar Appleton are coming over along with my dear friend Sarah White and her new husband, Peter. We're going to celebrate on East Coast time, however, as no one wants to stay up until midnight.

I assume you and Joey will be going to the Elks as usual. I hope he's not driving. He'll kill you both! Forgive me for being a bossy big sister, but really, dear, I think it's time to take away his car keys.

Gerald's calling me. I'd better close. Happy New Year!

Love,
Justine.

Chapter Thirteen

Loud as the roar of the cascading water was, Colin felt sure he could hear Rebecca Cane whispering over it. *Every choice has a consequence. In the end, the only one to blame is yourself.* He didn't need the lost bride to tell him that. He'd learned it firsthand.

Colin returned home from his disastrous visit to New York with a chip on his shoulder. No, make that a log. Hell, make it a tree, an entire forest. Furious, hurt, unhappy, there was no word big enough for the giant thing inside his chest.

Mia had once said that all she wanted was him. Obviously, that wasn't true. She'd decided she could do better with some rich frat boy who threw around hundred-dollar bills like they were tens. His dad probably owned some monster company and had a whole pack of lawyers just like Dad working for him. How could Colin compete with that?

The answer was simple. He couldn't.

His family did okay and that had always been enough. *He'd* always been enough. Until now.

The memory of Mia throwing her arms around Arthur in front of her dorm had kept him company as he waited for his flight. He'd tried to shake it off with Jack Daniels, drunk too much and gotten sick on the plane. He'd slept fitfully, and that hadn't improved his mood. Starbucks had gotten him through the long drive from SeaTac airport to Icicle Falls. What was going to get him through the rest of his life?

Dad, ever the touchy-feely guy, ignored his thundercloud scowl when he walked in the door, and when he opted out of going over to Gram's for Sunday dinner merely said, "Suit yourself."

Left alone, he spent some time tormenting himself by watching *The Princess Bride*, which he'd found when he was surfing the cable channels, sniveling all the while like a five-year-old. Guys didn't do that. They went out and punched something. Sitting around watching an old movie you and the woman you'd loved had watched when you were kids—it was such a chick thing to do. All that was missing was the quart of ice cream.

He turned it off halfway through and went for a run, sweated and swore up a storm, told God how pissed off he was. Then he went to the orchard and sat under a tree to feel sorry for himself.

The apples were long gone now, and the trees were nothing but empty branches. He'd never really stopped to think about what a desolate place the orchard was this time of year. It hit him now, though. All these trees, stripped down to nothing, mirrored his soul. He, too, was down to nothing. He was never going to find another girl like Mia.

Maybe that was a good thing, since Mia had just chopped his heart into a million pieces. Remembering how she'd thrown her arms around that dopey Arthur made him grind his teeth. *Just friends.* Yeah, right. How stupid did she think he was, anyway?

It wasn't only Arthur, though. Colin had seen this coming, had felt it approaching like an avalanche. She loved school, loved the city. She hadn't simply fallen for a guy; she'd fallen for a new life, one that didn't include him. Back there, he'd been nothing more than the redneck country kid from Valley Community College, a nobody lost in a sea of city sophistication. Her new life was a puzzle to him, and he couldn't make himself fit into it.

Memories of the times he'd spent here with Mia danced around him like ghosts, taunting him. Then came the biggest ghost of all, the memory of when Dad had caught them here together half out of their clothes and so absorbed in each other that they never heard him coming. Some events in a guy's life seem comic in retrospect. This one might have, if it hadn't humiliated Mia so much. Maybe she'd always had issues and he'd never noticed, maybe the interrupted moment that should have rocked their world was the final push that had made her look at herself differently. Who knew? All *he* knew was that afterward she had to do more, be more. It wasn't enough that she had a 4.0. She had to go away to an impressive college, rule the world.

Well, now she could. She'd rule it from New York City with her new friends. With Arthur.

New York, what a place—overcrowded, overpriced,

overhyped. He couldn't believe she liked it so much. Okay, so it had parks and museums. What work of art could compare to the sight of the Wenatchee River sparkling in the sun or the mountains buried and silent under snow? One bite of the Big Apple, and she'd fallen into some goofy hypnotic state that uprooted her from the people and place that should have mattered most.

Well, screw New York and screw her, he thought bitterly as he left the orchard. She could keep her museums and her parks and her fancy restaurants and her frat boys.

Back in the house he showered, grabbed a bag of corn chips and then settled in the family room with his favorite *Mission: Impossible* movie. Mission: Impossible, that about summed up his visit to New York.

He was halfway through the movie when Dad returned. He sat down next to Colin on the couch and watched as Tom Cruise saved the world. "Nobody runs like that guy."

Colin nodded and shoved a handful of chips into his mouth.

"So, I guess things didn't go well in New York," Dad said.

Colin answered with a grunt.

"Competition?"

"There shouldn't be any competition," Colin growled. "We're as good as engaged. Well, we were," he amended.

"So you guys broke up. I figured as much."

Colin locked his jaws tightly together, determined

to keep his emotions under control, and they both sat there staring at Tom, running for his life.

"That man's had his share of woman trouble," Dad finally said, accentuating his statement with a shake of his head. "Can you imagine losing Nicole Kidman?"

Now here it came, the fatherly lecture. That was the downside of living at home while you went to college. Colin braced himself.

Sure enough. "He doesn't have any trouble finding new women," Dad pointed out.

"I don't want to find a new woman." There was the problem. Angry as he was, Colin still wanted Mia. The fact that he couldn't have her anymore was irrelevant.

"I guess you'll be stuck where you are, then."

What was this, shock therapy? "Like you?" Colin retorted. Okay, that had been a crappy thing to say, but who'd asked Dad, anyway?

"I'm not stuck, son. I moved on."

If he'd moved on, how come he was by himself?

"Shit happens, and it happens a lot with women. She's found a new life. You need to do the same."

What kind of new life would it be without Mia?

"It's up to you to decide what it'll look like," Dad continued as if reading his mind. "She's going places. You can, too. Don't let this stall you."

The old man wasn't getting it. "Dad, I love her." They'd always been a part of each other's lives. How could she break them apart like this?

"I understand. Mia's a great girl. But if she wants to go, you've got to let her. Hanging on will only make you miserable." Dad stood up and laid an encouraging hand on his shoulder. "Tom's got it right," he said. Then he left Colin to keep Tom company while he finished saving the world.

It was the deepest conversation they'd had since Mom had first eased back into his life, wanting to visit him when he was nine. That one had been equally short. "I'll take you to Seattle if you'd like to visit her. I know you're curious. But remember, she's not the woman who raised you. She doesn't get to wear the Mommy badge. That belongs to your grandma and Aunt Beth. Got it?"

He did get it, and while he'd managed to grow a shallow relationship with the woman who'd abandoned them before he was old enough to say *Mama*, he'd known where his loyalties lay. Mom had disappointed him a few times, canceled weekend meet-ups, and her on-and-off attempts to snag a larger piece of his life often confused him. But she'd never been able to hurt him badly, probably because she wasn't that important to him. Now he saw that she had been to Dad what Mia had been to him. While Dad talked a big talk, he himself was still stuck in the same leaky love boat. There was a part of his life that was missing. Mom had hurt him badly, and his heart had atrophied.

What, Colin wondered as the days bled out, was going to happen to his heart? Was he going to end up like his old man?

Hell, no, he finally decided two weeks later. This was all wrong, and he needed to fix it. Mia had been drunk, and he'd jumped to conclusions. That was all. He'd apologize and they'd make up. She'd come home for Thanksgiving, just like they'd planned, and everything would return to the way it should be.

He called at a time when she'd probably be in her room studying and waited impatiently for the phone to stop ringing so he could hear her voice.

Another voice, much lower than hers, answered.

"Who is this?" Colin demanded. As if he didn't know.

"What, are you back to hurt her all over again? You didn't do a good enough job the first time around?"

Rage roared inside Colin, started a buzzing in his ears like a thousand hornets. "What are you doing there?"

"None of your business."

Colin could hear Mia's voice in the background. "Let me talk to Mia," he said through gritted teeth.

"No way. She doesn't want to talk to you."

Then the voice was gone and Mia was on the phone. "Colin, why did you leave?"

Why? Seriously? She was asking that when the reason was right there in her dorm room. "What's *he* doing there?"

"Some of us are going out to eat."

"Some of us," Colin sneered. "Why didn't you ever call me?"

"After you ran off for no reason and left that awful note?" She sounded hurt. Offended.

Well, he was the one who'd been hurt, and now he was the one who was offended. "No reason? Are you kidding? You and your pal Arthur gave me plenty of reason."

"I can't believe you'd trust me so little," she said, her voice shaky.

"I was coming back when I saw you through the dorm window wrapping yourself around that douchebag!" And here he'd been trying to tell himself that he'd jumped to conclusions. His eyes hadn't lied.

"I was just thanking him! Honestly, Colin, if you can't trust me, why are we together?"

"Good question. Why are we? You know, I called thinking there was a chance for us, but I was wrong."

She didn't argue, didn't protest. Instead, she greeted his accusation with a long silence. All he could hear was his blood pulsing in his ears. He opened his mouth to say never mind, that he'd been stupid, that he didn't care what she had going with Arthur, that he loved her, anyway.

Too late. "I'll send back the ring," she said. Then the connection died.

He started to call her back but stopped halfway through. Like his dad had said, Mia was moving on. Without him. Friday night and she was going out with *some of us*. He'd be staying in with Jim Beam.

He found nothing to be thankful for as Thanksgiving approached. The ring he'd given Mia came back, and he learned she wouldn't be. She was probably going to spend the holiday weekend with Arthur, he thought bitterly.

Both Gram and Aunt Beth were convinced this separation was temporary. "Your grandfather and I had a little tiff when we were young, but then he got drafted and that brought everything into focus," Gram said.

"Things will come into focus for you and Mia, as well, I'm sure of it," she added, patting his arm.

He'd made the mistake of asking for seconds on pumpkin pie, and while Dad and Uncle Mark were already out in the living room watching the ball game, he was now trapped at the kitchen table with her and Aunt Beth, the cheering squad for Team Colin and Mia.

"You two were meant to be together," Aunt Beth insisted.

Yeah? Then how come Mia had never called or emailed after he'd left? How come she'd given back the ring? History, that was what they were. He needed to move on. And he would. There were plenty of cute girls out there.

The problem was that none of them were Mia.

The lost bride was right. There was only one person to blame for the fact that he and Mia were standing here side by side but not together. "Do you ever wish you could go back in time and do something over?" he asked, studying her face for some sign of regret over how their story had ended.

She bit her lip and moved away from him.

"How come you're not with someone?"

"Maybe I don't believe in settling for just anyone."

He felt the jab. "You think I'm doing that with Lorelei?"

"Are you?"

"I don't know," he admitted. "I don't know about a lot of things."

She said nothing to that, merely stood with her arms wrapped around her middle, frowning at the waterfall.

He pointed off to the side. "Do you remember where we made love?" he asked softly. That seasoned her expression with wistfulness. "It was the first time for both of us. You saw the lost bride," he couldn't help adding.

"You didn't," she said with a sigh.

"I wish I had. Maybe it would have doubled our chances of…" He stopped himself. What was wrong with him, anyway? What was the point of talking like this? They'd both turned their lives in other directions. She was a hotshot, climbing the corporate ladder, and he was stuck in limbo. With Lorelei.

For a moment he thought she was going to say something. And if she did…

Instead, she began looking for their next clue.

Yeah, there was no point in thinking about it. Just like there was no point in this treasure hunt. What the heck had Gram willed them, and was it worth all this aggravation and…pain? There was no other way to put it. Hanging out with Mia and reliving their past hurt. He glanced at the falls one final time. He'd never come back here again.

As if to mock him, a shadow moved behind the cataract. The bride? No, couldn't be. He stared harder. Yes, that sure looked like…something. He squinted. Yes, it looked like a woman. Wow. Really? He blinked.

And then there was nothing. Well, that was the power of suggestion for you.

Shaking his head, he turned to help Mia search, peering under the little picnic table to see if there was a pink envelope taped there. Nothing. He straightened and saw that she was looking at the falls.

"Did you see the bride just now?" he asked.

Mia shaded her eyes. "It's easy to imagine you see something."

He didn't think he'd imagined the bride, but maybe he had. Either way, what did it matter?

Mia turned her back on the view and swept one hand under the bench. "Here it is!" A moment later she'd pulled out the envelope containing their next clue. She sat down, opened it and read, "'I hold your next clue but you'll have to shake me to see something new.'"

"She's making them harder," Colin said.

"No lie."

"What do you shake?" he mused, sitting down beside her on the picnic bench. "Maracas. Cocktails." He could use a drink about now.

"Salt? Maybe the clue's in a salt shaker at one of the restaurants here."

"Maybe," he said. "But what about the rest of it, the part about seeing something new? What do you shake and end up seeing something new?"

They sat in silence for several minutes. Mia was probably thinking about their clue, but all Colin could think about was her. Being in such close proximity had him wanting to grab her and kiss her and never come up for air, made him wish he hadn't been such a fool when they were young, made him wish he wasn't being such a fool now.

What was he doing with Lorelei, anyway? She was cute and fun, inspiring with all that ambition and energy. But how did what he had with her measure up to what he'd once had with Mia?

Mia again, he thought. He had to stop using her as the gold standard by which he measured all other relationships. If only all those old feelings weren't coming back in force.

Stick with Lorelei. She'll never give you heartburn the way Mia did.

She brought him out of his reverie with the snap of her fingers. "That's it!"

"What's it?"

She was already off the bench and headed for the trail. "Come on. We need to go to Christmas Haus."

"Okay, what am I missing here?" Colin asked as they walked back down the trail.

"There's only one thing I can think of that you can shake and see something new."

Then it hit him. "Duh. Of course, a snow globe."

"Yep. Shake it and you get a snowy winter scene. And the place to get snow globes is…"

"Christmas Haus," he finished with her. "Ivy's probably saving one for us with a message on the bottom."

An hour later, walking inside the popular gift shop that carried all things Christmas triggered an avalanche of memories for Colin. He could still see himself at ten, chasing Mia all over Gram's house with the ping-pong popgun he'd gotten from Dad. He'd gotten the latest Mario incarnation, too, and for the next two weeks they'd done nothing but play Nintendo. Then there'd been their first Christmas together as boyfriend and girlfriend. The minute the decorations had gone up at

Aunt Beth's house, he'd kissed Mia under the mistle-toe, thinking no one was watching.

It had been a kiss full of anticipation and joy. The New Year was full of promise. She'd be graduating. He'd give her that ring. They'd be together for the rest of their lives.

"Ha! Caught ya," Uncle Mark had teased, making Mia pull away, blushing. But the way she'd looked at Colin said it all. *I love you.*

That December he'd given her a tree ornament, a glass angel holding a little banner that read *Love*. Mrs. Bohn had wrapped it for him and he'd walked over to Aunt Beth's house that same day, insisting Mia open it right then, even though it was only the middle of the month.

"It's beautiful," she'd said and hung it on the tree. "Our first ornament. Let's get one every year, so when we're married, we'll already have decorations for our tree."

He'd liked that idea. She'd run out and bought him an ornament, too, a Santa Claus.

She'd also bought him something else. On Christmas Day she gave him a copy of *Wuthering Heights*. She'd tucked a picture of the two of them inside, and on the title page she'd written, "We're Cathy and Heathcliff, the happy-ending version."

After they broke up, he'd come home and smashed the Santa, burned the picture, and torn the book to shreds and dumped it in the recycling bin. Then wished a hundred times over that he hadn't been so impetuous.

He'd wished the same thing when she came home

for Aunt Beth's birthday, engaged to Arthur. If only he hadn't been such a shit that day in New York. Heck, if only he hadn't broken up with her, he wouldn't have had to see her wearing another man's ring. But the ring said it all. In the end she wanted someone else, something more.

What did she want now? Probably her life in the big city, the fancy job and the big bucks. He, on the other hand, had no desire to go any farther than Icicle Falls. Mia, he supposed, had always been meant for bigger things.

But if that was the case, why did it feel so right having her back here?

Christmas Haus was one of Mia's favorite shops, a veritable indoor Christmas-tree farm lit up for the holidays all year round. Every tree on display wore a different color and displayed a different collection of ornaments. There were trees done up in gold, trees in red and ones looking pretty in pink. Some wore elegant oversize balls and ribbons, others offered whimsy, decorated with fairies or princesses or ornaments shaped like old-fashioned candies and strung with plastic popcorn. One tree modeled Santas, while another held hosts of angels.

She tried not to look at the tree with all the angel ornaments. It made her think of the ornament Colin had given her the Christmas everything was perfect between them. She still had the angel. She never brought it out, though. Initially, the idea of seeing it hanging on her little tree was simply too depressing. And then she'd gotten together with Arthur, and it hadn't seemed right to display it.

She and Arthur started dating in December after Colin had broken up her. He'd taken her to see *A Christmas Story* at the beginning of the month. She'd felt almost disloyal to Colin at first, but then told herself not to be stupid. They were through and that was that.

"Stay here this Christmas," Arthur urged. "If you go home, you'll have to see the jerk and he'll make you feel bad all over again."

He had a point. Why should she go home to Icicle Falls and let Colin make her miserable when she could spend the holidays in style with Arthur's family in up-state New York?

"We'll have a great time," he predicted.

Arthur would never have made it as a fortune teller. The moment they pulled up in the circular driveway in front of the massive brick Tudor, she was asking her-self what the heck she was doing there.

"Here we are, home, sweet home," he said cheer-ily and bounded out of the car to open the passenger door for her.

He was such a gentleman. He'd be a good husband. If he asked her to marry him she should say yes. It was either that or mope around over Colin for the rest of her life. She liked the East Coast. She and Arthur could get jobs with companies in New York or Chicago, move up the ladder, have the requisite two children and some-day buy a house in the burbs like this one.

No, not like this one. This was too big. She wanted a cute little Craftsman or a Victorian or a log cabin like the houses in Icicle Falls.

She didn't have to move to Icicle Falls to find a cute house, though. They had lovely houses out here. And nice people, too. She'd be perfectly happy living the rest of her life here. Yes, she would.

The Cavanaughs' home was as impressive inside as it was outside, with cathedral ceilings and an entry hall big enough for the Mormon Tabernacle Choir. Curving staircases flanked each side and made their stately way up to a landing, where she saw a giant flocked tree decorated with purple balls and gold bows. An entry table bore an elaborate candle arrangement wafting the scent of evergreens toward her, and drifting out from another room came music, the Mormon Tabernacle Choir—ha!—singing "O Come, All Ye Faithful." More like O Come, All Ye Wealthy, Mia thought as Arthur led her into the house, calling, "We're here."

They found an assortment of well-dressed people lounging in an enormous living room with a Douglas fir decorated all in red standing in one corner, presiding over more presents than she'd ever seen in one place in her life. A fire blazed in the river-rock fireplace, and candles sat on the mantel. A middle-aged couple was sitting at a small game table, playing cards. The others, some Mia and Arthur's age, others older, lolled around on leather furniture, enjoying drinks.

"Well, look what the cat dragged in," said a tall fortysomething man with the same curly brown hair as Arthur's. He rose from the sofa, cocktail glass in hand,

and gave Arthur a big, slapping hug. "About time you got here, son."

And right behind him came a woman wearing gray wool slacks and a black cashmere sweater, her ash-blond hair caught up with an expensive-looking gold clip. The diamond on her left hand seemed too big to be real, but judging by the house, it was.

"You must be Mia," she said, taking Mia's hands between her slim, white ones. "Arthur's told us so much about you."

"He has?" Oh, for heaven's sake. Could she sound any more gauche?

"All good," Arthur said with a grin, putting an arm around Mia and pulling her close.

It was only natural. They were dating now. Still, she felt her cheeks warming, feeling several pairs of curious eyes on her.

"Glad to have you with us, Mia," said Arthur's father. "We're a motley crew but we're usually good for a chuckle."

The motley crew consisted of an aunt and uncle and a couple of cousins who were taking in her nondesigner clothes, a portly grandfather with the heavily veined face of a dedicated drinker, a slim grandmother with long silver hair, a beautiful Botoxed face and a haughty smile. A chuckle? That would probably happen as soon as she left the room.

"Joyful and triumphant," warbled the choir from who knew where. Hidden speakers? Maybe they were out in the kitchen, singing. That was undoubtedly big enough to house them.

"Let's get you settled," Mrs. Cavanaugh said, and led Mia and Arthur out of the living room. Up the stairs they went and down a lengthy hall. "I hope you two will be comfortable in Arthur's old room."

The two of them? Together? They hadn't gotten that far in their relationship. Mia turned desperately to Arthur, who'd been looking hopeful.

He got the message. "Uh, Mom, can you put Mia in one of the guest bedrooms?"

His mother had just opened the door to Arthur's room. It was huge, like everything else in this house, all done in shades of brown. The bed was enormous, but Arthur would have no trouble finding Mia in it.

She wasn't ready to be found. "We're not, er, we haven't..." She stammered to a halt, her face flaming as if she was standing in front of that river-rock fireplace in the living room.

Mrs. Cavanaugh's eyes widened in surprise but she recovered quickly and patted Mia's arm. "Actually, I'm glad to hear my son is being a gentleman and not rushing you. Abstinence hasn't been in style for a long time."

"I hope it won't be in style much longer," Arthur murmured, giving Mia a wink.

Mrs. Cavanaugh moved farther down the hall. "Let's put you in here," she said and opened a door on another room big enough for an entire family. Cream-colored carpet, eggshell walls, a bed with a sage-green bedspread and a million pillows, and of course it had a fireplace. "I hope this will do."

How could it not? Mia thanked her, and she left the

couple alone, saying, "Get settled and then you can join us downstairs for drinks. Dinner's at seven."

"Do you like your room?" Arthur asked.

"It's beautiful. The whole house is beautiful."

"So are you," he said, closing the distance between them and kissing her. Arthur was a good kisser. He would probably be an equally good lover.

"We'd better get downstairs," she said.

Dinner was slow-roasted beef tenderloin, bread fresh from the local bakery, along with herbed leek gratin, shiitake mushroom–tomato bisque, and a caramel-nut tart for dessert. Conversation started with reminiscences of favorite holiday trips to London and Lucerne. And wasn't that cruise to all the Christmas markets in Germany fun? Then, of course, politics had to be discussed—if you could call everyone deciding that any outsiders who held a different opinion were idiots a discussion. Mia kept her opinions to herself. No one asked, anyway. And why did Grandma Botox keep looking at her as if she should be waiting the table instead of sitting at it with the rest of them?

It snowed Christmas day and the fire roared in the big fireplace. The presents were extravagant—gold money clips, hundred-dollar gift cards thrown around like oversize confetti, expensive jewelry, the keys to a new car for Arthur's mom—a little something from Daddy Claus. Mia had been allowed to share the bounty, too, receiving a couple of those hundred-dollar gift cards herself, as well as a Marc Jacobs purse from his parents and a pretty gold locket from Arthur. All she'd brought was a modest twenty-five-dollar iTunes gift card for Arthur and Sweet Dreams chocolates for his parents, which his mother shared with the other women while Mia kicked herself for not bringing more.

Although it would've been wasted on Grandma Botox, who tried one and said, "It's not Vosges, is it?"

What, Mia asked herself, was she doing here?

Moving on, that was what.

"My family loved you," Arthur said as they drove back to the city.

Well, his parents seemed to. Maybe his grandmother would like her, too, if she changed her chocolate allegiance.

The months slipped away like thieves, and her relationship with Arthur became something more serious than casual dating. It wasn't what she'd had with Colin, but so what? What she'd had with Colin had obviously only been a storm of youthful passion that had blown itself out. Arthur was sweet, and she was happy with him. He was good for her and she could be good to him.

On Valentine's Day he took her to the Russian Tea Room for dinner and proposed. She surprised them both by saying no. "It's too soon. I'm not ready yet. I'm sorry."

He didn't look her in the eye. Instead, he looked at the ring sitting in its little box on the table between them. "It's Colin, isn't it? You're still not over him."

"I am," she lied. "I'm just not ready for a serious commitment. I need to concentrate on school."

Arthur nodded and frowned, and she felt like a heartless bitch. She reached across the table and laid her hand on his. "I'm sorry, Arthur. Maybe we should take a break from each other."

Now he did look at her. "Is that what you want?"

She didn't know what she wanted anymore and said as much. "I think I need to sort out my feelings." *Call Colin, try to work things out.*

But she never did gather the nerve to call him, not after their last conversation. She couldn't bear to get slapped away.

That summer she got an internship at an ad agency and stayed in the city, and the distance between her and her past grew. Come fall, she and Arthur were hanging out again, and that December when he took her to his parents' house for Christmas, they shared his bedroom. After that, of course, the next step was to move in together.

She told Aunt Beth she was seeing Arthur, but she didn't tell her she saw him when she went to sleep at night and when she woke up in the morning. She knew both Aunt Beth and Grandma Justine were disappointed that things hadn't worked out with Colin. There was no point in disappointing them further with the news that she was living with someone.

"When are you coming home for a visit?" Aunt Beth kept asking. "It's been ages since we've seen you."

Not since she and Uncle Mark had gone to Mia's graduation. Arthur had taken them all out for dinner and gotten tickets to a Broadway show. They'd been polite and appreciative, but Mia felt sure they were wondering what she was doing with this new man.

"I'm so busy with the new job," she always replied.

"We all knew you'd go on to do great things," Beth had said in their latest conversation.

All except Dylan, Mia thought.

"But don't forget us."

"How could I?"

She was sure Colin had forgotten her, though. She wanted to ask about him but chickened out. What was the point?

"I know Grandma would love to see you," Beth continued. "We all would."

Did that include Colin? He wasn't in Icicle Falls anymore, either. He'd moved to Seattle. What was he doing there instead of in the town that was so much a part of him?

Probably the same thing as she was, making a new life.

When Mia did finally come home to Icicle Falls to visit, she was wearing an engagement ring, but she didn't keep it on for long after she returned to New York. "I'm so sorry," she told Arthur. "I can't marry you. It's not fair to you. It's not fair to either of us."

"Was he at your aunt's party? Did you get back with him?" Arthur demanded.

"No." She never would now. She knew that.

"Then I don't understand."

"Neither do I," she said sadly, and placed the ring in the palm of his hand, closing his fingers over it. "You're a wonderful man, Arthur. You're funny and kind and smart."

He managed a half smile. "I sound like a pretty good deal."

"You're a *great* deal." Just not for her.

Things were over between her and Arthur, and it was over between her and New York, too. She landed a terrific job in Chicago with GF Markets and made a whole new set of friends. And the following Christmas, she decorated her new apartment and cried when she hung the little angel Colin had given her on the tree.

January 12, 2006

Dear Emmaline,
We're at sixes and sevens after Gerald's stroke.
Dylan and Bethie have been a great help, and we
got him settled in a very nice care facility. I'm
hoping he'll recover and be able to come home.
He's such a dear, not a word of complaint. It's
hard for him to speak, and I suppose he doesn't
want to waste his energy on that. I do love him so!

I wish I knew what to do about the orchard. It
would kill Gerald to sell it. But we may need to if
he has to stay where he is indefinitely. As I said
when we talked on the phone, I'm going to trust
God that this will all work out. There's no point
in borrowing trouble from tomorrow for today.
Right now I'm simply trying to focus on being
there for him and on counting my blessings. I
have so much to be thankful for—my family and
friends who are all being so supportive, and my
health, and, of course, all the wonderful years
Gerald and I have had together. I'm thankful I
still have him and I do hope he recovers enough
to come home. The house is lonely without him.
Meanwhile, I'm visiting him every day.

That's all for now. I must dash. Gerald will be
wondering what's become of me.

Love,
Justine

Chapter Fourteen

As she stood among the displays in Christmas Haus, Mia scowled at the tree full of angel ornaments. All that moping around over an immature, untrusting man—what a waste of time! She could've been happily married with a couple of kids by now. When she got back to Chicago, she was going to dig out the stupid angel Colin had given her and break its wings.

"You look pissed," he observed. "What are you pissed about?"

"You and your stupid angel ornament, that's what."

"You still have it?" He sounded pleased, almost cocky.

She wanted to kick him.

"Mia, Colin, hi." Ivy Bohn approached, wearing a red dirndl, the standard uniform for both owners and employees of Christmas Haus. Ivy fell in the category of owner. Her parents had the shop before her but had retired and left the business of keeping the holidays all year round to her and her sister.

"I've been expecting you," she said.

Mia erased the irritation from her face, putting on

a polite mask. "I bet you have." She pointed to the corner where a variety of elaborate snow globes were shelved. "Do you, by any chance, have a snow globe set aside for us?"

Ivy grinned. "I do. Justine came in and picked it out herself. I've got it over here." She walked to the cash register, where her loyal assistant, Nicole, was ringing up a sale, and produced a gift bag stuffed with red tissue paper. "I can hardly wait to hear what you find. Knowing Justine, it'll be something unique."

They thanked Ivy. Then, as more customers were approaching, they moved to the snow-globe neighborhood and checked out theirs. The scene inside the globe showed a little mountain chalet surrounded by fir trees. In front of it stood a couple in the traditional German garb, the man in lederhosen and the woman in a dirndl. Mia gave it a shake, and the couple was immediately engulfed in a snowstorm—Colin and her, before and after.

"Turn it over," he prompted.

She did and there, folded several times and taped to the base, was the pink stationery. She pulled it loose, unfolded it and read, "'For your next clue something sweet awaits you.'"

"Well, that's easy," Colin said. "It's gotta be Sweet Dreams."

Of course. The town's favorite source of chocolates.

"Does it say anything more?" he asked.

Mia's eyes misted. "She wants me to keep the snow globe, to remind me of Icicle Falls. 'Once an Icicle, always an Icicle,'" she read. That was so true. You could take the girl out of Icicle Falls, but you couldn't take Icicle Falls out of the girl.

"I keep hoping you'll move home," Grandma Justine had said to Mia when she'd come back for Aunt Beth's birthday.

Mia had been engaged to Arthur then. "We'll probably stay in New York," she'd said, and that had made her sad. What kind of crazy woman got sad about starting her married life in New York?

The kind of crazy woman who belonged in Icicle Falls. With each new stop on this treasure hunt, Mia felt the pull more strongly. She was the tide, and this town was the moon, drawing her back.

"I think you're meant to be here with us," Grandma Justine said when Mia had called to cry on her shoulder after she broke up with Arthur.

Maybe she was. Someday she'd come back, bring her family, settle down. She and Colin would see each other at Christmas, perhaps run into each other at Bavarian Brews. By then all the passion and anger would have finally burned itself out. They'd ease into friendship, reminisce. *Remember how we thought we were in love? Dumb kids. Glad that's all behind us.*

"Fine," Colin was saying. "You keep the snow globe. I'll keep whatever we find at Sweet Dreams."

"Oh, no, you don't!" she said, snapping back into the present. "Share and share alike."

She stowed the snow globe in his car and they strolled down Center Street to the Sweet Dreams chocolate shop.

"So you kept the angel," he said. "I wish I'd kept the Santa."

"You didn't?" He hadn't kept it. Even though it shouldn't have mattered, Mia felt hurt. "What did you do with it?"

His mouth turned down. "Stomped the shit out of it. Then kicked myself for being such a tool. I've kicked myself for a lot of things."

"What a coincidence. So have I," she murmured.

They were barely inside the company's popular shop when Mia spotted Colin's girlfriend checking out the bags of chocolate-dipped pretzels and potato chips. She glanced over as the sound of the bell above the door jingled, then, seeing Colin, she gave a guilty start and stepped away from the junk food like a shoplifter caught with her fingers hovering over the goods. "I thought you were looking for clues," she greeted them, her tone accusing.

"We have been," he said.

She rolled her eyes and grabbed a bag of chocolate-dipped pretzels.

He pointed to it. "I thought you didn't eat that stuff."

"Sometimes a woman needs chocolate." She marched over to him. "Like when her boyfriend's ignoring her and searching for *clues* with another woman."

Heidi Schwartz, who worked in the gift shop, glanced from one to the other, her eyes big. Boy, they were better than reality TV.

Meanwhile, here was Colin, the man who faced bullies single-handed, backing away from the Lorelei assault. "Come on, Lorelei, don't be like this."

Lorelei's eyes became slits and she narrowed the gap between them. "Like what?"

Colin backed up some more, bumping into a display tower of chocolate boxes. The tower teetered and he whirled around to steady it. Several boxes dove for the floor and his face turned red.

"Like. What?" Lorelei repeated. Any minute her head was going to spin right off her neck and shoot off for parts unknown.

"There's no need to be jealous," Mia put in, hoping to defuse the situation.

"I'm not jealous," Lorelei spat. "I just think it's odd that you two are here in a candy store when you're supposed to be looking for clues to some buried treasure that probably doesn't even exist."

"Of course it exists," Colin said, picking up the boxes. "Why would I lie?"

Heidi cleared her throat. "Actually, I do have something for you guys."

"See? I told you," he said, shoving the chocolate boxes back into place.

"Could we have it?" Mia asked, stepping away from the happy couple.

"Sure." Heidi reached under the counter and produced a two-pound box of Sweet Dreams truffles.

"Oh, the garden collection." Mia's mouth watered at the thought of dark chocolate filled with lavender-chocolate ganache and the unique combination of white chocolate and rose water.

She took it and turned it over. No clue taped to the bottom of the box.

Now Colin was on one side of her and Lorelei on the other. "Maybe your clue's inside the box," Lorelei said.

"Lorelei, you can't help," Colin told her.

"Just saying," she shot back as Mia opened it.

No pink paper was visible.

"Yeah, that's some clue," Lorelei scoffed.

"Maybe it's under the liner," Mia said and set the box on the checkout counter. She carefully lifted the liner, balancing all the little candies in their paper holders.

One fell on the floor and Colin grabbed it and popped it into his mouth. "Two-second rule."

"Yuck," Lorelei said, wrinkling her nose. Then she helped herself to a white-chocolate truffle. "Are these vegan?" Before Heidi could answer, she said, "Never mind," and popped it into her mouth.

Meanwhile, Mia had found the pink paper with their next clue. "'Her words are valued,'" she read. "'Let her tell you some of my story.'"

"Okay, what does that mean?" Lorelei muttered, helping herself to another truffle.

"Damned if I know," Colin said. "Her words are valued?"

"Aunt Beth?" guessed Mia.

"Works for me," Colin said.

"*Now* where are you going?" Lorelei asked.

"We're following where the next clue leads," Colin said, starting for the door.

"Make sure it leads you back to me for dinner." Lorelei, grabbed him by the arm and kissed him.

His cheeks were russet when they left. Lorelei

seemed to have a real talent for embarrassing him. And she sure seemed demanding.

"She's a little, uh…" Mia began, then stopped herself. She didn't need to be pointing out his girlfriend's flaws.

"What?"

"Nothing."

"I know what you were going to say. She can be kind of high maintenance."

"Some women are," Mia said diplomatically.

"You never were. You were always easy to be with." His brows knit and once again his cheeks reddened. They were back at the car now and he got into it like a man diving for cover.

Yes, this was hardly an appropriate conversation to be having. Like so many of their conversations. It was true, though. Whenever Colin had wanted to go fishing, she'd been happy to go along. If he'd wanted to hang out with the guys, she'd gone out with her girlfriends or did something with Aunt Beth. She'd never been demanding. There was no need to be, because they'd enjoyed each other's company. They were comfortable together, and happy.

Was Colin happy now with Lorelei? And if he was, why were the sparks still flying between them, waiting to ignite?

She got in on her side and turned to him, and the nosy words slipped out. "Are you happy?"

He blinked. "Yeah, I guess. Well…shit. I don't know," he said and seemed suddenly very focused on starting the car and pulling onto the street. "I mean, there are things I'd like to do."

"Like own an orchard?" He'd so badly wanted to take over his grandfather's.

"Someday."

She wanted to ask what Lorelei thought of those goals, but she decided she'd asked enough probing questions. Instead, she picked her flower up from the floor. It was looking sad and droopy. She'd put it in water when they got back to Aunt Beth's and hope it wasn't too late to revive it.

They found Aunt Beth in the middle of altering a dress for Hildy Johnson, but she was happy to take a break and offered them some lemonade.

"Poor Hildy," Beth said as she took glasses from the cupboard. "She's gone up two sizes. She's too cheap to go out and buy a whole new wardrobe. She's probably going to faint when I give her the bill."

"Speaking of giving people stuff," Colin said as Mia filled a vase with water, "do you have a clue for us?"

Aunt Beth set two glasses of lemonade on the table. "I already gave you a clue. Remember?"

"So, you don't happen to have another?"

She poured herself some lemonade and sat down. "Nope. Are you stumped?"

"A little," Mia said, joining them. She set the vase in the center of the table.

"What one are you on? I can see you found your clue at Lupine Floral. Poor thing." She shook her head at the sick-looking rose.

"It's had a long afternoon," Mia explained.

"So have we," Colin added.

"We're on the clue that talks about a woman whose words have value," Mia said. "We thought that was you."

"Well, thanks for the compliment, kids, but it's not. There are other women in Icicle Falls whose words have value."

"Grandma Justine's did," Mia said, and a tear slid down her cheek.

So many Grandma Justine sayings were filed in her memory, lined up like library books. *There are people who will let you down, but for everyone who does, God brings along someone else to lift you up.* This after her father had so bitterly disappointed her on her thirteenth birthday. *Remember how special you are and you won't waste your valuable time and energy on being jealous.* That one came after the great syrup attack, along with another bit of wisdom. *Don't waste good syrup when water will work just as well.*

Her favorite Grandma Justine saying was the one she'd written in Mia's college graduation card. *Be true to who you are, and you'll wind up exactly where you're meant to be.*

She hoped she was following that advice, although sometimes she wondered. Was she being true to who she was? And that raised the question of who she was. Growing up, she'd been a girl who loved her adopted family, enjoyed hiking and playing in the orchard. She'd been content to sit on a blanket on the bank of the Wenatchee River or Icicle Creek and read. She'd been just as happy helping Aunt Beth and Grandma Justine sell apples at the fruit stand or canning applesauce.

But she'd also enjoyed college and living in the city. And working hard and being successful made her feel good about herself. If she sometimes questioned what she was working so hard for, well, that was probably normal. Everyone felt like that once in a while. No one had a perfect job or a perfect life.

Grandma Justine seemed to have come close—pursuing hobbies, helping her community, watching over her family. Building a life with the man she loved. Hmm.

"Yes, she was a wonderful woman," Aunt Beth said, and now it looked like she, too, was going to cry.

Colin felt ready to join them. "How many more clues are there, anyway?" he grumbled.

"Not many," his aunt assured him. "You're coming close to the end, and the most important part. Pretty soon you'll learn what a truly remarkable woman your grandmother was."

He already knew how remarkable Gram was. She'd been the cornerstone of their family and an inspiration to half the town.

"We're at a loss here," Mia said. "Can't you give us a hint?"

"No outside help," Aunt Beth reminded her.

"Come on, have a heart," Colin begged. "We're stalled out."

"I'm surprised you're having so much trouble with this," Aunt Beth said.

"A woman whose words have value and who can tell us some of Grandma Justine's story," Mia mused.

"Think literally," said Aunt Beth. "That's all I'm going to say."

"Value, as in money?" Mia asked.

Aunt Beth was now a sphinx.

"Words with value. What words have literal value?" Mia tapped her chin. Did she have any idea how cute she was when she did that? "Words in a book?" She looked at Aunt Beth.

"You're getting warmer. Now, that's really all I'm going to say. I have to get back to work."

"Words in a book," Mia mused as Aunt Beth left them to finish their lemonade. "As in a writer. *Her* words have value."

"So, that means it's a woman," Colin said.

"If we're talking about a woman writer, there's only one person who fits, and that's Muriel Sterling."

"Now, why didn't I think of that?"

"I don't know. Why didn't you?"

"Because I'm not as smart as you."

"No, because two heads are better than one. You know, teamwork?"

Yes, they made a great team. He should never have let her go. Damn it all, why was Gram torturing him like this?

He didn't want to think about it. He gulped down the last of his lemonade and pushed away from the table. "Okay, let's go."

Luckily for them, Muriel Sterling was home. "Colin,

Mia, how nice to see you," she said, opening the door to her little house by the vineyard. "Come in."

"I'm wondering if you know why we're here," Mia said as they stepped through the door.

"I believe I do. Oh, and I just happen to have some lavender cookies from Bailey's tea shop."

Colin liked cookies, but what he really wanted was to get their next clue and move on. He opened his mouth to say they were in a hurry, but before the words came out, Mia was saying, "That sounds great." So in they went and settled on the sofa, and Muriel disappeared into the kitchen to fetch goodies.

He had to admit, being in Muriel Sterling's house was good for the soul. It wasn't the big kick-ass house she'd lived in when she was married and half the town came to her New Year's Day open houses, but there was something restful about looking out the living room window at all those leafy green vines with clumps of grapes dangling from them like giant earrings. Inside, she'd decorated with framed photographs taken by her oldest daughter, Samantha. A vase of daisies sat on the dining table, a testament to the difference between men and women. Nothing ever sat on his table except junk mail.

"This is such a pretty setting," Mia said, gazing out the window. "Someday, I'd love to have a house just like this."

"In Chicago?" he asked. No city would give her this kind of view.

She didn't answer. Muriel was back now with a tray

bearing a plate of cookies and two glasses. "I think you'll like this lavender iced tea."

"Ooh, is that something Bailey offers at the tea shop?"

"It is, as a matter of fact. I hope you'll have time to visit there before you have to leave," said Muriel. "How long are you here?"

Mia cast a glance in Colin's direction. "I'm only here for as long as it takes to puzzle out this mystery of what Grandma Justine left us. I have to get back to Chicago."

There it was again, a reminder that they were now leading very different lives.

"I'm glad you could at least come for the funeral," Muriel said. "And I'm glad you're making time for this treasure hunt. Justine was such a clever woman. And quite the mover and shaker here in Icicle Falls. But her reach went farther than taking in kids and starting the information booth. Did you know she helped me with my first book?"

"Gram was a writer?" This was news to Colin.

"At one time, yes, she did some writing. She even sold a story to *Redbook* back in the seventies. She acted as my editor, helped me pull my thoughts together. Without her encouragement, I don't think I'd ever have sold my first book. And I wasn't the only one she helped. She encouraged Olivia Claussen to keep going with the Icicle Creek Lodge after her first husband died and sent I don't know how many people her way. She also helped a lot of businesses in town, thanks to that information booth." Muriel opened a drawer in the buffet table and pulled out a small cloth-bound notebook. "Just as she worked with me on my story, I helped her a little with hers. She wrote down a few things she wanted you two to know, and this time I was her editor. Here's the final version." Muriel handed the notebook to Colin. "I'm going to sit on my back patio. When you're done, I'll give you your next clue."

She walked quietly out of the room, leaving Colin and Mia on the couch with the little book of reminiscences. He opened it and they began to read.

Even though I grew up in Pittsburgh, I think I was always a small-town girl at heart. But I didn't know that until I got to Icicle Falls.

Gerald and I were high school sweethearts and we never dreamed we'd leave Pittsburgh. We figured he'd work in a factory like his father had. We'd raise a family, go to church, pay bills, all the normal things you expect to do once you're married. Those plans got delayed. The Korean War came along, and Gerald got drafted. I prayed every day that God would keep him safe and bring him home to me. I knew if he didn't come back, I'd never marry. I'd never find with anyone else what I had with Gerald. We were so alike in what we wanted from life. We enjoyed the same things like drives out into the country or a stroll around the neighborhood in the evening, card games, going to a movie once in a while. We were both big Jimmy Stewart fans. I could hardly wait to get married and start a family. Needless

*to say, I was distraught when Gerald left. Like
every other woman whose sweetheart was gone,
I prayed every day for his safety. I never figured
out why he came back and others didn't. All I
could do was be thankful.*

*As you know, he didn't escape unharmed. Ger-
ald was badly wounded in Korea. He lost the
sight in one eye. But he came home to me and
that was all that mattered. We were married and
lived with my parents for a time so Gerald could
get back on his feet. War had taken its toll. He
was nervous and had trouble sleeping. We finally
decided he needed a change.*

*He had a friend who'd been stationed out west
at McCord Air Force base and had moved out
there. The friend told him how great Washington
was, all blue skies and green on the western side,
orchards and farming on the east. A great place
to build a life, said his friend. I loved the idea of
owning a little farm, but I wasn't so sure about
leaving home. Still, Gerald was really taken with
the idea of starting our married life in Washington, so I agreed to move. His father lent us some
money and we packed up and came out here,
looking for peace and quiet for Gerald and a
place to build our life together.*

*Washington was lovely and there was plenty of
green in the northwest part of the state. Plenty of
rain, too, so even though we could have bought
a dairy farm up north toward the Canadian bor-
der, we headed over the pass to where the sun-*

shine was. The mountains were so beautiful they took my breath away, and as we drove down the other side I had the strong impression that we had found our home.

We set up housekeeping in a small house in Yakima, and Gerald worked in a packing plant. We hoarded money like misers, saving for that farm we wanted. Bethie came along in 1954 and then Dylan in 1957.

We quickly learned that children are an expensive hobby. I began to think maybe we'd never save enough money to make our dreams come true. Gerald was already working so hard. There was nothing more he could do, so I decided to pitch in. I'd been pretty good in English at school. I applied to the local paper and got a job writing a food column. It wasn't a lot of money, but it helped. And from that I branched out and gave cooking lessons to young brides. I even entered a cooking contest. My butterscotch biscuits won me five hundred dollars, a real fortune back then.

By 1960 we were ready to take advantage of the GI Bill and put some money down on a place. We'd heard that Icicle Falls was in the process of reinventing itself and thought there might be a future there, so we went to take a look. We were checking out sale properties, and that was when we saw the orchard and the old farmhouse. We didn't even need to talk about it. We both knew as we walked among all those trees that we'd found our future home. We bought it and got to work. Maybe I worked a little too hard. In 1961 I lost a baby. And I lost a piece of my heart.

But I reminded myself to be grateful for what I had, and I pushed on. When your soul is in the desert you have to push on or you die. I still think about Gretchen, though. Sometimes I dream about her. I'm looking forward to meeting her when I get to heaven. I hope she won't hold it against me that I didn't take better care of myself.

After that loss I needed something to occupy my mind. Icicle Falls was growing now, with lovely little hotels and shops and restaurants springing up all over. We were starting to get visitors. Looking around, I realized that we needed an information booth, a central location where people could come and get brochures and maps and hear about all there was to do here in the mountains. So I decided to get one up and running.

There wasn't much money in the town's budget but we eventually managed to find a location. Gerald and one of his friends built the booth, and in the summer of 1963 we were in business. That miniature chalet was an instant hit. I loved working in it, welcoming people to Icicle Falls.

I loved welcoming children into our home, too. Thank God that Gerald felt the same way. I like to think we helped most of the kids who came through our doors. There were one or two we couldn't save, but what's the point in dwelling on that?

We had a good, full life, and that orchard was our pride and joy. But it was also a lot of work. Still, we hung on because we loved it.

I suppose there comes a point when you either let go of something and swim for safety or it takes you down. I tried to hang on to the orchard, but after Gerald's stroke I realized I couldn't keep it, just like I couldn't keep him at home. I had to let go of so much. It was either that or get taken down.

Of course, I'd hoped it could stay in the family. Colin, I knew how much you loved it. I knew you had your own dreams for it, too, but I couldn't hang on any longer. Your father had his law practice, and Beth and Mark had their company. There was no one to keep the place going. Anyway, I needed the money to pay the care facility. I cried all day when I put the orchard up for sale.

Colin remembered that painful time. Some people from the city who figured it would be fun to get back to nature bought the orchard. Nobody told Gramps. There was no reason to upset him. Everyone knew he was never getting out of that place.

Colin went to visit Gramps every afternoon that summer, up until the day the old man died, staying until he thought his chest would burst form all the pain he was holding in. When the end of August came and Gramps started asking how the harvest was going, Colin would lie and say, "Great. Don't worry, we've got it covered."

He had thought many times of calling Mia, sharing the grief, but he never did. He knew she knew about Gramps. Aunt Beth had told her and she'd called Gram several times. When Gramps died she'd sent Gram a card with a note inside, telling her what a special man Gramps had been—in case Gram wasn't aware of that?—and had sent flowers to the funeral, but she hadn't come back. It had been one more thing to hold against her.

Gramps asked about her once when Colin came to visit. One side of his face drooped, and his speech was slurred. He couldn't see out of one eye, so Colin always made sure to sit on Gramps's good side.

"How's Mia?" The words had come out slowly, painfully. Mia was now history, but Gramps seemed to be getting lost in the river of time.

Answering was as painful as hearing her name. "She's busy with school," he'd said. Then he'd switched to a subject he knew both he and Gramps would enjoy, spinning out a tall tale. "We just finished picking the apples. A bumper crop this year. That reflective material we put down really works, Gramps. And the newer trees we trellised are doing well. It's a much better way to grow fruit."

Colin had suggested that back when he was seventeen. He'd been doing some research and had read several articles on growing trees in a V shape, which allowed more sunshine to the apples on the lower branches and easier access for the grower. Gramps had been taken with the idea, and he and Colin had worked together on it.

They'd always worked well together. Colin appreciated his grandfather's easy smile and his love of the land. "Growing food and growing a family, the two best things a man can do with his life," Gramps used to say. He'd done a good job of both.

He ate up Colin's lie with a spoon, nodded and slurred, "Keep…it up."

When Colin left, the old man was making that half smile, showing himself well pleased with his grandson's visit and the news of a bountiful harvest. It was a joyful delusion.

Frowning, Colin read on.

But I reminded myself to be grateful for all the years we'd had the place and to be thankful that I still had my family and friends. And I was so happy when I found my new house. It wasn't very big but it was sweet and it had an apple tree. When I saw that, I knew it was for me.

I worked hard to give my family more happy times in that little house, and I think I succeeded. If there's one thing I've learned it's that living and loving together is what makes life worthwhile. It's not so much where we live but how we live. Cultivating lifelong friendships, making a difference where you are, and, of course, finding a life partner who truly knows you and

*will stand by you, no matter what. Those are the
things that are truly important.*

*Never giving up, that's important, too. After
I lost my dear Gerald, I was sorely tempted to.
But to stop living when your heart's still beating
and your brain still works is an insult to God.
So I kept going and had a few more adventures.*

*Now that's all I'm going to say. You'll learn
about the rest of my adventures soon enough.
The rest of this journal is blank. I'm leaving it
to you to fill the pages.*

Mia was crying now and Colin was feeling squirmy.
Gram's words about living and loving together had
poked a nerve. And what about never giving up? He
had done just that, tossed his dreams out the window
the minute he exited the freeway in Seattle. After reading about everything his grandma had accomplished,
well, failure was too kind a word for him.

His cell phone rang. *Guess who.* He answered reluctantly.

"I'm going to visit with Muriel," Mia said as Lorelei asked, "How's it coming?"

"I…" *Have got to make changes in my life.* Okay,
this wasn't the time for that conversation, and this
wasn't the person to have it with. He and Lorelei had
to have a serious conversation of their own, but now
wasn't the time for that, either.

"You've found the treasure?" she asked eagerly.

Not yet. *I'm still busy finding myself.*

* * *

Mia joined Muriel at the café table on her back patio, where Muriel was sipping iced tea. "Are you done reading?" she asked Mia.

Mia nodded. "Colin had to take a call, so I came out here."

"He must have a very important job if they're calling him on the weekend."

"No, he has a very important girlfriend," Mia said, frowning at the sun-drenched rows of vines laden with grapes.

"Ah."

Ah? That was the only comment she was going to get from the wise Muriel Sterling?

"You know we once..." Mia stopped herself. Everyone in town knew they were once an item.

"Youth can be both a blessing and a curse," Muriel said with a smile. "Don't you find it interesting that neither of you is married yet?"

Mia didn't find it interesting. She found it depressing.

Muriel continued before she could frame an answer. "Sometimes, when we're young, we don't quite grasp the important things in life. It's like trying to grab an apple that's out of reach."

"If it's out of reach, maybe you're not meant to have it," Mia said. And maybe that was why things had never worked out between Colin and her. They weren't meant to be together.

"Or maybe you need to stand on tiptoe and try again?"

"So you think Colin and I should try again?"

Muriel turned and studied her. "Do you still love him?"

Mia's face flamed. "I don't know." *Liar!* "No one's ever affected me the way he does. Did," she quickly corrected herself. "But he's with someone else now."

"It's not serious, though. Justine told me that was a condition of the will. Neither one of you could be in a serious relationship."

Mia gnawed on her bottom lip. That might be what the will stipulated, but here was Colin always on the phone with this other woman. And yet when he was with her... Oh, she didn't know what to think.

"Mia, would you take a little friendly advice?"

Right now she'd take any advice, friendly or otherwise. She nodded.

"I've had two husbands, both wonderful men. And if there's one thing I've learned, it's that true love is rare."

True love? Did she and Colin ever have that? If their love was so true, why didn't they stay together? She couldn't help remembering how quick he'd been to break up with her. And how quickly she'd moved on. Except her move hadn't taken her where she wanted to go.

"Oh, there's the kind of love you settle for," Muriel continued. "But the gold standard kind of love, the soul-searing, true-love variety, that's pretty rare. It's also fragile. It bruises easily. The pain can be as large as the joy. And it can be snatched from you in an instant," she added, her voice almost a whisper.

After being widowed twice, Muriel would know.

"You have to fight for it, Mia," she said, laying a delicate hand on Mia's arm. "It's worth fighting for. Don't give up, and don't settle."

She'd done both years ago. The only thing she'd stuck with was her job. Granted, it had its rewards—a nice, fat paycheck and a feeling of accomplishment—but when she compared her life to Grandma Justine's and Aunt Beth's and Muriel Sterling's, she didn't feel she'd accomplished very much.

She reminded herself that she still had time. But—

"What's worth fighting for?" Colin asked, coming out onto the patio, interrupting her thoughts.

"Love," Muriel said. "I was just telling Mia what a rare commodity true love is."

And easily traded away, Mia thought sadly.

"But enough of me philosophizing. On to your mission. Let's send you to your next destination. I've got it inside."

They followed her back into the house and she produced yet another pink envelope. "I think what you find next will prove very inspiring."

They thanked her, then went out to the car, Colin getting behind the wheel, Mia in the passenger seat, opening the envelope.

"Okay, now what?" he asked.

"'You'll find more words than you can ever read here,'" Mia read. "'You'll also find your next clue.'" She tapped her chin. "More words. It's got to be either the library or the bookstore, don't you think?"

"For sure. Which one do you want to try first?"

"How about the library?"

He nodded and turned the car toward the Icicle Falls Public Library. Millie the librarian was on duty. She'd been ruling over the library shelves, silencing chatty patrons, since Mia and Colin were kids.

She smiled at the sight of them. "Mia and Colin, I haven't seen you two in here in a long time," she said in her muted librarian's voice. "I'm sorry about your grandmother. She was a lovely woman. Helped out with all our Friends of the Library sales, right up until the week before she died, God rest her soul."

Was there anything Justine Wright *hadn't* been involved with in this town? Mia hoped that when she reached her golden years, she could do even half as much as Justine had.

"Thanks," Colin said, keeping his voice library-low. "She's actually sent us on a sort of hunt for something. Did she, by any chance, leave a clue for us?"

Millie shook her head. "I don't think so. What kind of clue?"

Obviously, the library hadn't been part of the treasure hunt. "It must be hiding somewhere else," Mia said. "Thanks, anyway."

"You're welcome," Mille said, looking thoroughly puzzled.

"So I guess it's the bookstore," Colin said, and they crossed the highway and ducked down into the main part of town where Mountain Escape Books was located.

Please, God, this has to be the last clue, Colin thought as he and Mia made their way to Mountain Escape

Books. Lorelei was getting restless and trying to pin him down on a time he'd be meeting her for dinner and the promised dancing, and that was making him antsy. He wanted to be done as much as she wanted him to be. This crazy treasure hunt needed to be over, and Mia needed to be gone. Out of sight, out of mind.

Except she'd never really been out of his mind. Every time a woman tried to get close to him, he remembered the hurt and rejection he'd experienced when he lost her and wound up backing out of the relationship. When he was between girlfriends, he thought of her and wondered what she was doing. How she was doing. He feigned a complete lack of interest if Aunt Beth mentioned her, but grabbed any scraps of information she dropped, eager as a crow.

Now here they were together, running all over town, visiting various landmarks of their past, and like Lorelei, he kept asking, *When will this be done?*

He was so busy turning everything over in his mind, he didn't hear his old pal Billy Williams calling his name until Mia nudged him. He looked up to see Bill Will galloping toward him, cowboy hat pushed back on his head and a Bavarian Brews coffee in his hand.

"Dude, I've been hollerating at you for half a block," Bill Will said once he caught up to them.

"Sorry," Colin said. "I didn't hear you." And they gave each other a bro hug complete with back slaps.

Bill Will turned his attention to Mia. "Hi, Mia. What are you doing in town?" Then understanding dawned. "Aw, shit, of course. Hey, I'm sorry about

Grandma J. I woulda come to the funeral, but I had to work. Let me take you guys out tomorrow night for a beer. We can have a wake."

"Thanks," Colin said, "but I don't know if I'll still be here."

"Well, damn. I'd haul you off tonight. I bet you guys have plans, though. Just like old times, huh? Are you—"

"No," Colin and Mia both said.

"I've got a girlfriend," Colin added.

Bill Will nodded, taking that in. "Is she up here? Maybe we could all go out tonight. Andy and me and his girlfriend and whoever else I can scare up are going to the Red Barn. Right now I'm working on a hot little redhead I met over at Bavarian Brews. She's got this shit of a boyfriend who keeps ignoring her."

Redhead, shit of a boyfriend… "Where is she now?" Colin asked.

"Over there." Bill Will turned and waved at the hot redhead seated in the gazebo in the little town park.

She was wearing tight jeans and a low-cut black top and holding a drink. Even from where he stood, Colin could see that her smile was meant for him and it said, *Take that, you shit.*

"That's my girlfriend," Colin said in disgust.

Bill Will's eyes bugged. "*You're* the shit?"

Yeah, when it came right down to it, that about described him.

Bill Will watched as she came over. He blew out a breath and shook his head. "Man, I didn't know. Honest, Col."

"No worries," Colin assured him. "I see you met one of my buddies," he said to Lorelei when she joined them.

"I guess this is a small town," she said, slipping an arm through Colin's while smiling at his friend. "Billy was telling me about what you all do for fun up here."

Billy was frowning now. "You didn't tell me Colin was your shitty boyfriend."

Lorelei had the grace to blush, but she brazened it out. "You didn't ask me. So this Red Barn sounds like fun. Is that where you're taking me dancing?" she asked Colin.

At the moment he wasn't sure he wanted to take her anywhere. But he'd promised. "Yeah," he said reluctantly.

"Well, then," she said to Bill Will. "I guess we'll see you there. You can teach me how to two-step."

"Colin knows how to two-step," Bill Will said. "Mia, you going, too? Save me a dance, okay?" Then he clapped Colin on the back, tipped his hat to Mia and hurried off down the sidewalk.

"Were you flirting with him?" Colin demanded. Jeez, was there a woman anywhere on the planet who could be trusted?

"So what if I was?" she shot back. "You've been ignoring me ever since I got here."

Mia stepped away, taking a sudden interest in the novelty hats displayed in the shop two doors down.

"I don't know how many times and how many ways

to say this, but Mia and I are sharing an inheritance and we're trying to find it."

"So go find it already," Lorelei said, shooing him away with a flick of her hand. "Then maybe we can finally do something and I won't die of boredom."

"Well, I guess if you get too bored, you can always pick up another one of my friends," he said, and turned his back on her. "Come on, Mia, let's get over to the bookstore."

"Yeah, you're gonna find buried treasure in a bookstore," Lorelei sneered.

Mia was nice enough not to comment on the latest Lorelei incident as they walked away, but he could imagine what she was thinking. It was the same thing he was thinking. *What are you doing with her?*

Pat York, the bookstore owner, came out from her little back office to greet them. She had a few more wrinkles these days, but other than that she looked the same as she always had, tall with that auburn hair, wearing a black skirt, turquoise blouse and a necklace made of blue-and-green stones. She had to be over sixty now, but she still looked classy.

She seemed especially delighted to see Mia, who had been a regular customer back when she lived in town. "How have you been?" she wanted to know. "Do you like it on the East Coast?"

Of course she did. Otherwise she would've come home.

"I do. It's a little faster paced than here."

"I can imagine. Beth tells me you've been very successful."

Unlike him. He prayed Pat wouldn't ask him how his life was going.

"I must say I do love the rich history the east has, but I think we have the best of all worlds right here in our little mountain town," Pat said.

"Yes, you do," Mia agreed.

"And Colin, it's nice to see you back in town."

Now she was going to ask him how he was doing. *Ask me in a couple of years. Maybe by then I'll have my shit together.*

"You still like living in Seattle?" Pat asked.

He hadn't found his inheritance yet, but he had discovered one thing. He didn't belong in Seattle. He belonged here with the people he cared about. "I think I'm ready for a change." More than ready.

"Change is good," Pat said. "And at your age, life is still in flux."

Was that what you called it? Anyway, that sounded better than not knowing what the heck you were doing.

Chitchat finished, Pat got down to business. "Is there something I can help you with?"

"I think so," Colin said. "Do you have anything for us from my grandma?"

"As a matter of fact, I do." She went behind the checkout counter, which was loaded with all manner of merchandise like pens and bookmarks, and pulled out—surprise, surprise—a long pink envelope and gave it to Colin. "You might want to open that here," she suggested as he turned to leave.

"So our hunt is in here somewhere?" Mia asked.

Pat leaned her elbows on the checkout counter and smiled.

Colin opened the envelope and read, "'Talk to Pat.'"

Well, dear, I'm settling into the new house just fine. I should have enough money left from the sale of the orchard to pay for Gerald's care and keep this little place. Bethie would rather I moved in with her, but I want to hang on to my independence as long as possible. She already does so much for me. She doesn't need me underfoot day and night on top of that. I'm sure I wore her and Dylan to the bone moving me out of the old place.

It was hard to lose the orchard and our old house. We made so many happy memories there. But you can take your memories with you wherever you go, and the family will make new ones here. I'm attaching some pictures of my new digs. Don't you love how fast and easy it is to share pictures by email? I'm so glad you kept after me to do this.

I know it broke Colin's heart to see the orchard go, but what else could I do? I'd gone through our savings. Anyway, a very nice couple has bought the place, and seeing how excited they are takes away some of the sting of losing it. We haven't told Gerald. There's no point, since he's not getting any better and will probably remain where he is. If I told him, it would only upset him. If he does get well enough to come home, I guess we'll cross that bridge when we come to it.

I'm glad to hear Joey's operation was a success. The pacemaker should solve his problems.

That's it for now. I have more boxes to unpack and I need to get over to the nursing home to see Gerald.

Love,
Justine

Chapter Fifteen

Talk to Pat. That was simple enough. "It looks like you're our next clue," Colin said.

"It so happens that I am. I knew your grandmother for years. She was quite the woman."

Yeah, she was. And now she was gone. She'd never see him get married, never meet his kids, never see him…go somewhere in life. That made him feel doubly sad.

"And she thought you were quite the special young man. She bragged about you, about what a help you were to your grandfather with the orchard, how you pitched right in when the men were putting the addition on your church."

A lot of the teen boys had helped. That was nothing special. And all this talk about his grandmother was making his chest hurt. "No offense, Mrs. York, but could you just give us our next clue?"

"No offense taken. I'm sorry, though. I can't. Your grandmother warned me you wouldn't have the patience to stand around and talk. However, I'm afraid that's what you're going to have to do."

Colin frowned, feeling both chastised and annoyed. Out of the corner of his eye he could see Mia biting back a smile. He sighed. "Okay, what else are you supposed to tell us?"

"A little more about your grandmother. How much do you know of her life after your grandfather died?"

What was there to know? She hung out with the church ladies, baked apple pies and asked about his love life every time she saw him. He shrugged.

"Funny how easy it is to think of old people as not really having a life. Their job is to exist on the periphery of ours, to cheer us on and admire our exploits. But your grandmother wasn't the kind of woman to sit on the sidelines, even after she reached an age when people might have thought that was all she was good for. Your grandmother had her share of losses, as we all do if we live long enough, but she never stopped living life to the fullest. Two shop owners here in town are still in business because she lent them money when they were struggling. And she was writing a cookbook with Beth. Did you know that?"

"No," Mia said. "I wonder why Aunt Beth hasn't told me."

"Well, she's had other things on her mind lately," Pat said. "Anyway, they were going to self-publish it and sell it here in the store. I do hope Beth completes it."

"I do, too," Mia said.

So did Colin. All those delicious things Gram made—it would be great to have them in writing so they didn't get lost. More than that, though, it would be like keeping part of her alive and with them.

"And she had a secret," Pat continued.

"What kind of secret?" Mia asked.

"I can't tell you yet. But I *can* tell you that you'll get closer to learning it if you look in the nonfiction section," Pat said, pointing to a far corner of the store.

"So our clue's in one of those books?" Colin asked.

"Yes, it is," said Pat.

"That's a lot of books."

"Yes, it is. Don't make a mess while you're looking."

"If you want to take off, I can look and then call you when I find something," Mia offered. "I know this is complicating things for you."

Things being Lorelei. He wondered what she was doing now. And who she was doing it with.

But tired as he was of the game, there was no way he was leaving it. Anyhow, he wanted to know what Gram's big secret had been.

"Come on," he said, and trudged to the nonfiction section.

"If you start at the top, I can start at the bottom over here," Mia said, pointing a couple of shelves over. "Then we can meet in the middle."

"Works for me," Colin said, and took a cookbook from the shelf. Gram writing a cookbook. Who knew?

There was nothing in the book. He picked up another. Nothing in that one, either, or the next three.

He moved on to books on knitting and struck out there, as well.

Now he understood the meaning of that old saying about looking for a needle in a haystack. Mountain Escape Books carried books on every imaginable subject—gardening, health, money management, business, how to lose weight, how to gain confidence. Several shelves were dedicated to biographies of everyone from Nikola Tesla to Charles Dickens, not to mention the latest reality show celebs. One of these books would have a folded piece of pink stationery between its pages. The cookbooks and gardening books were probably the best bet. Hopefully, he'd stumble on it in a few minutes.

Half an hour later, he'd gone through every cookbook, gardening book, sewing book, do-it-yourself book and self-help shrink book on the shelves, and nothing. Mia wasn't having any luck, either. And, checking the time on his phone, he saw they were down to fifteen minutes until the store closed.

He was about to return the phone to his pocket when Lorelei called. "Are you still in that bookstore?" she demanded.

"Yes."

"Well, are you about done?"

"No." He was never going to be done. He was going to spend the rest of his life wandering around Icicle Falls looking for clues, like some old miner searching for El Dorado.

"Well, how much longer?"

He could feel a pain starting behind his eyes. To match the pain in the butt at the other end of the call. "I'm not psychic, Lorelei. I have no way of knowing." Why did he feel that every time they talked they were covering old ground? "I told you not to come."

"Yeah, and I think you did that so you could mess

around with some old girlfriend," Lorelei snapped. This from the woman who was picking up guys in Bavarian Brews?

Patience, never Colin's strong suit, vanished. "Damn it all, Lorelei, it's enough that I have to deal with losing my grandma and wandering all over town remembering things I'd like to forget. I don't need you ragging on me on top of everything else."

"Ragging on you? *Ragging* on you?"

Maybe that reaction had been a little extreme. "Okay, I'm sorry."

"Well, sorry doesn't cut it. I've about had it with you."

"Yeah? Well, I've about had it with you, too." The words were barely out of his mouth when he realized he'd just committed romantic suicide.

"Are you breaking up with me?" Lorelei's voice was dangerously quiet.

This wasn't how he'd meant to have that important conversation. But they'd been edging toward it ever since she came up here, ever since he'd looked around his hometown and started opening his eyes. And his heart. He and Lorelei didn't belong together. If he was going to be honest with himself, he'd have to admit that, deep down, he'd known it for some time. He'd blamed his reluctance to buy a ring on cold feet. Not ready to give up his freedom, wanting to be sure. Blah, blah. That wasn't really the problem, though. He'd liked Lorelei a lot. Okay, maybe not so much since she'd come to town and started driving him nuts. But liking wasn't the same as loving. He was only hanging on for something to hang on to. Dumb. And unfair to her.

He softened his voice. "Lorelei..."

"What?" Not the sweet, soft voice of reconciliation.

That was just as well. "It's not working between us, you know that."

"It was until you came up here," she insisted.

Yeah, it sort of had been. But in the end they would have split. They were destined to go down different paths in life, and regardless of what he found or didn't find on this crazy hunt, he knew his path led back to Icicle Falls. And Mia. Always Mia. No matter what he did, no matter how he tried to escape the fact, he was bound to her, heart and soul. Time and distance hadn't changed that. So hanging on to one woman when you were in love with another—not the right thing to do.

"Look, I'm gonna end up here. You want to be in Seattle. You want a gym, I want an orchard."

"A what? Since when?"

"Since I was a kid."

"You never told me."

There was so much he hadn't told her, whole sections of his life she had no idea about. He'd never told, she'd never asked. What did that say about them? "We don't belong together." He looked at Mia as he said this. She was kneeling in front of a row of biographies. She had a book open and was staring at it. Was she hearing what he was saying? Did what he was saying matter to her?

"I came all this way for you," Lorelei said as if she'd

followed him to another country instead of a couple of hours across the state.

"I'm sorry. It looks like you wasted your time."

"A lot of it. You are such a loser, Colin."

Yeah, he was, but he was hoping to change that. "I'm sorry I hurt you."

"You know what? I don't need you," Lorelei informed him. "I've got executives hitting on me at the gym all the time. Executives! And I bet one of them will want to invest in a fitness club."

"I hope you find one who does," he said, and he meant it. Even though he didn't want to be with her anymore, he still wanted her to be happy. He wanted both of them to be happy.

She made one final snort of disgust and then the line went dead. He pushed End and shoved the phone back in his pocket.

Mia looked at him. "Did you just break up?"

"Seems that way." Lorelei was right. He really was a shitty boyfriend.

Mia frowned.

"What?" What was she thinking?

"Nothing. That seemed a little sudden is all, kind of like a volcano erupting. Are you sure you want to do that?"

He'd hated wounding Lorelei's pride—but yes, he was sure. "Volcanoes don't erupt suddenly," he said. "It only looks like it because you don't see all the stuff building under the surface." And there'd been more building under the surface than he'd wanted to admit.

Mia's gaze shifted away from him. "Is that what happened with us?"

He squatted down next to her. "I honestly don't know. Sometimes I look back and try to sort it all out, and it's like a maze I can't find my way through."

"You might wind up thinking that about what just happened with Lorelei, too." Now she did look up, her expression earnest. "You don't want to do something you'll regret. Call her back, tell her you made a mistake. Go meet her for drinks. I can finish here."

He shook his head. "No, that would only drag things out. We weren't right for each other. It wouldn't be fair to keep stringing her along."

"Are you *sure*?"

"Yeah. I've made lots of mistakes, but this isn't one of them. Want me to tell you how I know?"

She bit her lip and nodded, her gaze locked with his.

"Because I'd rather be here with you than hanging with Lorelei." He winced. What man in his right mind hit on his ex the minute after he'd broken up with his girlfriend?

Mia pressed her lips together and returned the book to the shelf.

"I know that sounds bad," he said, "but it's the truth." She still didn't say anything so he pressed on. "Have I just been imagining something happening between us these last few days?"

"Colin, I don't want my heart broken again."

Wait a minute. *He* was the one who'd had his heart broken. He was about to say so when Pat approached them. "Closing time, you two."

"But we're not done," Colin protested.

"You are for today."

"Can't you stay open a little longer?" he pleaded, offering his most ingratiating smile.

She smiled back.

Good. Success.

"Afraid not, even for you. We have a big wine-tasting party over at D'Vine Wines and I promised my husband I'd be there. I'm afraid you'll have to come back on Monday. I'm sure you two can find something to do over the weekend."

Wouldn't you know? The bookstore was one of the few shops that wasn't open on Sundays. But maybe that wasn't such a bad thing. There was no Lorelei waiting for him now. Colin was free to spend the rest of the weekend with his family. And Mia. Most important, Mia.

"Monday?" Mia repeated weakly. "I have to be back at work on Monday. I'm supposed to fly out tomorrow."

Pat looked surprised. "So soon?"

"I left Chicago on Wednesday."

"I would've thought you'd be able to take a week," Pat said. "I give that much to my employees when there's been a death in the family."

Mia was shaking her head.

"You must have some vacation time," Pat persisted.

"I can't afford to take time right now. We're working on an important project."

"I'm sure your boss would understand," Pat said gently. "I know I would."

"You couldn't let us in on Sunday for a while?" Colin asked.

"Sorry, I really can't. Ed and I will be in Seattle for my daughter's birthday, and I know all my employees have plans. If it'll help, you can come in before we open on Monday. I'll be here at eight." She looked at her watch. The store phone rang and a moment later Theresa, her right-hand woman, called, "Pat, Ed wants to know if you're on your way."

"Tell him yes," said Pat. "Sorry, kids. I hope you can work this out."

So did Colin. How were they going to finish their search if she had to leave? How were they going to put their lives back together?

Mia reluctantly took her phone out of her purse. How did you tell your boss that you wouldn't be back in the office on Monday as promised because you were in the middle of a treasure hunt? It sounded so crazy. And even if she was searching for a million dollars, she wasn't sure Andrea would understand. As far as Andrea Blackburn was concerned nothing was more important than the marketing of GF Markets products. Mia knew she needed to show her own dedication, especially now that she was in charge of marketing Sprouted Bliss.

"If you can't stay, don't worry. I'll finish the search and split whatever I find fifty-fifty," Colin said.

"Really?"

He nodded.

"But we're supposed to do this together."

"We have been. In fact, you've figured out most of the clues. It's about time I pulled my weight. Anyway, if you've got to get back…"

She did. That shiny new job on the next rung of the corporate ladder could be as easily caught by any number of people. Still…

"Then go. I promise I won't screw you over."

So there it was, permission to leave, to return to Chicago, to the life she was building, a safe life with no heartbreak. She liked Chicago. And so what if there was no man waiting for her there? She'd find someone— eventually.

Except that here in Icicle Falls, she'd found someone, the same someone who'd always been part of her life. What would the future hold if she stayed just a little longer? Was it worth the gamble? What if they hurt each other all over again? Colin seemed to have a habit of abruptly breaking up with women.

But…anything could happen. Mia made her decision. "No," she said. "I need to abide by the stipulations of the will."

He smiled and, oh, there went the tingles. "Okay, then."

Mia called Andrea's extension at the office and got her voice mail. There was the beep. She took a deep breath and plunged in. *Keep it vague*, she decided, *and hope you don't get fired.* "Andrea, I'm afraid we've run into a snag with the will, and I'm going to be delayed getting back. I'm so sorry. I'll check in with you on Monday. I'm sure I can be in the office by Wednesday."

"You really didn't have to do that," Colin said.

"I know." But she'd wanted to. And oh, dear, what did that say about her?

She hoped they could wrap this up quickly on Monday. If she could fly out by Tuesday, she'd probably be fine. Things happened. Life didn't always go according to plan. Her boss was hardworking and driven and yes, she expected everyone else on her team to be the same, but she wasn't like Miranda Priestly in *The Devil Wears Prada*. She had a heart, and surely she understood the importance of family. She had a…cat.

Oh, boy. There was a reason many of the executives at the company were young and single. Most of them were married to their jobs.

Well, there was nothing she could do about this. No sense worrying. When it came right down to it she was glad she had a couple more days in Icicle Falls, a little more time to hang out with the Wrights.

And one Wright in particular. Colin was like a magnet. Even though her brain kept worrying that this was a relationship best left in the past, her heart was hopelessly drawn to him.

"I guess we've got the weekend to kill," Colin said as Mia put away her cell phone.

Her cheeks were pink, a sure sign she was feeling nervous. And attracted. What they'd once had was still there, like diamonds waiting to be dug up.

"What do you say we go to Zelda's, sit out on the back patio and have one of those wild huckleberry martinis?"

Now she was nibbling her lip, something *he'd* like

to do. "Okay," she said and he felt he'd scored some kind of major victory. "Let's stop by the house first so I can freshen up," she added.

"Okay," he agreed, but she looked perfectly fresh to him. In fact, she looked great. And he had her for another day. He didn't want her to leave Icicle Falls until they'd sorted things out between them.

"So you're stuck here for a little longer," Aunt Beth said when they returned to the house and gave her their progress report. The smile on her face showed how bad she felt about that.

"Looks like it," Mia said. Then to Colin, "Give me a minute to change and call the airline."

"Since you two have the rest of the weekend free," Aunt Beth said, "should I make dinner?"

"No. We're going to grab something at Zelda's."

His aunt smiled approvingly. "Good idea."

Beth had known it all along—those two were meant to be together. Something had shifted between them. She could see it in the way they looked at each other.

Mom, you're a genius.

As soon as they left, she couldn't resist calling Dylan. "Thought I'd report in on the treasure hunters."

"I'm right in the middle of something, Beth."

Curb your enthusiasm. "Fine. Never mind."

"You called. You may as well tell me."

"They stalled out at the bookstore. Now they're on their way to dinner."

"Together."

"Of course together."

The silence on the other end stretched out so long, Beth thought she'd lost the connection. "You still there?"

"Yes, I'm here. Did *you* suggest they go out to eat?" he asked suspiciously.

"No. I didn't need to. They came up with it all on their own."

"With a little help from you, I'm sure."

"I didn't need to help. They want to be together. They always have."

"If they had, they would've stayed together. I need to talk to him."

Her brother was such a dope sometimes. "Don't mess this up, Dylan."

"It's already messed up. Thanks to you and Mom."

She could almost feel the anger sizzling through the phone. "No, it's not. Let things run their course and it'll all work out."

"Beth, you live in a fairy tale. Things don't always work out. People get hurt. I know you helped raise Colin, but he's still my son. Maybe you could remember that."

And then he was gone.

"And maybe you could remember that he's a grown-up and gets to make his own decisions without any interference from you," Beth muttered. Honestly, when it came to love, her brother suffered from terminal blindness.

It was only five thirty when Colin and Mia walked into the popular restaurant, but the place was already filling up. He asked to be seated on the huge patio. It was a relatively new addition to the restaurant and featured tables with umbrellas and a spectacular mountain view.

Rita Reyes brought them their drinks. "It's about time you came back," she said to them. "Nobody really leaves here for good, you know," she teased.

"So I hear," Colin said. And he understood the reason for that. Was there a better place on earth to replant your roots, regrow your life…climb right back into the pit of love you fell into when you were a teenager?

Mia sipped her drink and stared at the mountains. She hadn't made eye contact with him since the bookstore.

"You have to look at me at some point," he said.

She set down her glass, turned her head and met his gaze with those gorgeous big brown eyes. "I'm looking."

"You seem nervous."

"I *am* nervous. What are we doing?"

Starting again? "You tell me." He hoped she'd agreed to go out with him for the same reasons he'd asked her.

"I don't know. You just broke up with someone."

He took a slug of his drink. Too damned sweet. He set it down. "I told you why. It was all wrong. Every woman I've been with since you has been wrong."

"Still…"

"Okay, let's think of this as a dinner between old friends. Nothing wrong with wanting to be with an old friend."

"No, there isn't," she said. "Why don't you call Andy?"

"Because Andy doesn't have breasts."

Okay, that hadn't gone over well. She scowled at him and stood.

He caught her arm. "Come on, Mia. Please. Stay. I was being a smart-ass. Let's hang out like we used to." *About a million years ago.*

She gave a long-suffering sigh and dropped back into her chair. "We could get hurt all over again."

"Maybe," he acknowledged. "Or not. Maybe we, no, make that me—maybe I could grow up and not be so quick to jump to conclusions. I could change."

She half smiled at that. "Yeah?"

"Yeah. And maybe you could forgive me for all the times I've been a shit."

The smile was still there. "I'll have to think about it."

"Think about it over dinner."

She nodded. "Okay."

For dinner they enjoyed trout and truffle-baked potatoes, and memories of the fun they'd had in their childhood. They only basked in the good memories, leaving the door closed on the darker times and the misunderstandings. Conversation flowed easily, washed along by a nice Riesling. For dessert they split a piece of wild blackberry pie with ice cream.

There was something so intimate about digging forks into the same plate, and watching her lick her fork was torture. His biggest barrier—Lorelei—was gone and now he was ready for bed. With Mia. Totally inappropriate, considering the fact that he'd just broken up with someone. As she'd pointed out...

But what about going dancing? Was that inappropriate? They didn't have much time before she flew back to Chicago. He needed to make the most of it. "You know, I was supposed to go to the Red Barn tonight."

She stopped her licking and studied her fork. "You could still go."

"I don't want to go by myself."

She set the fork down and looked at him. "You just broke up. Remember?"

Yes, and he wished she wouldn't keep reminding him of that. "Which makes me a free man."

"Which makes you a mess."

"I told you, I've been a mess ever since we split, and that's the truth."

She leaned back in her chair and regarded him. "Do you know how different things could have been?"

If he hadn't been such a fool. Oh, yeah, he had a pretty good idea. "Let's go dancing."

The Red Barn was actually an old barn, converted to a honky-tonk. It had a huge wooden dance floor, a long bar that served plenty of beer, whiskey and tequila, as well as soft drinks for the serious dancers. It also had a life-size plastic Jersey cow stationed inside the front entrance and framed photos of old barns hanging on the walls. If the name of the place hadn't been enough of a clue, the cow sure was. No one came in here expecting anything but rockin' country music.

Fortified with bottles of Hale's Ale, they made their way to a corner table. The band wasn't due to come on for another hour, but the place was packed, and the jukebox was cranked up. "Hey," she said, "there's Bill Will and Andy."

Colin's old pals sat on the far end of the dance floor, at a table for four. Bill Will was a pretty good-looking guy, and since he worked on a guest ranch, his jeans and Western shirt and boots were a perfect fit on all levels. Andy, not so much. He'd lost some weight since Colin last saw him, but he still looked like a nerd playing dress-up in his Western outfit. The little brunette with him didn't seem to care. She laughed at something he said and gave him a playful swat on the arm.

Bill Will caught sight of Mia and Colin and waved, and next thing Colin knew, his old pal was on his way over, towing along a scrawny blonde wearing tight jeans and an even tighter top that really showed off the merchandise. Andy and his plump little brunette followed in their wake. Then it was greetings all around.

"Glad to see you guys made it," Bill Will said to Colin, slapping him on the back. He leaned over and lowered his voice. "And sorry about, you know."

"Not your fault," Colin told him. "We broke up, so if you want her number…"

Bill Will frowned. "No, that's okay."

Colin nodded. Good call. Bill Will was even less of a match for Lorelei than he'd been. And he sure didn't have any money to invest in a gym.

"Look at this. We're all here just like old times," Bill Will said. With that, he pulled up a chair, introduced his new friend, Cookie, and made himself at home. Andy followed suit and suddenly Colin's cozy twosome was a sixsome.

The only time he was going to get Mia alone would be on the dance floor.

Still, it was good to see the guys. The last couple of times he'd been to town, he'd been too busy to call. At least that was what he'd told them. Really, he'd been too embarrassed to hang out with them and have to confess that he still didn't know what the heck he was doing with his life. Bill Will was happy playing cowboy, and Andy was selling insurance and making a bundle.

"So, have you heard about Neal?" Andy asked as they guzzled beer. Colin shook his head and Andy continued. "Just made partner at that law firm down in California. The youngest one there. I guess he set some kind of record."

"Cool," Colin said and picked at the label on his bottle. Happiness for his old pal mixed with frustration over the fact that he'd accomplished nothing with his life so far, and that made for a cocktail that wasn't pleasant to swallow.

"How's it going in Seattle?" Bill Will asked. "And when are you coming back here?"

"Soon, I hope." Maybe Gram was leaving him enough money for a down payment on a little house somewhere in town or a cabin in the woods. And if so, then he'd…what? Go to work in another warehouse?

Dad had expected more of him, he knew it. He'd hoped Colin would become a lawyer, but Colin had never wanted to draw up wills and power-of-attorney documents, or spend hours cooped up in some office, preparing legal briefs. Even Dad admitted that lawyers were a dime a dozen.

Still, he'd been disappointed to see Colin get a college degree and then go nowhere with it. "Son, you're single and unencumbered. You could do anything you want. Don't just settle."

"I won't," Colin had assured him. "I won't be working in a warehouse forever."

He hoped he hadn't been wrong about that.

The band was on stage now, plugging in their guitars and tuning up. Watching them, Colin couldn't help thinking of Jake O'Brien, a hometown boy who'd stayed true to his dream of becoming a country music songwriter. Jake was rapidly working his way toward becoming a big name, touring with the likes of Dierks Bentley and Jason Aldean.

Meanwhile, Colin was waiting for life to throw open the door to success and say, "Come on in." He needed to stop standing at the door and waiting for it to be opened. He needed to kick the damn thing down.

The band consisted of four guys—one on drums, one on bass and a couple playing guitars. They were a motley collection of locals who, when they weren't playing, drove forklifts and swung hammers.

"Hey, there, everybody," one of the guitar players said into his mike. "You all here for a good time?"

There was plenty of hooting and clapping. Bill Will stuck his fingers in his mouth and whistled.

"Then let's get this party started." The drummer counted the others off, and the band broke into a fast country song.

"Hey, we can do the Kick-Ass to this," Bill Will declared, jumping up from his seat and grabbing his date's hand. "Come on, Mia. You can pick this one up right away."

She, too, got to her feet. "Come on, Colin," she said, and headed for the dance floor, assuming he'd follow.

He didn't. He didn't know very many line dances. Never was into them. After all, what was the point if you couldn't hold the girl? He opted to nurse his beer and watch.

Mia was well worth watching. She was still wearing a short denim skirt and it showed off her legs. She wiggled her butt, did a couple of kicks and a fancy turn, right in sync with everyone else as if she'd been dancing that particular dance forever instead of learning it on the fly. Man, she was cute.

The guy who'd positioned himself next to her thought so, too. He was a big beefy guy with a snake tattooed on his arm. He grinned down at Mia, and Colin frowned. Then he put his hands on her waist and tried to turn the dance into a couple's affair.

That was it, no more sitting and watching. Colin left his drink and quickly got out on the floor, just as a twirl separated Mia from her erstwhile partner, managing to insert himself between her and the slab of cement with legs.

"Hey, pal, what do you think you're doing?" the guy demanded as they all grape-vined three steps to the right.

"Dancing with my girlfriend," Colin said, trying to master that butt-shaking kick thing.

"I didn't see her out here with you," said the guy, and gave Colin a shove.

He was in the middle of a turn, and the shove sent him spinning. Great. He'd invented a new step, the turkey shuffle. He was vaguely aware of Mia saying, "Hey, don't you be doing that."

He righted himself just in time to see her kick the guy in the shin. Wow. She'd come a long way from the timid kid she'd once been.

She left the dance line and came over to Colin. "Let's dance."

He was about to spin her into a classic swing step when the oversize pest limped past, using a very ungentlemanly term about Mia.

Okay, nobody talked to a woman like that, especially a sweet woman like Mia. Colin grabbed him by the arm. "What did you say?"

"You heard me," the guy growled and shook off his arm.

Colin grabbed it again. "You apologize to the lady."

"The hell I will," said the mountain.

"You'd better if you don't want to wind up eating your teeth," Colin snarled. He worked out at the gym. He could take this guy.

If he could keep his balance. The mountain gave him another shove, sending him into a dancer behind him. "Hey, watch it!" The guy shoved Colin back to the mountain, who was ready for him.

Next thing Colin knew, he was swinging wildly, hoping to connect with the big ugly's jaw, and Bill Will had entered the fray, along with the dancer Colin had crashed into. Then Andy was in there, risking life and limb and glasses. Fists were flying and so were a couple of beer bottles, and then someone even bigger than the mountain had Colin by the shirt collar and was reminding him where the front door was. And Mia was running along behind, protesting that Colin hadn't started it.

"We don't care who starts it," said the bouncer. "Our job's to finish it."

Finish it they did, with all three couples, as well as the mountain and a few other brawlers, suddenly out in the cold.

"Dude, that was fun," Bill Will said as the mountain stomped off to his truck.

"I was so worried you'd get hurt," Andy's little brunette said, clutching his arm.

"It takes more than a punch or two to hurt me," Andy said, puffing out his chest. His glasses were bent and his hair was sticking out in all directions, but he was smiling. This was probably the most excitement he'd had in years and, judging by the way his date was looking at him, there'd be more excitement to come.

"Hey, let's all head over to Zelda's," Bill Will suggested.

That could go on all night. Colin had wanted to dance with Mia, get a chance to hold her in his arms. At the rate the evening was going, *that* wouldn't happen. "Another time, guys," he said. "Thanks for jumping in back there," he added, and gave both his old pals a parting bro hug.

"Anytime," Andy said, making the most of his moment of macho.

"So what was all that about?" Mia asked as they walked to the car. "Don't tell me you were jealous."

"What do you think?"

"I think some things never change." Her smile wasn't quite so teasing.

He didn't want an argument about their past coming between them, not tonight. He decided to give it the boot. "I guess I was always a little crazy where you were concerned. And stupid," he added before she could say it. "I'm over being stupid." She was leaning against the car now, looking up at him. He put his arms around her. "We never did get to dance."

"We were kind of busy."

"Yeah, but I really wanted to dance with you." He opened the car door, reached inside and turned on the radio. Sam Smith was singing "Stay With Me." Colin held out a hand. "How about a dance right now?"

She let him draw her against him and they started swaying. Someone left the Red Barn and the music leached out the open doors. The band was singing "Love You Like That," and suddenly lyrics about love were all around them. "You still feel so good in my arms," he whispered and tightened his hold.

What would have happened, Mia wondered, if she'd flown back to Icicle Falls all those years ago and refused to leave until they had everything ironed out between them?

Never mind that. She had *now*, and now was what

mattered. She slipped her arms around his neck and laid her head on his shoulder. With every step, every breath that ruffled her hair, the connection grew stronger, along with the pull to forget about career success and come home. And yet she'd worked so hard for it. She needed it, needed to finish what she'd started. Surely Colin would relocate for a few years.

She decided not to bring up the subject. Tonight was perfect. Why risk ruining it?

The dance ended and, for a moment, she thought he was going to kiss her. She was sure she'd felt the brush of his lips at her temple. Instead, he whispered, "Let's go."

They didn't go home, though. The car seemed to have a mind of its own, taking them to Memory Lane, that little road hidden from the world. Colin turned off the engine and faced her. He reached out a hand and played with a lock of her hair. "I want to make it work this time."

So did she. She almost said it. Almost. But first they needed to get something straight once and for all. "You know why it didn't work last time. You didn't trust me. I never cheated on you with Arthur. Never. And the only reason I wound up with him was because, well, he hung in there and you didn't."

"I was a fool," he said.

"In the end, though, I couldn't marry him. I guess it was like with you and Lorelei. We weren't a fit." His hand slid down to her neck, gently brushing her skin. *Ooh, do that some more.*

"It's always been you," he said. "I've tried to find

someone else. What a waste of time. I'm tired of wasting my time, Mia. Tired of wasting my life. I want to get things right. I want to do something worthwhile, and I want to do it with you."

He was already coaxing her toward him for a kiss but his words stopped her. "What exactly do you mean by that?"

"What do you mean, what do I mean?"

"How do we make that work?" Did she give up her job and come home an almost-success and hope that was good enough?

"We'll find a way," he said, and kissed her.

She closed her eyes and tried to imagine what their life would be like. All she could see was his father's disapproving face.

The next day the family, with the exception of Dylan, went to church. More people wanted to hug and commiserate. Some simply wanted to make sure they had the inside scoop on what was going on with the Wrights.

"Colin, you rascal, we haven't seen you at church in ages. I hope you're not planning on following in your father's footsteps," said Hildy Johnson. "It's important to stay connected to the Lord."

"Yeah, but probably not with some of his followers," Colin said, and it was all Mia could do not to snicker. Hildy was one of those sheep that only the Good Shepherd could love. People had been hoping for years that she'd get lost, but she showed up every Sunday.

She turned her attention to Mia. "And Mia, it's been far too long since we've seen you. Your aunt told me you got a promotion. I guess you'll never come back to Icicle Falls now."

Mia was aware of Colin's gaze and the question behind it. *Will you?*

"I could have moved," Hildy continued. "Thought about going to art school in Seattle after high school. I've always had quite a flair for art." She shook her head, making the slack skin at her chin wiggle. "But you know what they say, love comes in the door and a woman's plans go out the window. So here I am, my talent wasted. But Nils couldn't live without me." She lowered her voice. "I swear, if he didn't have me, that man would put his pants on the wrong way. Ah, well, men will gobble up your life like an anteater gobbles up ants." She gave Colin's cheek a playful pat. "So beware."

"Is there a right way to put on your pants?" Colin whispered when Hildy turned to talk to Aunt Beth, negotiating for a discount on a coat she wanted let out.

"I guess so," Mia replied. Poor Nils. He had to be the most henpecked man in Icicle Falls.

"Maybe while she's at it, Aunt Beth could sew the old bat's mouth shut," Colin muttered.

Hildy did have a gift for irritating people, but Mia suspected there was some truth in what she'd said. Perhaps it didn't matter if plans went out the window. Perhaps, no matter what she planned, it wouldn't ever be good enough.

The ushers finally herded the congregation into the sanctuary, where they settled in and started singing their first hymn, "It Is Well with My Soul." Mia knew the words. She wished she meant them.

She found it difficult to concentrate on the sermon. It was too hard to keep her thoughts in the present when they kept wandering into the future.

After church there was more visiting to be done, more people wanting all the latest on Colin and Mia's lives, as well as speculation over what they'd find on their treasure hunt, which was the talk of the town.

"I think this is why Dad doesn't like to come to church," Colin said as they left. "He'd be fine with God if His people weren't such a pain in the ass."

"They're not all bad. Most people ask about you because they genuinely care."

"Yeah, I guess you're right," he said and placed an arm around her. "As usual," he added with a grin.

Bailey called Mia at Beth's just as the family was walking in the door from church. "You're still in town."

"I am," Mia said.

"I'm sure you're getting ready for a big family dinner, then. I have to go over to Mom's in a little bit, but I thought we could have a quick latte first. The shop's closed on Sundays and Todd's over doing some stuff at the Man Cave, so I actually have some time to breathe. I'd love to see you."

"Same here," Mia said. It had been far too long since she'd hung out with old friends.

"Go ahead," Aunt Beth encouraged her. "Dinner's a couple hours away."

"Looks like I can make that work," she said to Bailey. "I'll see you at Bavarian Brews."

"I've got a better idea. Come by the tea shop and I'll show you around."

Ten minutes later Mia was walking up the steps of the old Victorian that housed Tea Time, Bailey's tea-shop and tearoom. Bailey was waiting to let her in and swung the door open with a flourish. "Welcome to my kingdom of tea."

"It's adorable," Mia said, taking in the tables with their linen tablecloths and bone-china settings, the lace curtains at the window and the shelves displaying chintz teapots and saucers.

"As you can see," Bailey said, leading her into the shop area, "we carry Sweet Dreams chocolates." She pointed to a shelf filled with glass Mason jars containing loose tea, all tied with lavender ribbons. "I'm making a lot of my own tea now. The chocolate mint is a big seller." She pulled one off the shelf and gave it to Mia. "A little welcome-home present."

"Really? Thanks."

"I have ulterior motives," Bailey said with a grin. "Give people a sample and they're hooked. Once you've tried this, I'll have you for life. Come on upstairs. I've got our lattes ready."

She led the way up a wooden staircase with a carved banister. The top landing had a little sitting room with a love seat, coffee table and a couple of chairs. Two large, steaming mugs sat on the coffee table, along with a plate of cookies.

"This is so cute," Mia said, looking at the bookcase with its candles and a wedding photo of Bailey, the old Tiffany-style lamp. "Is this extra seating?"

"Extra seating for Todd and me. We live up here." She handed Mia a mug. "I assume you still like white-chocolate lattes with extra foam."

"Oh, yes." Mia took the mug and glanced around. "It's cozy."

"It'll do for now. We have our master bedroom in the back, and we use the second bedroom as an office. The third one's going to be the nursery," she added with a sly grin.

"You *are* pregnant! I wondered."

Bailey patted the bulge under her top. "I am."

Mia leaned over and hugged her. "I'm so happy for you."

"We're excited. I wasn't in a hurry to get pregnant, you know. I mean, I've been having so much fun with the tearoom. And between that and the Man Cave, we've been superbusy. But I'm ready for a new challenge. And a baby Todd, what's not to like about that?"

"So you know what it is?"

"We're pretty sure it's a boy."

"Wow. I bet your mom's excited," Mia said, trying to ignore the little stab of jealousy. Was she ever going to have a baby bump? She shoved away the thought. Who invited her biological clock to this party, anyway?

"Oh, yeah. She's totally into the grandkid thing. And between Samantha and Cecily's kids, our baby will have lots of cousins to play with." Bailey took a cookie, then slid the plate closer to Mia, who managed to resist the temptation. Barely. "Enough about me. Tell me about you. How's the job?"

"Great. We're marketing a new product and I'm in charge of the campaign."

"You'll probably be president of the company some-day." Bailey picked up the plate and held it in front of Mia. "Come on, you know you want one."

"Or course I do, but I have to say no to *something*. Aunt Beth is stuffing me full of goodies."

"Okay, I'll have to eat yours. I'm eating for two now."

"You've always eaten for two," Mia teased. "I don't know how you stay so skinny."

"Great sex," Bailey said. "Speaking of sex, have you met anybody in Chicago?"

Mia hedged. "I've made some friends."

"Friends with voices lower than yours?" Bailey persisted.

"Maybe I will have a cookie," Mia said. She grabbed one and took a bite. "Oh, wow. This is cookie heaven."

Her feeble attempt to change the subject failed. "So there's nobody amazing in Chicago?"

"There are lots of amazing people in Chicago." Bailey frowned. "I mean men."

"There are. I just haven't found the right one."

"How hard are you looking?"

"Not very," Mia admitted. "Honestly, I'm so busy with work, I don't have time."

"That doesn't sound good."

Mia shrugged. "Well, in a way it is. I'm really doing well at the company."

"I'm glad." Bailey chose another cookie. "I hope

you can come back and visit more often, though. You know, hop on your private plane."

"I'll be sure to do that."

"Seriously, everyone would love to see more of you."

"Don't worry. I plan to make more visits in the future."

"And when the baby's older, we'll come see you in Chicago and stay in your penthouse." Bailey gave her shoulder a playful nudge. "How's the treasure hunt going?" she asked.

"It's been awkward," Mia admitted, "but…" She could feel her cheeks burning. "But good."

"Good as in something's happening between the two of you?"

"Maybe." Hopefully.

"Cecily was right! Did Colin tell you he ran into her in Bavarian Brews?"

"No."

"Well, he did. And she said she had this feeling that you two might get back together."

"Maybe we will," Mia said. Maybe this time things really would work out between them.

They chatted for another twenty minutes, Bailey catching Mia up on how her sisters and their families were doing and Mia talking about life in the corporate world.

"I don't think I'd want your job," Bailey said. "Sounds stressful."

"It's hard work, and I still get nervous when I have to give a presentation, but it's satisfying, too. I like seeing a product I've helped promote catch on."

"Well, I'm going to check out Sprouted Bliss," Bailey promised.

"And I'm going to like Tea Time on Facebook," Mia said. Then she sobered. "I'm sorry I haven't done a better job of keeping in touch."

"That's okay. We've both been busy. We'll do better in the future. And who knows? Maybe you guys will end up moving back here."

"Maybe," Mia said again. Right now that word summed up her whole life. *Maybe*. Maybe at some point, she'd figure out what she was doing.

She returned to Aunt Beth's and joined the family for Sunday dinner—ham and baked beans and coleslaw and a peach pie for dessert. Uncle Mark complimented her. "That was the best dinner this side of heaven," he said.

"Great meal, sis," Dylan agreed, passing his plate to Colin, who was clearing the table.

"And now it's time we got serious," Mark said. He walked to the kitchen junk drawer and produced a pack of cards. "Hearts."

Oh, yes, just like the old days. Except Grandma Justine and Grandpa Gerald weren't there. For a moment Mia wanted to cry. But then the play began and soon she was caught up in the challenge of not taking any points and even shooting the moon, dumping points on her opponents. There was smack talk and laughter, and it felt as if she'd stepped back in time. Until she saw Dylan looking speculatively at her. Oh, yes. Just as if she'd stepped back in time, and not in a good way.

Did anyone tell you I got a raise? Will I ever be good enough for your son?

After a couple of games, Colin suggested a walk and Dylan decided he needed to go home. Uncle Mark was saying something to Colin, and Dylan pulled Mia aside and lowered his voice. "Don't break his heart again."

What about *her* heart? "I wasn't the one," she began.

Dylan stopped her. "I know the story. Just remember, you women have more power than you realize."

Colin was looking at them now and Dylan dropped the subject, along with Mia's arm, kissed his sister and hurried out the door.

"What did Dad say to you?" Colin asked as they went down the front steps.

Part of her wanted to tell him, but that would be tattling, and she didn't want to cause problems between Colin and his father. "Nothing. He just said not to give up on the hunt." He'd probably like nothing better than if she did give up, if she went away and stayed away. His son loved her. Why couldn't he?

Thank you for the beautiful flower arrangement, dear.

The funeral was lovely. So many people turned out to honor Gerald. I was quite overwhelmed. And now I'm quite exhausted. I feel as though I've lost my anchor, and I'm adrift with Gerald gone and another family harvesting our Galas. But life goes on, doesn't it? One set of players leaves the stage and a new cast begins a new story.

As for the rest of my story, I have no idea what it will be. The thought of making a new life is overwhelming, but thank God I have the children. We're all helping each other through this difficult time. Please pray for me.

Love,
Justine

Chapter Sixteen

It was a perfect evening for a walk, the mountain air fresh and cool, making it easy to forget the heat of the day. Colin took Mia's hand as they strolled away from Aunt Beth's house. Neighbors were out on their porches, enjoying the evening, and called out greetings as they strolled past.

"You know, that's one of the things I like about this place," he said. "People know you. They care about you."

"No one cares about you in Seattle?" she teased.

"Don't get me wrong. It's a great city. Lots of stuff going on—the Seahawks, the Mariners. But this…" He wasn't sure he could put it into words. There was something about this place that made him feel connected, as though his life somehow mattered.

"I know what you mean. Icicle Falls is special."

"As special as Chicago?" Did she actually prefer the city to this?

"More special," she admitted. "But Chicago's where my job is. I can't just quit."

Maybe Mia didn't want to quit at all. She was going

places. How far could she go if no one held her back? She deserved to find out. He sure didn't want to be the one to stop her.

He remembered what Hildy Johnson had said. Did all women end up feeling that way, as if men had somehow messed up their lives? Would Mia feel like that if he asked her to come back to Icicle Falls?

There was no point in asking. It wasn't fair. She was the one with the big important job.

"I have a nice apartment," she ventured. "It's right downtown."

"Downtown," he repeated. Not much room to spread out in an apartment. He'd found that out living in Seattle. Of course, he didn't have much to spread—a minimal amount of furniture and his kick-ass sound system, a mix-and-match mess of dishes, some books on horticulture and a couple of Stephen King novels, his bicycle. A guy alone didn't need much space.

But a man with a family, that was different. A man needed tools and a garage and a yard where he could toss the ball with his son. Most of Colin's ball tossing had been done with Uncle Mark, but his dad had gone out with him occasionally. He wanted to be able to do the same thing with his own kids someday. He wanted to help them build a tree house, too. You couldn't build a tree house without a yard. You couldn't have even one measly apple tree without a yard.

How far his life was drifting from what he'd had growing up.

He could adapt. He'd get a good job and they could save up for a house. He had a degree. People didn't care what your degree was in as long as you had one. The important thing was to build a life with Mia.

"What are you thinking?" she asked.

"Huh? Oh, nothing."

"You can't think nothing," she reminded him.

That again. Okay, what *was* he thinking? "Downtown Chicago. Great nightlife." They could go dancing and go out to eat. He'd found places to ride his bike in Seattle. He'd find places to ride in Chicago.

He wouldn't find any orchards, though. No farms, no ranches. There would go the last of his dreams. That realization was like being in a small plane with a failed engine. Here came the ground.

But never mind. You didn't get to keep the life you had as a kid. That was what being a grown-up was all about. He could let go of those old dreams, find new ones. He'd never find another Mia. He brought her hand to his lips and kissed it. They could live in the city and come back to Icicle Falls for holidays.

Only holidays. Yes, he could do this. He offered her a smile.

She was looking pensive. "Okay, now what are *you* thinking?" he asked.

"I'm wondering if we *can* start over. Maybe we've… grown apart."

He stopped and pulled her to him. "Do you really believe that?"

"I don't know," she said. "Just because we were friends growing up doesn't necessarily mean we were meant to be a couple. Maybe we got it all wrong and it was for the best that we broke up."

"I don't believe that," he said. "If we were supposed to be with other people, don't you think we would be by now?" He hurried on before she could answer. "Breaking up was the dumbest thing we ever did. I'm not gonna be that dumb again. I'll get a job in Chicago. We'll make it work this time."

"You told Lorelei you wanted an orchard."

"I want you more." And to prove he meant it, he took her face in his hands and kissed her. Ah, Mia's lips. They were why kissing had been invented. He caught the faintest whiff of her perfume, and it was headier than alcohol. He would follow her to Chicago, to Timbuktu, to the moon.

He kept her standing there on the sidewalk for long minutes as he savored the taste of her mouth, the smell of her hair, the feel of her body pressed against his. There was nothing more important than being together, and he wasn't going to waste time on anyone or anything else.

She was smiling when they finally ended the kiss. Seeing her smile, he felt a swell of emotions that was almost too big for his chest. That feeling, he'd only ever experienced it with Mia. He'd never felt it with Lorelei or with any of the girls he'd dated since they broke up. They were definitely meant to be together.

They turned back to Aunt Beth's house and settled on the porch swing, holding hands and talking the night away, remembering all the good times from their childhood and reliving the highlights of high school.

They didn't go too far into the future, simply agreeing that they'd be together. No matter what, that wasn't going to change.

He gave her one more kiss before finally going home, running his fingers through her hair, imagining that hair spread out on a pillow. Her next to him in bed every night for the rest of their lives. Waking up beside her every morning. Starting weekends with great sex. Oh, yeah. He'd make breakfast on Saturdays—pancakes, his specialty. They'd find some crazy old Formica table like Aunt Beth's to eat at, stick a vase of flowers in the middle of it. Then, someday, there'd be a couple of kids sitting at that table, a boy and a girl. The girl would look exactly like Mia. They'd be happy.

He was smiling when he walked back down the street and turned the corner to his dad's house, smiling when he strode up the front walk, smiling when he let himself in the door.

Dad was in his library, seated in one of the leather chairs, a book in his lap. He looked up at Colin and he wasn't smiling. "Long walk," he observed. It wasn't a pleasant observation.

"Sort of," Colin said evasively, then he started for his room before the bad vibes could devour his happiness.

"Stay a minute," Dad said.

Less than a minute. He sat on the edge of the chair opposite his father. "Dad, whatever you're going to say—"

"You don't know what I'm going to say."

"I can guess."

"You remember how it was the last time you and

Mia broke up. You want to get on that merry-go-round again?"

It didn't have to be a merry-go-round. They'd both grown up. "I love her. I always have."

"I loved your mother. Love's no guarantee."

"It is for us," Colin said and stood. He clenched his jaw and tightened his fists.

Dad looked at him with his usual sober expression. "I'm not saying this to piss you off, son. I'm saying this because I want you to think carefully before you act. I don't want you to make the same mistakes I did. I don't want to see you hurt."

The fight went out of Colin as quickly as it had entered. "I understand that, Dad. But things didn't work without her. I tried."

"Maybe you both know what you want now."

"I think we do."

Dad suddenly took a great interest in studying the bookcase on the opposite wall.

"It's your life. You have to live it."

These last words were hardly a vote of confidence, but they were said with fatherly love, and Colin could at least appreciate that. "Yeah, I do." Then he laid a hand on his father's shoulder to show there were no hard feelings and went upstairs to bed.

He wondered if his father realized that one of his biggest mistakes might have been not giving love a second chance. There were many things he admired about the man—his smarts, the way he looked like he'd stepped right out of the pages of *GQ*, his commitment to his family. Dad had always been busy with work, but he'd also found time to help when he was needed. Colin could still remember him and Uncle Mark up on the roof of the old orchard house for several weekends, laying shingles in the summer heat. He'd helped Gram find the nursing home for Gramps, managed to get Colin through school. And Colin knew he'd helped some of the older people in town, often pro bono. Heck, Dad could've stayed in Seattle and become a hotshot trial lawyer, could have made partner in some firm and pulled in a butt load of money. Instead, he'd come back to Icicle Falls to make sure his son had a good childhood. Yeah, he'd done a lot of things right.

But not love. Dad knew about broken hearts but he knew nothing about mending them.

Mia lay in the old brass bed, watching as the moon and the trees outside cast a shadow puppet show on the ceiling of her old room. A summer breeze danced into the room, tickling the lace curtains at the window and caressing her cheek, whispering, "Welcome back."

What an incredible turn her life had taken. She'd returned to Icicle Falls, her heart laden with grief, and now, tonight, she was brimming with happiness. She touched her fingers to her lips in an effort to bring back the memory of Colin's kisses. His words floated gently at the back of her mind. *We'll make it work this time.*

Of course, he hadn't said *how* they'd make it work. What if they couldn't?

Don't think about that, she told herself. Not tonight. She wasn't going to let so much as a drop of doubt contaminate the way she was feeling now. It had been a long road back to love, and the last thing she wanted was to put up a roadblock just when everything was working out. "More adventures lie ahead today," Aunt Beth said the next morning as they sat at the kitchen table, enjoying early-morning lattes and scones.

Mia finished her scone and Aunt Beth nudged the plate of goodies closer to her. At the rate Mia was going, she'd soon be standing in line behind Hildy, asking Beth to let out her clothes. But now wasn't the time to worry about that, she decided, and helped herself to another.

"Are these going in your cookbook?" she asked.

"So you heard. Pat must have told you."

"I think it's a lovely idea," Mia said. "I hope I'll get a copy."

"You'll get the first one," Beth promised. "It's been great having you back, sweetie."

"It's been great to be back."

Aunt Beth toyed with the rim of her mug. "Would you ever consider moving home for good?"

"After I've had a chance to prove myself with the company."

Aunt Beth nodded. "Ah, yes. The promotion."

The way she said it made it sound more like an inconvenience than an accomplishment. "I worked hard for it," Mia said, stung. Aunt Beth had always been her biggest fan.

"Of course you did."

Maybe she was worried that Mia was somehow deserting Colin. "Colin would be willing to move," she added.

"So, you two have already gotten to that point, have you?"

Mia could feel a flush creeping up her neck. She nodded.

Aunt Beth laid a hand on her arm. "I'm glad. You belong together." She gave a decisive nod. "Whether that means on the East Coast or out here, you'll have to decide." She took a sip of her latte. "I don't think he's meant for the city, though."

"He lives in a city now," Mia pointed out.

"He's drifting in a city now. That's not the same thing."

The sunshine streaming through the kitchen window suddenly didn't seem as warm. Mia sat back and regarded her. "Is there something you're trying to tell me?"

"No. Not really. I suppose, when it comes down to it, Colin's drifting has nothing to do with his location. He needs an anchor and that anchor is you. His grandmother tried to tell him as much."

Obviously, he hadn't listened.

Aunt Beth smiled. "My mother always saw what was best for people long before they did. She also knew what was important."

What did Aunt Beth mean by that? Mia didn't get a chance to ask because her phone rang. Glancing at caller ID, she tensed. She'd been dreading this call, afraid her voice-mail message wouldn't be enough. It was nine in Chicago. She was surprised Andrea had waited this long. She excused herself and left the kitchen, saying a leery hello on her way to the front porch.

She opened the door and found Colin standing there, about to knock, a grin on his face. He looked good enough for a Vanessa Valentine book cover, casual in jeans and boots and a brown T-shirt that lovingly hugged a fine set of pecs.

"Hi," he said just as Andrea said, "Mia, I got your message. What on earth is going on? We expected you back in the office today."

"I know. I'm terribly sorry." She stepped aside to let Colin in.

"Not as sorry as I am. We put you in this position because we thought we could depend on you."

"You *can* depend on me," Mia assured her.

"This is a company that's going places and we expect our employees to be dedicated enough to stay on for the ride. You are dedicated, aren't you, Mia?"

"Of course I am." The way Colin was studying her made Mia feel like a bug being dissected in front of an audience. She turned her back on him. "But there are extenuating circumstances..."

"Someone new has died?"

"No. But like I said, the will—"

Andrea cut her off. "Has, I'm sure, been read by now. Whatever you need to handle can certainly be handled by email."

"Well, not exactly. It's complicated."

"Life is not that complicated when your priorities are in place, Mia, and the only people who make excuses are the ones who aren't team players. Now, are you a team player or aren't you?"

"Yes, I am. Of course I am." Hadn't she proved it these last five years?

"Good. I'm sorry for your loss and I'm glad you were able to see your family, but now I expect you back here. Find a flight that's going out later today. I need you in the office tomorrow. Actually, I needed you here today."

"T-tomorrow?" Mia stuttered. How was she going to make that work? They still had clues to follow. "I don't know if I can do that."

"Then I don't know if we can have you in charge of the Sprouted Bliss campaign."

Andrea would remove her just like that? After she'd worked so hard for the company? After all those sixty-hour weeks?

"I stuck my neck out for you, Mia. Don't let me down. Don't let GF Markets down."

"I won't."

"Good."

Mia could hear the smile in her boss's voice. At least someone was happy. She ended the call and started searching online for cheap flights out.

"I guess your boss doesn't get it, huh?" Colin said.

She kept her eyes on her phone screen, not wanting to look at him. She wasn't sure what she'd see in his eyes, but she plainly heard disappointment in his voice.

"I was supposed to be back today."

"Things happen."

"Try telling that to my boss."

"That's the downside of working for someone else."

She did look up and saw that he was frowning. "Colin, everybody works for someone else."

"Gramps worked for himself. No one told him what to do. He mapped out his own day, his own life."

"We can't all own an orchard," she said, and that deepened his frown. What a dumb thing to say, considering how much Colin had loved the orchard. "I'm sorry. That was thoughtless of me."

"But true," he said.

The conversation suddenly stalled. Where to go from here?

Nowhere, she decided, and went back to her internet search. "We have to finish this hunt today. I've got to fly out tonight." Oh, good. There was a flight leaving at five. Surely they were on their last clue. They could find whatever Grandma Justine had left them, figure out what to do with it and then she'd roar off to the airport, turn in the rental car, get back to Chicago and rescue her job.

And hope Colin would follow her. She booked her flight, reserving one of the last remaining seats.

"How long do we have?" Colin asked.

"Just this morning."

"And then you leave."

"Not for good, not forever. And you're coming to Chicago, right?"

"Absolutely."

It was the correct word, but she still felt as if a giant shadow had cast itself over the day.

It's not like we won't ever be back, she reminded

herself. That didn't help. In the end, Chicago wasn't Icicle Falls. And her job wasn't as secure as she'd always thought. Success could be snatched out of her hands just like that. Reality was a cold bitch.

"We should get going if we're going to solve this puzzle," Colin said, opening the front door.

Mia hurried down the front walk with him, wishing that instead of money or whatever trinkets Grandma Justine had left, they'd find a magic bottle complete with the requisite genie. Then...

What would she wish for? To become instant millionaires? That wouldn't make Dylan like her any better. To turn back the clock? How far back would she have to turn it? To some time before her mother got sick and her dad took off? To the idyllic time when what she and Colin had felt like the rock of Gibraltar? No. All you could rewind were movies you'd recorded on TV. Anyway, going back didn't make you smarter. You probably did the same stupid things all over again.

They didn't have to do the same things over again this time. They could work out their issues. They'd already worked out the biggest one, where to live.

So why did she not feel right about it?

She didn't want to look for an answer, not yet. One search at a time.

February 14, 2016

Dear Mother,
I know it's silly to be writing a letter to someone who's no longer with me, but I miss you and this helps. Here it is, Valentine's Day, and I must confess I'm feeling a little alone. It's been so many years without Gerald you'd think I'd be used to being a widow by now, but I'm not. I wonder if you ever get used to it. I never thought to ask you.

I'm not sitting around moping, however. I had some ladies over today for a little Valentine's lunch, widows like me. Muriel Sterling-Wittman and Dot Morrison. Then there was my old friend, Sarah. She found the nicest man last year, dear Peter Gabriel. So sad that he died only a few months after they were married. She barely had time to get her new name printed on her checkbook! She's talking about finally retiring and selling the hair salon. I'll believe it when I see it. Anyway, they all came over. Bethie picked up a salad and some cupcakes from the grocery store for me, so it wasn't the most elaborate lunch, but it was all I had the energy for. The ladies enjoyed themselves and it made a nice diversion. Bethie wanted me to come to her house for dinner tonight, but I told her Valentine's Day is for sweethearts. I'm glad I said no. I'm tired.

I'm tired a lot these days. I don't think I'm

going to be around much longer. While I'm ready to meet the Lord and see you and Daddy and, of course, dear Gerald, I'm also a little sad to go. I would've loved to see Dylan find someone, although at this point in life he probably won't.

I'm especially sad to see Colin so unsettled. I don't think he's happy in work or in love, the two most important sources of a man's contentment. I still don't know what happened between him and Mia, but it's a shame. The last time she came home to Icicle Falls it was plain that he's still crazy about her. I think she loves him, too. Neither of them has found someone and I'm sure that's because they only want each other. They simply need a little push. I wish there was something I could do to help them. I have a few affairs of my own to settle. I'm wondering if I can do it in a way that will help both Colin and Mia. I need to think about this.

Now I'm going to bed. Perhaps I'll see you in my dreams. I miss you terribly.

Love,
Justine

Chapter Seventeen

"Welcome back," Pat said, letting Colin and Mia in.

"I guess this qualifies us as your best customers," Colin joked as they entered the bookstore.

Colin had never been Pat's best customer, but he did remember the time she'd helped him pick out a book for Mia's birthday. He'd gotten her a copy of *The Princess Bride*. Aunt Beth had shown them the movie, and they'd both liked it, for different reasons. He'd loved the action and the funny bits. She'd been taken with how romantic it all was. No way was he ever going to run around saying, "As you wish," and he refused to admit that getting her the book was tantamount to the same thing. But he'd been secretly pleased when she'd opened his present at her thirteenth birthday party and let out a reverent gasp at the sight of it.

She'd been to the bookstore countless times since, investing in novels like *Pride and Prejudice*, *Jane Eyre* and, of course, *Wuthering Heights*. Now, as they made their way to the nonfiction section, she was gazing avidly around as if they hadn't been in only two days ago. He was sure she was going to get sidetracked by the display of new arrivals.

Instead, she plunked herself right back down where she'd left off on Friday and began pulling out books and leafing through them. Colin did the same.

They'd been searching for a few minutes when Muriel Sterling came in. Between having had several books published and the fact that her family owned Sweet Dreams Chocolate Company, she was the closest thing Icicle Falls had to royalty. "Thanks for stopping by," Pat said to her. "I have a case of books for you to sign."

Mia looked up and said hello to Muriel. "You have a new book out?"

"Just today," Muriel confirmed.

"Oh, you didn't tell me when we were at your house," Mia said.

"That visit wasn't about me. It was about you."

No doubt about it. Muriel Sterling-Wittman was a class act.

"Yes, but I always like hearing when you've got a new book out," Mia said. "I have every one."

Muriel picked up a book from the pile Pat was stacking on a table. "Well, then, we must continue that tradition." She scribbled something on the title page and handed the book to Mia, who thanked her as if Muriel had given her a hundred bucks.

Colin glanced at the cover—a single candle glowing in the window. *Love Never Fails.*

He hoped that was true.

"You're welcome," Muriel said. "I hope you find it helpful."

"I'm sure I will," Mia said, reverently running her hand over the cover.

Yep, Mia and books. She'd always had her nose in one. There was probably a correlation between that and the fact that she was class valedictorian in high school.

She'd been scared spitless to give her speech at graduation. Gram had counseled her to pretend she was working at the information booth, telling visitors about Icicle Falls. Uncle Mark had said to picture everyone out there in the audience in their underwear and wearing red clown noses. Aunt Beth had given her Saint-John's-Wort. Colin had given her a kiss for courage and told her to look at him.

She had, and she'd smiled. She told him later that she couldn't have gotten through the speech without him, especially when she pictured him with a red clown nose.

She carefully set Muriel's gift aside and returned to searching through the ones on the shelves. The process sped up considerably in comparison to their Friday-afternoon inspection.

Colin, too, was aware of the minutes flying past. What kind of jerks made her come back even though she'd explained that there'd been a problem with the will? And why would she want to go back? Was there any place as great as Icicle Falls?

Yes, he reminded himself. Wherever Mia was, that was as great as Icicle Falls. He pulled down a thick paperback, *Stock Investing for Dummies*. And lo and behold, he found a pink envelope inside. "Got it!"

Mia scrambled to her feet. "What was it in?" she asked and he showed it to her.

Pat ambled over. "I see you finally struck gold, so to speak. Are you wondering why your clue's in a book like that?"

It did seem kind of weird. "Yeah," Colin admitted. "I thought it would be in something on gardening or cooking."

"There's a reason she hid it in a book on stock investing," Pat explained. "Stocks were how she turned herself into the proverbial millionaire next door."

"Millionaire?" Gram?

"Grandma Justine was a millionaire?" Mia asked. "Seriously?"

"I don't get it," Colin said. "She had to sell the orchard to pay for Gramps's nursing care."

"I know," Pat said. "Your grandmother had such a fighting spirit, just like many of the other people who worked so hard to bring this town back to life in the early sixties."

"But how?" Okay, how had Gram gone from a poor widow to a millionaire?

"She came into the store one day and asked me to recommend some books on personal finance and investing. Your grandfather had a small life-insurance policy that paid out, and she still had some money left from selling the orchard. She thought maybe she could find a way to do something with it. She took a gamble and invested her nest egg in the stock market, investing in companies she liked, such as Apple and Starbucks." Pat smiled. "I don't know how much you follow the stock market, but I remember when Apple was selling for around eight dollars a share in 2005. I wish I'd bought some then, or even when your grand-mother did. It was still a bargain. It's worth a great deal more than that now. I'll leave it to you to imagine the profits on a thousand shares of Apple stock alone."

Colin shook his head, hardly able to believe his ears. "She never said anything."

"She wasn't one to brag," Pat said.

Yeah, but still.

"Is this the last clue?" Mia asked.

"Yes, it is," Pat said with a smile.

The final clue, the end of the line. After this, he'd have to let Mia leave. But, he reminded himself, he'd be joining her soon. Whatever Gram had left them was bound to help them make a new start. Maybe there'd be enough money for a down payment on a house.

He handed the envelope to Mia and let her do the honors. She opened it and there was another letter from Gram, along with a hand-drawn map that looked like something out of *Treasure Island*.

Colin peered over her shoulder and read silently.

Dear Ones, if you're reading this, then your treasure hunt is about to come to an end. This is your final clue.

By now Pat will have told you how I came to escape becoming a poor widow. Although, really, even if I'd never gotten my hands on another cent, I'd have felt rich. There have been times in my life when money was tight—when Grandpa and I were first starting out, when the children were little and we were trying to make a go of the orchard, and of course when I had to put the dear man in that nursing home. That ate through our money in a hurry. But you know, I've always been blessed in the things that mattered—good family, good friends, my health, and above all, having a true and faithful love. Really, if a woman has all that, she has everything.

Still, after Grandpa died, I found myself feeling down, feeling as though I'd failed somehow. I'd lost the orchard and it had meant so much to him. To me, too, and to all of you. That's not to say I didn't love my little house. I did, and we made some lovely memories there. But whenever I thought of home, I thought of the house on Apple Blossom Road.

You're both young and have many years ahead of you, plenty of time for your hearts to find that special place you call home. Perhaps what I'm leaving you will help.

So, here are your instructions. Take the map to Apple Blossom Road. It's where my happiest times were, and it's where you'll find my final gift to you.

"This is it," he said to Mia. "Looks like we'll be done in plenty of time for you to catch your flight."

"You're leaving?" Muriel asked, sounding disappointed.

"I have to get back to Chicago," Mia explained. "My job."

The look Muriel and Pat exchanged wasn't hard to interpret. *What are you two doing?*

"I guess we should get going," Colin said. "Thanks for the clue."

"You'd better pick up a shovel on your way," Pat said. "You'll need it."

So Gram really did have them digging for buried treasure. And in the apple orchard. Either old Garvey was a real sport to have given permission for them to go digging around there or Gram had bribed him. She'd sure gone to a lot of trouble for them. But then, that was Gram. Colin couldn't help smiling.

The smile did a vanishing act when he remembered that soon their time together, here in Icicle Falls, would be at an end.

This was it. Within the hour, she and Colin would have their inheritance. Mia would just have time to run home and gather her things. Then she'd have to get back in her rental car and drive over the mountains to SeaTac airport. She hated having to say goodbye to Aunt Beth and Uncle Mark. Dylan not so much. As for Colin, she hated to leave him again for even a day. Although they'd worked things out, the underlying fear that he'd change his mind and not come to Chicago lurked beneath the surface of her mind like the Loch Ness monster, waiting to grab her newly found happiness and devour it.

But that was silly. Colin was right; they were meant to be together. Hopefully, whatever they inherited would smooth out any bumps in the road ahead. Maybe

it would be enough for Colin to start a business or…
something. Whatever it was, they could pool their re-
sources. She'd prove Dylan wrong. She'd show him
that she was worth keeping. Maybe she'd even show
herself once and for all.

They stopped by Aunt Beth's house and Mia waited
in the car while Colin got a shovel. Pat must have called
Aunt Beth, because she came out to the car. "This is
it, huh?"

Mia nodded. "And a good thing, too. It turns out I
have to fly back tonight."

Aunt Beth lost her *let's party* expression. "You do?"

"I'm afraid so. I can't wait any longer."

"But we're going to need to sign a few things, sort
out some details."

Mia gnawed her lip. "I may have to do that from
Chicago. My boss is pretty mad that I'm not already
back in the office."

Aunt Beth frowned. "I guess that's the curse of success. Your boss doesn't sound very understanding."

Right now Aunt Beth wasn't being very understanding, either. No one in Icicle Falls understood the corporate world. "She also has someone to answer to," Mia
said in Andrea's defense.

"The advantage of being self-employed," Aunt Beth
said, "is that the only person you have to answer to is
yourself. But I understand," she added.

No, she didn't.

Colin was back now. He put the shovel in the trunk
and came around to the driver's side.

Aunt Beth leaned down and said through Mia's window, "Come on over here when you're done. I'll be waiting."

He nodded and put the car in gear and they were off. Neither one of them spoke, and that was okay with Mia. She was too busy digesting what Aunt Beth had said. Since when was success a curse and not an accomplishment?

She was still chewing on that when they turned onto Apple Blossom Road. There was the orchard, all the trees lush and green and lovely and holding more than apples. So many memories lived among them. How appropriate that Grandma Justine would send them here for their treasure.

Following the map, Colin pulled off at the old fruit stand and onto the dirt road that paralleled the orchard on the eastern side. In the distance Mia could see the same old truck they'd seen at the farmhouse, which meant Butch Garvey, the man they'd met when they first started their hunt, was around somewhere, possibly culling the apples with blemishes from the trees. The irrigation system was going, small hoses giving the trees their early-morning drink of water. Mia got out of the car and inhaled the mountain air. Today it smelled of damp earth and growing things.

She could almost see her younger self darting in and out of the trees, playing tag with Colin. She'd taken a walk with her mother through this orchard before Mama died. It had been a slow and labored stroll, with Mia holding tightly to her mother's hand, hoping fervently that if she just held on she wouldn't lose her.

She'd learned at an early age that just holding on didn't work. Maybe that was why she hadn't fought for what she and Colin had.

He took the shovel out of the trunk and came around to her side of the car. "Okay, let's see what we can find."

She opened the map and they studied it again.

"Starting from the northeast corner, we have to go down ten rows," he said. He counted the rows of trees and pointed. "Three more rows to the left."

She nodded and they fell into step. Mia realized her heart was beating faster.

They reached the designated row and consulted the map again. "Twenty trees down that way," she said.

Mist from the sprinklers drifted on the air, landing on her face and arms. The morning was already warm, and the cool spray felt good.

A little more walking, a few more paces counted off, and they saw a fresh mound of dirt in between two trees. It looked like a small grave, and Mia swallowed down the sad memories of losses both distant and recent.

"Jeez," Colin muttered, and she knew he was having the exact same thoughts. "Well, let's get digging," he said with determination.

Soon a fine sheen of sweat covered Colin's face and arms, and his T-shirt was damp. He stopped digging and wiped his forehead with one arm. "Poor Uncle Mark if he had to dig this hole. They must've said shoot for China, 'cause I think we're halfway there."

"It can't be much deeper," Mia said, squatting at the edge of the hole.

"I hope not. We're in hard pan now and this stuff is tough digging."

"Want me to take a turn?"

"And get all dirty and gross right before you have to leave? No way." He jammed the shovel into the ground again and brought up some more earth. A few more shovels full and he struck something hard. "This is it."

Now Mia's heart was galloping. She caught her lip between her teeth and held her breath as he scraped earth off some sort of steamer trunk.

"A real treasure chest. Leave it to Gram," he said, and started scraping away more dirt from the edges.

Another few minutes, and she and Colin were lifting out the chest. He brushed the dirt off the old leather top, undid the hasps and raised the lid. And there inside, in a large sealed plastic bag, was a large manila envelope.

He looked at Mia. "Well, here goes." Then he pulled it out and offered it to her.

She shook her head. "You open it." Her hands were shaking too much to do it, anyway. Once more she found herself holding her breath as he opened the bag and took out the envelope. She watched as he opened it and pulled out a document.

His eyebrows drew together, and then he blinked several times in an obvious effort to hold back tears. "Oh, my God," he said faintly and sat down hard on the damp ground.

August 3, 2016

Dear Mother,
Gerald came to me again last night. He promised to be right there at heaven's gate waiting for me.

I'm ready to go. This morning I feel awful. I'm perspiring as if I have the flu and I have a horrible headache and a terrible pain in my arm. I think I'd better call Beth.

Chapter Eighteen

Colin stared at the deed. How could this be?

Mia was kneeling next to him now. "What is it?"

"It's the deed to this place." His eyes were seeing it, but his brain was having trouble processing. The home that held so many memories was now theirs? He felt overwhelmed with gratitude, but it came wrapped in disbelief. He had to be dreaming.

"Oh, my," Mia said faintly.

He heard the sound of heavy footsteps and looked up to see the man he'd assumed now owned his grandmother's house.

"Saw your car," Butch Garvey said. "I see you found what you were looking for."

"I thought you owned this," Colin said.

Butch shook his head. "Nah. I've just been the caretaker. Got a little place over on the other side of town I've been renting out to my cousin. Your grandma hired me six years ago to keep the place running for her. If you want, I'll stay on and help you with it."

"She bought it six years ago? Who knew about that?"

Butch shrugged. "Your dad, I guess, since he's the lawyer."

Colin opened the accompanying piece of folded pink stationery and read.

If you have any questions, you can ask your Aunt Beth. I love you both,
Grandma

Any questions? Yeah, he had a ton of them! Who knew about this besides Aunt Beth, Uncle Mark and Dad? Why had Gram kept it a secret from him? Why hadn't she moved back? Then there was the most important question of all. What were he and Mia going to do now? He looked at her and saw her wiping away tears.

"I think we need to go see Aunt Beth," he said.

She nodded and they got up and started for his car.

"Be talkin' to you," Butch called after them.

Gram had left them the orchard. More than that, she'd left him his dream. And a house, and a chance for a new beginning.

But Mia was leaving for Chicago. He was supposed to move to Chicago. "I don't know what to do," he said. He knew what he *wanted* to do, but that was something entirely different.

"Like you said, we go talk to Aunt Beth."

He'd half hoped she'd say that they should get married and move into the house on Apple Blossom Road. But she didn't. Maybe all the implications of their inheritance hadn't registered yet. Or maybe she was so in love with her important corporate life that she didn't care. She'd been focused on success since high school. Growing apples probably didn't fit that definition.

So he could buy Mia out and continue what his grandparents had started. Or he could sell the place and go with her. He felt like the proverbial monkey with his hand stuck in the jar. *Let go of what's in the jar and you can keep Mia.* It was a no-brainer—he needed to let go of what was in the jar.

They didn't talk on their way back to the car. They didn't talk as they drove to Aunt Beth's place, either, and it wasn't a comfortable silence. They each had a choice to make. She, too, had her hand stuck in a jar.

They found Aunt Beth at her kitchen table, along with Dad, both nursing lattes. "So you found your treasure at last," she said.

Yes, he had, and the treasure wasn't that orchard, special as it was. The true treasure was Mia. He loosened his grip and pulled his hand free from the jar and was rewarded with a giant swell of love and joy. He put an arm around her shoulders. "Yep, we did."

"So you knew about this all along?" Mia asked. "Both of you?"

Dad wasn't smiling, but Aunt Beth was beaming. "Yes. Our mother was a very special woman."

Dad nodded. "Yes, she was."

"Once she made all that money, she was determined to get the orchard back. She knew how much you loved it, Colin, and she'd always felt a little as if she'd robbed you of your birthright."

Hearing this made him feel unappreciative, considering what he knew he had to do. "I never thought that." Yes, he'd been sad to see the orchard go, had envisioned it staying in the family, but he'd never felt *entitled* to it like some kind of prince or a rich kid waiting for his inheritance.

"I know. Still, selling it was such a blow. When she realized she had enough money from her investments, she approached the owners and made them a nice offer and they took it."

"Why keep it a secret? Why didn't she tell me?"

"She was going to," Aunt Beth said, "but you seemed to be happy in the city and she didn't want you to feel obligated to come home and take over managing it. So she hired Butch Garvey to run the place and simply sat on it for a while and just enjoyed having it. Then it became apparent that you were…drifting. After she talked with you on your last visit—"

The Fourth of July. She'd stuffed him with pie and grilled him about his job, the city, his love life, even Mia. He'd finally had enough of getting his sore spots poked and told her to mind her own business. Ugh.

"She knew she'd been right to buy back the orchard and that it needed to go to you. It was meant to stay in the family."

He didn't deserve it. He wanted to cry. "Why all this running around chasing clues, though?" he asked and saw the corners of his father's mouth slip farther down.

"Can't you guess?" his aunt asked.

Actually, he could. He looked at Mia and she was blushing.

"She'd hoped you'd find an even greater treasure than that deed."

"We have," Colin said.

His aunt's face lit up. "So…"

"So we're going to—"

"Talk about it," Mia said, and hauled him out of the kitchen.

"What's there to talk about?" he protested as she led him through the living room.

"What do you mean, what's there to talk about?"

"We need to sell it."

"Sell it!" Her frown was as deep as Dad's. She opened the front door and pulled him to the front porch swing, settling him on it. "You can't sell your family's orchard, not when Grandma Justine worked so hard to get it back for you."

"For us," he corrected her. "What use have we got for it if we're living in Chicago?"

Except, maybe they could keep Butch on to run the place. Surely someday they'd get back to Icicle Falls. Unless Mia kept rising in the company. Then what would they do?

She sat for a moment, looking at the mountains rising all around them, seeing something he couldn't. Then she suddenly stood. "Stay there," she said, and marched back into the house. What the heck?

"You're wrong, as usual," Aunt Beth was saying when Mia walked into the kitchen. She gave a start at the sight of her. "Oh. You're back."

"Could I speak to Dylan alone?" Mia asked.

Beth seemed surprised, but said, "Sure," and left the room.

Now it was just the two of them, Mia and the man who had never accepted her, and he was looking as uncomfortable as she felt. Her heart was at it again, banging so hard she felt it was going to push its way right out of her chest. Part of her wanted to turn and run, but she knew she couldn't. She had to have answers. She'd needed answers for years.

"Are you going to sit down?" he asked.

This wasn't a sit-down conversation. She remained standing. "Why don't you want me to marry your son?"

He blinked. "I never said that."

"You told me yesterday not to break his heart."

"And I meant it. You already broke it once before."

"He's the one who broke mine," she said. "*He* left *me*. Colin never told you that?"

"He told me you'd found someone else."

"He jumped to conclusions."

Dylan exhaled a world-weary sigh. "Mia, what's the purpose of this conversation?"

"The purpose is to find out why you don't like me."

He pulled back and looked at her in shock. "Whatever gave you that idea?"

Seriously? "I know you've never liked me."

"And you know that how?" Oh, yes, he was, indeed a lawyer. *Show me the evidence.*

Heat rushed up Mia's neck and exploded across her face. "I heard what you said to Colin in the orchard all those years ago." The most humiliating experience of her life, bar none.

He shook his head. "Mia, I have no clue what you're talking about."

The heat of embarrassment was so intense she was sure her face was going to catch fire and melt. She couldn't look Dylan in the face, so she focused on Aunt Beth's half-full mug. "You said, 'And Mia of all people.' That was when I knew I wasn't good enough. I was the little girl you all took in, just a hanger-on."

"Not good enough! Was that what you thought?"

She looked up to see him staring at her in astonishment. "What else should I have thought?"

"That I was concerned my son was taking advantage of you, that you were young and vulnerable. You'd been through enough, been hurt enough. Our family needed to be a safe place for you, and Colin needed to understand and respect that."

Now she did sit down, falling onto the chair and placing her hands on the kitchen table to steady them. "I thought…"

"I suppose you thought I was some kind of monster," he said. "Well, I'm not. I may not be as touchy-feely as my sister, but I care about this family."

"And what about me?" she asked.

"You've always been a member of the family."

He didn't exactly come out and say he cared about her, too. Maybe this was as close as he'd ever get. "Your son wants me to marry him."

"I figured as much."

Would it hurt Dylan to smile? "Are you okay with that?"

Oh, wait. What was this? A small stretching of the

lips, a slight upward curve. "Of course I am. I assume, since we're having this conversation, that you're going to say yes."

"I am if I'm wanted. If I've proved myself."

"You've never not been wanted, Mia. You should know that. And you've never needed to prove yourself, not to me, anyway."

She hadn't? She could feel tears welling up and her throat tightening.

He stood and opened his arms. "Welcome to the family."

The tears spilled over and she hurried to hug him. "Thank you," she managed.

He gave her back a pat and then stepped away. "I guess you and your husband-to-be had better decide what you're going to do with your inheritance."

She smiled at him, thanked him and then hurried out of the kitchen. She stopped to hug Aunt Beth, who was hovering in the living room, then rushed back out onto the front porch where Colin was waiting.

He was no longer sitting on the porch swing. Now he was pacing. He looked at her, brows knit. "What was that all about?" he asked.

"Just making sure everyone wants me in the family."

He frowned. "Of course everyone wants you in the family. And even if they didn't, I don't care. *I* want you."

You'll always have a family, her mother had promised. Mama was right. She'd lost some important things as a girl, but the Wrights had stepped in and filled the void. They would always be there for her, a rock-solid foundation on which she could build her life with Colin. And they could build that anywhere.

"I need to call my boss."

He nodded, lips pressed tightly together. He was willing to follow her to the ends of the world, or at least the other side of the country. She couldn't help remembering *The Princess Bride. As you wish.*

She wished for so much just now that her heart felt ready to explode.

Andrea answered her phone with a curt hello.

Mia's heart began to hammer in her chest again. "Andrea, I'm afraid I won't be able to make it into the office."

The silence at the other end was like the silence before the guillotine fell or the trap door opened and you wound up swinging by your neck. "Mia."

"I know. I know what this means. I'm only coming in to wrap things up. I'll be giving my two weeks' notice."

"Have you gone mad?"

"No, I've inherited a fortune."

"Well," Andrea huffed. "I hope you enjoy spending it. You've certainly left me in the lurch."

"I'm sorry. But I know you'll find someone to replace me," Mia said, and ended the call. Considering how many hungry ladder climbers there were at GF Markets, it wouldn't be hard. Really, there was only one person who considered her irreplaceable.

And right now he was looking at her as if she'd just chopped off her foot. "What was that?"

"That was me starting my new life." She closed the

distance between them and wrapped her arms around his waist, gazed up into those blue eyes, waiting for the smile to come and make them crinkle. "Colin Wright, will you marry me?"

"Babe, the sooner, the better," he said, and kissed her, his lips hard against hers, filling her with his energy and hope. A moment later he pulled back, brows knitting again. "Are you sure? I said I'd move to Chicago and I meant it."

"I don't need that job anymore."

"This isn't exactly a fortune."

"I don't need a fortune." And she didn't need some fancy job to prove her worth. "All I need is you."

Now it came, the smile that lit his eyes and made them crinkle at the sides. By the time he was fifty he'd have deep crow's feet. And he'd still look gorgeous.

"We can be us anywhere," she said softly, "but the best place to be us is right here in Icicle Falls, carrying on the family tradition." She didn't need to prove herself anymore. She simply needed to enjoy belonging.

She knew it. She'd always known it. Beth sauntered back into the kitchen, sat down at the table where her stubborn brother was finishing his coffee and picked up her mug.

She cocked an eyebrow at him. "Are you ready to admit Mom and I were right?"

"You were eavesdropping" he accused her.

"Of course I was. Honestly, Dylan, it's a good thing we all love you or we'd have to kick you out of the family."

"I had no idea she felt like that," he protested.

For such an intelligent man, he had a shocking lack of wisdom when it came to people. "I think you owe Mom and me an apology. Since she's not here, I'll accept it on her behalf."

He rolled his eyes.

"Come on, say it. Repeat after me. 'You were right.'"

"Yes, yes. It looks like, for once in your life, you were right."

"And maybe I'm right about a few other things. We got Colin squared away. Now, how about you?"

"That's okay. You should have enough to keep you busy interfering in Colin and Mia's lives."

"I never interfere…unless it's necessary."

He shook his head. "You're hopeless."

"No, hopeful."

He did smile at that. "Well, it looks like you pinned your hopes on the right couple." He downed the last of his drink, then gave her a hug. "Send them to me when they're ready to discuss the details of the inheritance," he said. Then he slipped out the back door.

Beth took a deep, satisfying breath. "Well, Mom. You did it." For a minute, it seemed as if the sun shining through her kitchen window was just a little brighter and she felt its warmth on her shoulders, as if a gentle arm was suddenly wrapped around them. People probably had better things to do in the afterlife than hang around and watch their relatives fumbling and bumbling down here on earth. But Beth was sure that Mom had taken time to enjoy this happy moment when her last wandering kids came home.

Home at Last

The late-September Saturday afternoon was warm, the sun shining its blessing on the new couple.

The wedding had been simple but elegant, held on the lawn of the house on Apple Blossom road with enough chairs set up to accommodate fifty guests. Lupine Floral had provided the flowers—white roses and asters—and the three-tiered frosted gingerbread cake, a gift from Cass Wilkes at Gingerbread Haus, had been decorated to match. The cake topping, a small sugar treasure chest filled with chocolate coins, had been a hit, especially since everyone present had known about the treasure hunt. Colin's dad had been his best man, and Uncle Mark had given the bride away. Bailey Sterling-Black had acted as maid of honor and Aunt Beth had sat in the front row and cried through the entire ceremony. The bride was resplendent in a mermaid gown, enhanced with seed pearls and sequins and made by Beth. In short, it had been a perfect wedding.

Colin and Mia hadn't gone farther than Seattle for their honeymoon and had run into Lorelei while they were eating at Wild Ginger. She'd come in with a very fit-looking fortysomething man and had happily snubbed them.

Now they were back, strolling hand in hand in the orchard. "I still can't believe this is ours," Colin said, taking in the rows of trees with their evening sunshine nimbuses.

"Me, neither," Mia said.

He looked down at her. She was so beautiful, with the sunlight making her dark hair glow. Heck, she was beautiful anytime of day. "You know what else I can't believe? That we're finally together for good."

"Believe it," she said with a smile.

He drew her to him and kissed her. Her lips were warm and she leaned into him, as solid and real as the trees surrounding them. Their history was here and their roots ran as deep as those trees. This was where they'd started out; this was where they'd ended up. This was where they belonged.

They stayed outside until the sun set, talking yet again of their plans for the orchard—all the new methods Colin was going to employ, the bees they'd be bringing in, new outlets they could find for their apples and complementary products they could sell.

Glancing around the orchard, Colin could almost see Gramps up on a ladder, trimming a tree, could see Dad in his jeans and T-shirt, pitching in to help with the harvest, could smell that apple pie baking in Gram's oven and taste her apple crisp. For a moment there he could've sworn he'd caught a glimpse of a boy who looked exactly like him chasing a laughing dark-haired little girl through the trees. This orchard was as much a part of his family as the people who'd tended and loved it. Everything they could ever need or want was right here.

And would be. Someday their children and maybe a foster child or two would play in this orchard, grow up to help with the harvest.

"You know, Dorothy was right. There's no place like home," Mia said as if reading his thoughts.

"Come on," he said, putting an arm around her shoulders. "Let's go inside."

They turned and made their way back to the house. Their house. It was time to make new memories.

* * * * *

Recipes from Gram

Beth has almost completed her mother's cookbook. Here are a few of the recipes from it.

Apple Crisp

Ingredients:
2 or 3 large apples, peeled and sliced
1 cup sugar
½ cup butter
¾ cup flour
1 tsp cinnamon

Directions:

Butter a large pie pan and arrange the apple slices on the bottom of the pan. Sprinkle with cinnamon. Work together the sugar, flour and butter until crumbly. Spread over the apples and bake at 350 for thirty minutes. Serve warm with whipped cream.

Blackberry Scones

Ingredients:
2 ½ cups flour (save out ¼ cup)
¼ tsp salt
¼ tsp baking soda
1 Tbsp baking powder
½ cup butter
⅓ cup sugar
⅔ cup milk
1 cup blackberries

Directions:

Mix together the dry ingredients, then cut in the butter. Gently add blackberries and then the milk. Form the dough into two balls and knead in the extra quarter cup of flour. Shape into two flat round pieces and cut into quarters. Bake on an ungreased cookie sheet at 425 for twelve to fifteen minutes. Cool on wire rack.

Peach Upside-Down Cake

Ingredients:
Upside-down topping:
¼ cup butter
½ cup brown sugar
3 fresh peaches, peeled and sliced (or 1 cup canned sliced peaches)

Cake:
1 ¼ cup flour
¾ cup sugar
¼ cup butter
1 ¼ tsp baking powder
½ tsp salt
½ cup milk
1 egg
½ tsp vanilla

Directions:

Put butter in a pie pan and melt over a stove burner on low heat. Add brown sugar and let it dissolve. Then arrange peaches over that. Mix the cake batter and pour over peaches. Bake at 350 for twenty-five minutes or until a toothpick inserted in the cake comes out clean. Serve warm with whipped cream.

Mulligatawny Soup
(Courtesy of Selma Moyle)

Ingredients:
3 large carrots, peeled and sliced
2 stalks celery, sliced
6 cups chicken broth
3 cups diced cooked chicken (2-3 boneless chicken
breasts, depending on size)
1 cup chopped onion (1 large onion should do it)
¼ cup butter
1 apple, peeled, cored and chopped
5 tsp curry powder
1 tsp salt
¼ cup flour
1 Tbsp lemon juice

Directions:

Cook carrots and celery in 1 cup broth for twenty minutes or until tender. Add chicken. Heat, cover and keep warm. Sauté onion in butter in a large pot or Dutch oven until soft. Stir in apple, curry and salt and sauté five minutes longer or until apple is soft. Add flour. Gradually stir in the rest of the chicken broth. Bring to a boil, stirring constantly, then reduce heat. Cover and simmer fifteen minutes. Add vegetables and chicken with the broth they were cooked in and bring just to boiling. Stir in lemon juice. Serve with rice or sourdough French bread.

Guten Appetit!

Acknowledgments

I'd like to thank Floyd Stutzman, owner of the Stutzman Ranch, for taking time to allow me a glimpse into the hard work and loving care involved in managing an orchard. I want to own an orchard! Well, maybe not. It's a lot of work. Instead, I think I'll just come and buy apples from Floyd. Thanks also to my friend Glenn Anderson at Edward Jones for letting me pick his brain about stocks. Wish I'd bought stock in Apple way back in 2005! I sure appreciate my loyal writing buddies who try to keep me on track—Susan Wiggs, Kate Breslin, Lois Dyer, A. J. Banner and Elsa Watson. Thank you as always to my agent, Paige Wheeler, who never fails me, my wonderful editor Paula Eykelhof for her insight and advice, and to all the dedicated staff at Harlequin MIRA for giving me such a lovely cover and so much support. I love writing stories and you all make it possible!

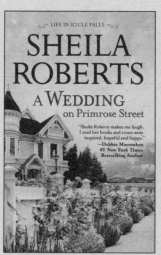

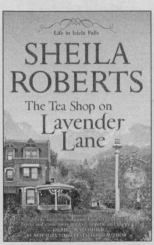

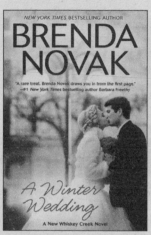

REQUEST YOUR FREE BOOKS!

2 FREE NOVELS
FROM THE ROMANCE COLLECTION
PLUS 2 FREE GIFTS!

YES! Please send me 2 FREE novels from the Romance Collection and my 2 FREE gifts (gifts are worth about $10). After receiving them, if I don't wish to receive any more books, I can return the shipping statement marked "cancel." If I don't cancel, I will receive 4 brand-new novels every month and be billed just $6.49 per book in the U.S. or $6.99 per book in Canada. That's a savings of at least 19% off the cover price. It's quite a bargain! Shipping and handling is just 50¢ per book in the U.S. and 75¢ per book in Canada.* I understand that accepting the 2 free books and gifts places me under no obligation to buy anything. I can always return a shipment and cancel at any time. Even if I never buy another book, the two free books and gifts are mine to keep forever.

194/394 MDN GH4D

Name _____ (PLEASE PRINT) _____

Address _____ Apt. # _____

City _____ State/Prov. _____ Zip/Postal Code _____

Signature (if under 18, a parent or guardian must sign) _____

Mail to the **Reader Service:**
IN U.S.A.: P.O. Box 1867, Buffalo, NY 14240-1867
IN CANADA: P.O. Box 609, Fort Erie, Ontario L2A 5X3

Want to try two free books from another line?
Call 1-800-873-8635 or visit www.ReaderService.com.

* Terms and prices subject to change without notice. Prices do not include applicable taxes. Sales tax applicable in N.Y. Canadian residents will be charged applicable taxes. Offer not valid in Quebec. This offer is limited to one order per household. Not valid for current subscribers to the Romance Collection or the Romance/Suspense Collection. All orders subject to credit approval. Credit or debit balances in a customer's account(s) may be offset by any other outstanding balance owed by or to the customer. Please allow 4 to 6 weeks for delivery. Offer available while quantities last.

SHEILA ROBERTS

31835	CHRISTMAS ON CANDY CANE LANE	___$7.99 U.S.	___$9.99 CAN.
31815	A WEDDING ON PRIMROSE STREET	___$7.99 U.S.	___$8.99 CAN.
31661	THE LODGE ON HOLLY ROAD	___$7.99 U.S.	___$8.99 CAN.
31470	MERRY EX-MAS	___$7.99 U.S.	___$8.99 CAN.
31432	WHAT SHE WANTS	___$7.99 U.S.	___$9.99 CAN.

(limited quantities available)

TOTAL AMOUNT	$ _____
POSTAGE & HANDLING	$ _____
($1.00 for 1 book, 50¢ for each additional)	
APPLICABLE TAXES*	$ _____
TOTAL PAYABLE	$ _____

(check or money order—please do not send cash)

To order, complete this form and send it, along with a check or money order for the total amount, payable to MIRA Books, to: **In the U.S.:** 3010 Walden Avenue, P.O. Box 9077, Buffalo, NY 14269-9077; **In Canada:** P.O. Box 636, Fort Erie, Ontario, L2A 5X3.

Name: _____

Address: _____ City: _____

State/Prov.: _____ Zip/Postal Code: _____

Account Number (if applicable): _____

075 CSAS

*New York residents remit applicable sales taxes.
*Canadian residents remit applicable GST and provincial taxes.

MIRA®

www.MIRABooks.com

MSR0416BL